Dear Alex

Dear Alex

MIRANDA SEYMOUR
& J-P JONES

First published in Great Britain in 2025 by
The Book Guild Ltd
Unit E2 Airfield Business Park,
Harrison Road, Market Harborough,
Leicestershire. LE16 7UL
Tel: 0116 2792299
www.bookguild.co.uk
Email: info@bookguild.co.uk
X: @bookguild

Copyright © 2025 Miranda Seymour & J-P Jones

The right of Miranda Seymour & J-P Jones to be identified as the authors of this
work has been asserted by them in accordance with the
Copyright, Design and Patents Act 1988.

All rights reserved. No part of this publication may be
reproduced, transmitted, or stored in a retrieval system, in any form or by any means,
without permission in writing from the publisher, nor be otherwise circulated in
any form of binding or cover other than that in which it is published and without
a similar condition being imposed on the subsequent purchaser.

The manufacturer's authorised representative in the
EU for product safety is Authorised Rep Compliance Ltd,
71 Lower Baggot Street, Dublin D02 P593 Ireland (www.arccompliance.com)

This work is entirely fictitious and bears no resemblance to any persons living or dead.

Typeset in 11pt Minion Pro

Printed and bound in Great Britain by CMP UK

ISBN 978 183574 1818

British Library Cataloguing in Publication Data.
A catalogue record for this book is available from the British Library.

From Miranda: To Mom, Dad, Becky, Ellie, Gwendy, and Ben

From J-P: For Mum, Dad and Amit

PROLOGUE

While I'm in the lift down to the Single Mingle, I stare at my reflection and rehash my alias, Anastasia Edwards. For once, I'm pretty pleased with how I look. My dark brown hair is behaving, staying remarkably frizz-free and glossy at the top and falling into gentle waves around my shoulders. I've managed to master the smoky eye look thanks to a new Insta account my flatmate, who is also my cousin, Adam, made me follow, and I finally seem to have found a foundation that doesn't make my pale skin look orange under strong lighting. Perfection.

As I retouch my lipstick (a saucy red I deem suitable for my new alter ego), I start having serious misgivings about whether I have the required mystique to pull off my new name. Almost immediately, though, the lift doors are opening in front of the registration desk. I know there's no turning back. I hastily stuff my lipstick back into my sparkly clutch and plaster on a smile. Trying not to think about what my best friend Bea would say if she knew I was here under such morally dubious circumstances, I announce my arrival to a beaming receptionist who hands me my badge. The sound of my name feels unfamiliar on my tongue, and I hope she puts the slight hesitation in my voice down to nerves.

Why did I go down the Russian royalty route?! When it came to an alias, I thought an exotic first name and boring surname was cunning. Yet, now that the badge is situated unflatteringly on the neckline of my dress, I'm less sure that I can carry it off. How can scruffy homebody Alex Taylor become elegant Anastasia Edwards for an evening? I might as well have gone for Charade Smith or Mysteriana Jones.

Past the registration desk, there's a huge bar space full of people awkwardly assembling into artificial little conversation groups. Oh God, I should have had that warm-up glass of wine with Adam before leaving. I knew it. Even more excruciating than the people desperately trying to make conversation are the hosts herding them into groups like rabid matchmaking sheepdogs.

OK Alex, I tell myself, stick with the plan. Sixty minutes maximum. Meet this shy Ryan guy. Give him a self-esteem boost. Maybe subtly give him a few hints to help with his future dating game. Easy. I'm a writer. I'm creative. I can do this. And I really have nothing to feel guilty about, I reassure myself, shushing Bea's voice in my head. I'm just making amends. And sure, that might involve assuming a fake identity and lying to a man I've never met, but it's for all the right reasons.

How am I even going to find him? There's an ocean of bachelors ahead of me, circling the groups of women like sharks. I determine that while I might make the night more enjoyable by linking up with one of these girl gaggles and lamenting the shallowness of the dating pool, I'll probably better accomplish my aim by being laser-focused on the task at hand: find Ryan, flirt shamelessly, and then leave, Cinderella-style, before the fairytale ends.

Steeling myself for an evening of awkward chat, I arm myself with a glass of courage from the bar and move in. *Thank God for name badges.* I discount a slightly sweaty Scott and a somewhat creepy-looking Robin. Robin has drawn a smiley face in the 'o' of his name, and I grimace. There are so many people here who could use my sage advice that I'm wondering if I should set up a dating advisory booth and charge. I keep scanning the room for Ryan. There's a Bruce in his twenties, who already seems to be relying heavily on the bar to keep his balance. Who is called 'Bruce' in this generation? I plot a course around him and consider whether my judgemental attitude is why I'm still single.

Suddenly, I spot him. The name on his badge is written in a scrawl, but I can make out the 'R'. He is exactly as I imagine him. A bland but not unpleasant face held in a slightly hopeless expression. Around thirty. A bit of a paunch. He's standing at the end of the bar, loitering for a bit and looking around the room before choosing his poison. *Probably to avoid making conversation with anyone*, I think, aligning this with the Ryan I know from his messages. I take a sip of my wine and head towards him.

"Hi, I'm Anastasia," I say, almost challenging him to disagree. He looks me up and down in a rather obvious way that doesn't really tally with my image of him.

"Can I get you a drink?"

I ponder the maturity of having a second glass of wine within twenty-five minutes of arriving at the event. How does this fit with my resolution to make good life choices?

"That's kind. A white wine spritzer, please," I say, smiling, while very subtly pushing my first empty glass away from me down the bar. "Just a small is fine," I add virtuously.

Watching Ryan order, I ponder all the gentle help I can give him, the womanly wisdom I can impart to help him up his game. I relish the boost I feel that comes from doing good, glowing with the anticipation of transforming shy Ryan into someone who strides out with twice the confidence he arrived with. Surprisingly, he launches straight into conversation. Something about the merits of beer over wine. Hmm, he's less shy in person than his letters suggest. Before I can come to the defence of my dear old friend, the fermented grape, he's already moved to the scarcity of good real ale pubs in central London.

"Hmmm," I mutter non-committedly, as I take two slightly hurried sips of spritzer. This isn't going quite how I expected. Ryan has now been waxing lyrical about breweries for five solid minutes. *When does this tongue of his start getting tied?* I think with an edge of panic. So far, I haven't had a single opportunity to jump in and coax him out of his shell. I try to rearrange my face into an interested expression–a tightrope between not wanting to encourage him and not wanting to make him think he's boring. Ryan seems completely unaware, however, and talks with the confidence of an expert about budget airlines, Mariella Frostrup, parking in Lambeth, tooth whitening, and the Isle of Sheppey. By the end of it, I'm almost as exhausted as my liver. Before I'm driven by sheer desperation to drink number three, I make a play for control of the conversation to steer into the more personal (surely the shyness will kick in then?).

"So, Ryan, what brought you here today?" I ask, smiling flirtatiously. Or at least my impression of flirtatiousness, which Adam tells me can also come across as 'perplexed while doing mental arithmetic'.

Ryan laughs, "Oh, it's Rich, not Ryan. That's my handwriting, soz."

Who says soz out loud? Before I can react and beat a hasty retreat, non-Ryan treats me to his next monologue, this time on handwriting, which I guess is at least partly responding to what I've said and therefore counts as conversation.

When he pauses to sip his carefully selected real ale, I jump in to start making my escape. "It's been a real pleasure speaking to you," I say brightly, "but I think…"

"Oh yeah. It's been great," he cuts in. "Anyway, look, you're really nice, but I'm looking for a more traditional woman. No offence or anything."

"Er…" I try to wade through the scrambled eggs inside my head for a response. I settle for saying "Er…" again. Which I think gets the point across.

Non-Ryan wishes me good luck before nodding over to a man called Clarke, who has mirror-shiny shoes and enough product in his hair to wax a boat. "He looks nice."

"Thanks," I say weakly.

I've repulsed the most boring man on the planet. Despite how uninterested in non-Ryan I am, the rejection dragon rears its fearsome head. I know

I'm going to be obsessing over what I did wrong, but logically I know this Rich character knows nothing about me, and I barely said a word. I've been this way since I dated Chris. Chris, who I haven't quite managed to shake my feelings for and who variously made me feel like the most loved, cherished woman on the planet and the most neglected. One day, I felt like his world, and the next, an afterthought.

I order a Diet Coke and try to press on with my mission, banishing the Chris thoughts to the depths of my psyche, where they will no doubt lurk until resurfacing at the most inconvenient time, usually the middle of a job interview, the ten minutes before I'm due to go on a date, or 3am on a Tuesday.

Moving through the room turns into a computer game. It's incredibly crowded, and some people appear to have needed even larger doses of courage than me. Meanwhile, like those ghosts in PacMan, the networking hosts keep prowling around. When they find their prey, they hook them by the arm and drag them off to the most unsuitable person in the room. I shudder. MUST AVOID. I did a fine job finding Rich all by myself anyway.

Having done several more circuits of the room, I'm finally set upon by one of the hosts, a steely blonde woman with the grip of a WWF champ. "Hello there, Anastasia. What a lovely name! Let me introduce you to some of the other guests."

I'm frogmarched to a far-off corner of the room. In this nest, she's stockpiled three other victims: a mortified-looking 20-something-year-old guy with a crew cut and tattoos, a cheerful but tipsy-looking woman my age, who under any other circumstances I would have liked to befriend, and Ryan!

Definitely Ryan. Very clear block capital letters. He's not what I expected and could not be more different from Rich. Six foot, if not more, with curly black hair and attractive, designer-looking stubble. Wow. This guy doesn't need the help of a drunken, non-traditional Russian duchess. I clock some pretty firm biceps in my speedy audit. I swallow hard and take a steadying breath, suddenly wishing I hadn't had quite so much courage-wine. I remember that for tonight, I am not Alex Taylor. I am graceful, charismatic Anastasia Edwards. It's time for those acting lessons I begged my mother for at sixteen to pay off.

He joins the others in a commiseratory nod toward me as the host disappears on her next prowl. There's an agonising lull in the conversation before the drunk girl takes charge, cheerfully relaying some of her more awkward moments from the evening so far. At the same time, the young crewcut guy surveys us and silently decides we're pensioners. I can see his brow furrowing as he contemplates his future life: drunkenly gulping back wine in the same bar a decade from now, fruitlessly searching for 'The One'. He murmurs something and disappears, presumably in search of youth.

I steal what I hope are surreptitious glances at Real Ryan, noticing the way he runs his fingers over the ridges in his glass. He looks nervous, and I can't say I blame him. I've never been particularly shy, but even I am struggling with the artificial nature of these forced interactions. Tipsy girl chats on, and I make a few interjections, trying to force a connection with Ryan. Ryan smiles and looks politely interested in the conversation, but he doesn't really contribute or give me anything to latch onto. I feel myself panic when Tipsy Girl drains the last of her cocktail and makes her way back to the bar. We're alone. Ryan seems happy enough to be sipping his beer in silence, but it's agonising to me.

"So, are you strong and silent or bored and restless?" I blurt out. I could not be less Anastasia if I tried.

"Sorry?" He looks momentarily startled.

I redden. "Oh, you're just… quite quiet."

He looks mortified. "Am I being horribly rude? I'm sorry. This place is a bit of a first for me."

"You're doing fine. First for me, too. What made you sign up?" I ask nonchalantly, hoping to hear something about the wisdom of *Agony Alex*.

"Oh, someone suggested it. Thought it'd be a bit out of my comfort zone, so I forced myself to do it."

"Oh, charming," I tease. "You're making me feel like a parachute jump."

He briefly looks mortified again (his expression is quite endearing) but then grins, taking a swig of his beer. "At least with a parachute jump, you get an instructor."

"Think of me as your instructor," I jump in. "Buckle up. Now, what do you need instructing in?" I cringe the moment the words are out of my mouth.

"Not too much. I haven't just escaped from an underground cult or anything…" he replies hastily with a laugh, "I guess, maybe a bit on small talk. Bit on flirting… Breaking into a group conversation. That sort of thing."

"Oh God. I hate those things too," I say, briefly forgetting my role as a life coach. "But er… I guess it gets easier with practice. I suppose everyone feels awkward at the beginning."

He nods over to a trio of guests loudly chatting like they're in an advert for Jacob's Creek chardonnay. "How would you break into that group over there?"

"Hmm. I'd march over and announce myself and just say, 'You all sound like you're having fun. Can I join?'"

He looks unconvinced as another braying laugh echoes from the corner. "Maybe I can build up to that. It might take work… What about you? Why are you here?"

"Oh. I guess I'm a little impatient with online dating. My thumb has RSI from swiping left, and I'm a bit fed up trying to condense my character into three paragraphs of hilarious prose."

I rattle on before realising that I'm pretty much just speaking as me, Alex, with the enigmatic Anastasia, Instructress in Love, temporarily forgotten. I switch back quickly. "Any other tips you'd like? You have full access to the mysteries of a woman's mind here."

He laughs, "Major conversational no-nos?"

"I'd say real ale, parking arrangements, and tooth whitening."

"I think that goes without saying." I can see his body start to relax slightly, and he seems to be genuinely enjoying our conversation.

"You would be surprised!" I say, nodding towards non-Ryan, who has collared the drunk girl from our happy band.

"Wow. Someone who needs more instruction than me," Ryan says.

"You don't really need instruction. Just a bit of a confidence boost," I say, deciding it's time to refocus on why I'm there. "You're funny; you have a nice smile. You're a good listener. Do you have any idea how unusual that is in guys? Most wouldn't have paid attention this long..." I trail off, realising the wine is making me over enthuse.

"Sorry, what were you saying?" he teases.

I swat at him playfully. Flirtatiously even. Eeek. That isn't part of the plan. It's time to evacuate.

"Haha. Anyway, make sure you remember – you ARE a good catch. I better go before my Uber turns into a pumpkin."

"Wait, wait. You're a terrible instructor. Three tips, and you're out of here? Can I at least buy you a drink sometime to say thank you?"

I suddenly feel flustered. My original mission feels like it's gone a bit off-piste. Shy Ryan has suddenly developed an obscene level of confidence. It must be the glow from the Anastasia effect. A drink. Does he mean a date? That would definitely complicate things. I was meant to disappear once my work here was done.

On the other hand, rejection now would totally undermine everything I did to boost his confidence. Surely it would be better to cement my work so far and have one date before I mysteriously move abroad? I could re-frame it as a coaching session and firmly remove any romantic element from it. It'd be good for him. And he is very handsome. However, as his coach, I shall retain a professional detachment and not consider the way a solitary dimple flashes when he grins or that his eyes are a gorgeous, rich brown that would be the envy of the contact lens industry. I will remain professional. I will just stick to the mission. And anyway, I'm sure I can spare an evening in my busy schedule of looking for jobs and disdainfully overseeing Adam's interactions with women to make time for such a noble pursuit.

He blushes deeply at my hesitation, and I'm so charmed by his shyness that I grab his phone.

"Sure, why not!" I exclaim and punch in my number before I have a chance to think better of it.

ONE

Two months earlier

"One of the main reasons a gecko might shed its tail is due to bullying; if this happens, remove the bullied gecko from the vivarium and isolate it until the tail has regrown in order to avoid infection."

I sigh. Now that I've reached the infectious lizard-skin-shedding bit of my writing marathon, I decide more wine is required. *Reptiles Monthly* pays well, better than any of my freelance writing. Still, it also involves building up an unexpectedly detailed anatomical knowledge of the mating habits of various types of turtles, scale-sores in grass snakes, and the less well-mannered aspects of a python's dining rituals.

I head to the kitchen to top up my wine mug. Yes, mug. The dishwasher's on, and I'm not Audrey Hepburn. I cast my mind back to my university self – the great aspiring film critic. All heavy eye shadow and faked attitude (and tan). To be fair, she'd probably be quite pleased with wine in a mug at 6pm on a Saturday. It's very Shoreditch. The penguin pyjamas, messy hair, and unicorn-shaped slippers, possibly slightly less so. As for the fact that instead of championing Iranian cinema to the masses, I'm wordsmithing the grooming needs of scaly pets for a little read periodical… well, probably better not to dwell on what she'd make of that.

The beginning of my spiral into self-judgement is mercifully interrupted by the melodious bells of my phone. My heart immediately betrays me, and I get that familiar little pang that it's Chris… that he's had a change of heart and decided to get back in touch finally. I hate how quickly I dive for my phone, my mind full of the happiest of memories while skilfully suppressing the bad ones.

It's my mother.

"Hello, Mother," I mutter ungraciously.

"Hi, darling! Have you been drinking?" Instantly suspicious, my mother has a knack for picking up on the smallest of slurs in my voice.

"No. I'm working," I mumble grumpily. "What is it?"

"I'm just phoning to say hello and, you know, check on how you're doing." Since Chris and I broke up six months ago, the awkward "How are you doing?" calls have significantly increased.

"I'm fine!"

She pounces. "You hesitated."

"Really, Mum. I. Am. Fine. Totally, 100% fine," I lie, wiping the corner of my eyes with my penguin sleeve. Why does someone asking how you are always weaken the floodgates?

Speaking of floodgates, it seems my mother's penchant for drama has been unleashed in a tsunami of maternal concern.

"Well, your father and I wanted to check you're OK. Being on the breadline in the world's most expensive city, you know… When are you going to start writing for a proper paper? I know you can do it. Chris managed it; why don't you give it a try?"

The reference to Chris and his fancy job as a sub-editor at *The Economist* is too much, and I let out an involuntary moan.

"Mum… Please don't bring Chris into this. He's a different kind of journalist."

"Yes, a salaried one. With a pension. Could you…?"

"No, I couldn't! His background and trajectory are totally different. I studied film. I want to write about film. It's not the same."

"Yes, but you're not writing about films, are you? You're writing about reptilian orgies or some such nonsense."

"Mum, that was a significant piece on the mating habits of the very endangered Tunisian Fringe-Fingered Lizard. They don't have orgies. It was a very important project to try and increase their numbers, and as a vet, I thought you would appreciate its importance! I can't talk to you about this anymore. I need to get on with my writing."

I manage to hang up five minutes later after promising to come home for the weekend soon to discuss My Future™ with her and Dad.

The thing is, I really loved Chris. We'd been together for five years, and I genuinely thought he was the one. God knows it was hard to meet new people in my hometown of Nowheresville, Cheshire, but when I met Chris, I just had this *feeling*. I knew. For most of my life, the only person I'd been able to talk to about writing was Bea, but everything changed after uni when I got a six-week internship at the *Knutsford Gazette*, our local newspaper, and Chris was at the next desk. Similar age, same dreams. I'd never really believed that sort of fairytale nonsense before (even though I'd faked it well during a brief stint writing horoscopes), but when he asked for my number in my final week, my stomach flipped. I knew, I just knew, that he wasn't going to ghost me or mess me around. It turns out our parents knew each other, too. He attended the private school in Chester, but my mother and his were in the Knutsford church choir, and his parents had even been to Mum and Dad's house for dinner. It was meant to be.

Everything was going so perfectly. We'd planned our big move to London and started excitedly making job applications. It was all so sweet and supportive; we'd read each other's applications and edit each other's writing samples. He was always just a bit ahead, but he was still my biggest supporter. And I didn't mind that he got the first job he interviewed for, the one I spent so many hours coaching him on that I neglected my own interview prep. He became a reporter for some small but worthy Ezine on environmentalism, while I ended up getting an admin job at a charity. It didn't matter, though; he still met me after my first day with prosecco and a smile like I'd won the Booker prize.

For me, the break-up came out of nowhere. He'd taken me to the Christmas markets in Krakow for the weekend to celebrate just after he'd got his foot in the door at *The Economist*, and I genuinely thought that now at least one of us had 'made it', he was going to propose. I'd spent all evening cooing at the wooden toys in the gorgeous little market stalls and squeezing his hand in mine as we walked through the winding streets, stopping to kiss at the beautiful displays of twinkling lights we passed. Every time we reached a secluded spot, I'd wonder: *Is this it?* Even when we headed back to the hotel, I still assumed he'd propose before our flight left the next day. I remember that evening so clearly.

When we got in, I started excitedly unpacking my shopping. I'd bought his mum a beautiful olive wood globe, and I showed it to him, thrilled. He seemed a little muted, but I assumed he was just tired, so I left him to it when he went to take a shower. When he got out, with wet hair and wrapped only in a towel, he seemed in a better mood, so I walked over to him and nuzzled into his chest. He pulled me close to him, telling me he loved me as he kissed trails down my body.

The next morning, I woke up and rolled into him, surprised that he was already awake. It was usually next to impossible to wake him in the morning unless you had a strong cup of coffee in hand and preferably a bacon sandwich. I ran my hand along his chest, hoping for a repeat of last night, but he didn't react. I started kissing him, but it was like kissing a statue, so I stopped.

"Chris? You OK?"

"Alex... I think we should break up."

It took me a minute to work out what he had actually said, and then I was immediately hit by a punch to the stomach. Sadness, fury, disbelief, disappointment, extreme hurt. For a second, I didn't know whether to cry or laugh, so I did both. I can't remember how long I cried for, but it felt like hours. In between shaking sobs, I remember him reassuring me that there was no other woman and that he cared about me. Still, he just didn't see things the same way I did or want the things I wanted, and now that he had his dream job, it was time to sort out the rest of his future, and he just didn't see that future happening with me.

When, a few weeks later, I saw pictures of a new woman on his Instagram, I felt like a fool for still crying into my cereal. The relationship had been over long before I'd known it was over. It didn't last with her, but the visceral pain I felt when I saw that picture will stay with me forever.

I was furious with him and humiliated. Angry with him for wasting five years of my life. Furious with him for doing this while I was far away from my family and friends. Humiliated that I, like an idiot, thought he was about to propose.

But then there was also that little voice inside my head whispering: *Why would he want to partner up permanently with me?* He was right. His career was going as planned, and he was smart, well-travelled and stylish. I still dressed like a student, spent my time lurching between all the freelancing writing gigs that no one else wanted, and putting my foot in it with Chris's similarly smart, well-travelled and stylish friends. *Who would want to marry this mess?*

I'm feeling pretty low after Mum's career pep talk and the memories it conjured up, so I take another slug of wine and contemplate my fate. Mum's right that I'm not doing what I always wanted to. Still, I am writing. It may not be startlingly original prose about cinema, but times are tough. Along with being the features writer for *Reptiles Monthly* (does what it says on the tin), I also manage the staff magazine for Sparkle Toothpaste, LLC. (that's a real page turner) and I had been ghostwriting the TV tie-in novels for the *Galactic Unicorns*™, the children's literature equivalent of Sunny Delight. Sadly, *Galactic Unicorns* had never completely captured the hearts of sprogs across the globe, and both the cartoon and the future books had been pulled two months ago. Not only will nobody ever find out if Loyal Majestic ever triumphed against Princess Gloom and her interstellar bats, but it also means that I am down a £15,000 contract for the year to keep the wine in my mug and me in my range of highly sexy pyjamas.

I top up my drink again and phone Bea, my best friend from home. Bea is thoroughly wonderful, the sort of best friend everyone needs. We don't see each other nearly as much as we should now that I live in London and she's still at home, working for the local branch of the RSPCA in Knutsford. She sees my parents more regularly than I do, a fact my mother never tires of reminding me.

Bea and my mum bonded over their mutual love of animals, Bea having once smuggled half the stray dog population of Cheshire into her dad's garden shed when she was eight. Even now, Bea always has a forlorn animal in tow that she's fostering, and my mother, being a vet, absolutely laps this up. Despite us now living in different places, nothing's really changed with Bea. She's the one person I don't speak to for weeks, and then we are able to pick up exactly where we left off. She never judges me, no matter what (although she often 'advises' me). She's the one person I've never felt the need to exaggerate to or withhold anything from.

She sometimes worries that I'll replace her with some Shoreditch-chic girlfriend or forget her as I lead my sparkling London life… if only she'd seen me try my conversational hot topics (*Murder She Wrote* and whether olives are zombie grapes) on some of Chris's female friends – all of whom seemed to speak five languages and know someone at *The Times* – she'd know she had nothing to worry about. I can't afford even the tiniest sparkle in London, let alone anything resembling glamour. My rent and bills take up most of my meagre income, and then food takes care of the rest. Also, not working in an office (thank God – neither my wallet nor my sanity could afford the rush hour commute) means that I have little opportunity to meet girlfriends, apart from the women my flatmate Adam brings home.

He's a blond and muscled personal trainer – so there are a few. While none appear to speak five languages, they're just as put off by my conversational gambits. Adam and I have lived together for three years now. He's also my cousin. He's my Aunty Sheila's – Mum's sister – son, and our mothers are super close, so Adam and I were pretty much brought up almost as siblings. He definitely pulls off the annoying older brother role with style.

Bea answers on the second ring. "Bea! I may have consumed the best part of a bottle of wine, half a pizza, and a multipack of miniature Mars Bars. And I'm in my penguin pyjamas. And I've just had a horror call from Mum. But apart from that, I am surviving!"

"Oh, my sweet darling," she says sympathetically, immediately seeing through my slurred bluster. "Tell me what's been happening."

I immediately unload the sorrows of the world upon her as she listens, occasionally interjecting with consoling noises and appropriate expressions of indignation. Even I manage to muster a small chuckle, and before I know it, I'm laughing away at her tales of scandal in Knutsford. Somehow, an hour has passed, and I'm feeling decidedly more cheerful.

I know Bea's worried about me though, because she offers to come down to London for the weekend. This is concerning for two reasons. Bea is a self-proclaimed 'small-town person' and is proud of it, but more than that, she claims to loathe Adam. Her feminist credentials don't allow her to be civil to someone who has occasionally been known to invent suave personas to seduce women at parties. Despite this, I've caught her eyeing his muscles when she thinks I'm not looking.

"I love you for the offer, Bea, but really, it's OK. I promised Mum and Dad I'd come down in the next few weeks, so why don't I choose a date, and then we can have a wine night?"

She agrees happily, and I briefly probe her knowledge of reptile keeping before we hang up. It's limited. Apparently, she prefers to rehabilitate cuddly pets and leaves the scaly ones to the others.

Having done all I could with linguistic flair in the world of reptile keeping, I look again at my emails.

Nothing from *Empire*, *Film* or any of the other magazines I've harassed recently. Optimism overthrowing cynicism for a moment, I check my junk mail. It's not full of ten increasingly desperate pleas from a major newspaper to find out why I am ignoring their requests to be their film critic. It's just the usual smattering of discounted Viagra and malware attempts. I'm not sure if it's just the surging return of my usual cynicism, but the wine mug's looking half empty instead of half full. I top it up again and bravely click through to the job sites for journalists and writers.

Some projects appear beyond me (*Galactic Unicorns* doesn't get you through the door at *The Guardian*), but I start to make a list of a few other jobs. *Saga Magazine* is looking for a consumer affairs writer, and then there's the usual array of small organisations looking to offer magic beans for a writer's sweat and tears. Nothing seems remotely close to keeping me in my high-falutin' lifestyle of a poor person living in a child's bedroom in zone three of the capital, but suddenly, I spot the gold at the end of the rainbow. A gig that promises more than even animated magic horses have ever coughed up.

I click on it and start reading: Ladditude Magazine *(circulation 200,000) is offering a contract for an engaging and empathetic writer* ("Check!" I hiccough quietly to myself) *to man an advice column for its readers.*"

"I give great advice," I mutter before realising I'm speaking to the wine mug. Excitement building, I continue reading: Ladditude's *new Agony Uncle will share his best tips and wisdom with* Ladditude's *diverse readership. Exploring everything from the pressures of being a modern man to health and fitness tips, the Agony Uncle will b brother voice of authority and compassion."*

Uncle? Brother? So much for the magic unicorn gold. Bloody men. I'm on the precipice of my 'down with the patriarchy' rant. The frequency of these rants (which count as some of my most original and surreal creative outputs) has seesawed in the six months since Chris and I broke up.

There's become something very *Academy Award* acceptance speech about them. I've taken to speaking dramatically into my wine mug microphone, complete with melodramatic gesticulations. However, I've reached the point where they've become circular and boring, and the imaginary Oscars musicians have started to serenade me off-stage right, so instead, I settle for bravely logging into my bank account. It's a torturous adventure into Mordor, an exploration of emptiness and desolation that has increased significantly since my rent went out of my current account yesterday. I still haven't quite seemed to grasp that this happens with a terrifying regularity every month, so it always feels like I've been sucker punched in the ribs when I log in and discover I'm down another £650. I keep hoping that one day I'll log in and be one of those people who mistakenly has £5 million placed into their bank account. Except in my case, they'll never realise, and I'll move to an idyllic Tuscan vineyard like in *Under the Tuscan Sun* and change my name by deed poll, and they'll never track me down. And then I'll fall in love with a sexy Italian man, and we'll ride off into the sunset together in his vintage car. I'm losing myself in blissful fantasy until I foolishly scroll further through my online banking app and notice the wasteland has got even bleaker, thanks in part to a karaoke night with Bea the night after the school reunion last month and an impulse buy of fresh lobster when I had delusions of Adam and I hosting a fancy party. And Häagen-Dazs. And prosecco.

The dangers of online shopping. Who even buys lobster online? Can I still cancel? I take a slurp from the mug and log in to my account to try and save myself from my impending bankruptcy by crustacean. As the evening has darkened and my £6 bottle of wine has grown tastier, my screen has grown correspondingly hazier. I jab at the app a few times optimistically before arriving at a 'Thank you' message. Buoyed by one task successfully completed, I consider my next productive step. The wine mug is helping me consolidate my life choices. As I scroll through more freelance gigs, I keep getting pulled back to the most lucrative one, *Ladditude's* Agony Uncle.

The sound of the key in the lock interrupts my productivity. The last thing I need is to bump into Adam's latest conquest, undoubtedly several years younger than him and several light years more stylish than me. I hear him doing what he thinks is his sexy voice, husky mockney, in the hallway. Something chirrups in response, and at first, I think he's lured home a cockatoo until I realise the sound is the titter of some early twenty-something.

He offers her wine, and then I hear the expletive when he spots the space in the fridge where the bottle had been. I glance guiltily at its new home on my desk. It *has* gone to a better place, to be fair. It's found a more deserving beneficiary than a twenty-two-year-old suspected member of the parrot family. In the living room, I hear Spotify on full blast. Deprived of wine, Adam has embarked on stage two of his seductive strategy – songs that his plentiful nightclub experience tells him make women want to writhe around sweatily against his torso. The cockatoo twitters with delight, and I just know it's going to be a long night. I take a few slurps of my contraband wine and crank up my Country & Western break-up songs list on Spotify. Two can play that game.

As I'm slow dancing with my dressing gown, swirling around the room and draping the arms around me romantically in what I presume is a majestic fashion, I open my laptop, and the following things might have happened:

- I check Chris's Instagram again, and after scrolling back through hundreds of photos accidentally like one from several years ago
- I start drafting a letter about sexism to *Ladditude*
- I check in to make sure my wine mug is well-provided for
- I start drafting an application letter to *Ladditude*
- I pass out gently on my bed, snug in my penguin pyjamas
- Audrey Hepburn reincarnated.

TWO

The invitation pops up in my email while I'm researching freelance gigs/watching videos of puppies meeting kittens for the first time:

"Position at *Ladditude*," I read.

Dear Mr Taylor,

Thank you for applying for the role of Agony Uncle at Ladditude. Our team were very impressed with your writing samples, and we would like to invite you to an interview on Wednesday at 15.00 via Zoom. As we are a small company, we do not have offices and tend to work remotely. Please let me know if this time is convenient and if you are open, in theory, to remote working. We look forward to meeting you.

Best wishes,
Stephen Lippman

Crap. While I admire my determination to take on the patriarchy after several glasses of wine, I'm feeling slightly less enthusiastic in the sober light of day. I wander into the kitchen and take a huge gulp of coffee, and slowly, the fog clouding my brain starts to roll back. I remember exactly what led to hitting the 'submit' button; the final straw was seeing one too many smug Instagrams of first homes and refitted kitchens. That got me dreaming of a regular gig rather than living hand to mouth for the privilege of writing for thirty people a month. Drunk me is hardly going to let a little thing like not being the preferred gender get in my way. Sober me, however, is arguably more sensible. I ponder the idea of being Agony Uncle for *Laddititude*, which a quick Google assures me is every bit as blokey as the name suggests, and discount it.

It's fine. It's all fine. I'll just write back to this Stephen Lippman person and tell him that I've got another job. It must happen all the time. There's nothing else I can do anyway. I mean, the email was very nice and complimentary about my writing, and I am a bit short of cash… but there's really no way I can get around the whole being a woman thing, so I'll have to let it go. Definitely, I will let it go.

Firm in resolve, I wander to the cafetière and top up my coffee. I'm sipping it thoughtfully when Adam slouches in, bare-chested and smug, with a girl who cannot be more than twenty-two in tow, confirming my earlier suspicions. He attempts to high-five me as if we're Little League buddies while she scrolls through her phone in the background.

"Alright, Alex?" he announces. "Big night last night?"

"Err… no… just a quiet one. I stayed in," I mutter, unwilling to confess about the Agony Uncle job in front of his fledgling.

"It sounded like you were having an interesting evening…" he trails off, chuckling, and I redden slightly.

I'm about to tentatively ask why he might have that impression when he decides to tell me anyway. "You were singing "Before He Cheats" by Carrie Underwood… over and over and over again. At top volume. Still working off some post-Chris rage?"

"I'm fine," I say, shooting daggers at Adam and glancing at the fledgling, trying to remember how developed female intuition is at twenty-two and wondering if she'll display some female solidarity. She seems more preoccupied with her iPhone, so I'm assuming not. God, I miss being in my early twenties.

She and Adam start making nauseating kissing noises, so I drain my coffee and grab my coat, leaving the flat before they induce any potential after-effects of my heavy night of drinking.

Typically, it's raining outside, but not enough to brave the love nest for my umbrella. "Get it together, Alex," I mumble to myself. "You're twenty-nine. Get a grip." I wander into a café for some shelter, and as I wait for my too-posh omelette to arrive, I realise I've gone into my overdraft again. Way, way into it. It's like that point in the cave where potholers intuitively realise that if they don't turn back now, they might not make it (I know this from my brief time at *Potholers Weekly*). I start to feel a bit frantic. Blood pressure rises, my heart beats faster, and I start to get sweaty palms, but the waitress is already approaching with my unaffordable meal.

I take a forkful of eggs, chewing distractedly while desperately combing through my memory, trying in vain to remember how I could be so overspent. In a panic, I start going through what funds have yet to go out of my account and what will come in. My rent has gone already, which is the biggest expense, but I still owe Adam for bills. I'll get some money this week from *Reptiles Monthly*, and I'll get my final paycheck from *Galactic Unicorns*, but that's it.

I need to stop going out for breakfast, I say as I take another bite of the posh omelette. With every bite of that flavoursome egg, I'm aware I'm standing in a burning building, striking matches. I take a steadying breath. OK. Let's focus on solutions. I need to start looking for new jobs. As soon as I get home, I will be laser-focused on my job hunt. No distractions. I'm a good writer with a broad enough portfolio; it can't be that difficult to find a job that pays properly. Adam was also going on about some book I should buy about self-control, which I absolutely will order next week.

Now that I've solved my impending homelessness, I ignore the dissenting voice in my head telling me that I've been unsuccessfully looking for a secure writing job for years and the whisper that cuts sharpest: wanting it isn't the same as deserving it. I CAN do this. It's just imposter syndrome. I'm versatile; I'm adaptable. Chris always said I was the stronger writer. I take myself firmly in hand before I can wander down a traumatic memory lane and settle my bill, leaving a tip I can't afford.

By the time I get home, I'm feeling decidedly better and more confident. I open the front door and wander into the kitchen. Adam is sitting at the kitchen table, sans fledgling, looking morose. "What's up?" I ask him, not overly concerned with his answer.

"Kristel's gone," he says glumly. "Thought she should date someone closer to her age."

"That's fine, isn't it?" I wonder. "You didn't want to date her, did you? You don't want to date anyone!"

"No, but I'm not used to being dumped. I'm usually the dumper. Especially not because of my age," Adam mutters darkly before stalking off to his bedroom to demolish some zombies on his Xbox.

I go and get my laptop and bring it back to the kitchen table, Googling writing jobs and thinking that I'll be available to talk if Adam does emerge. Next, freelance writing jobs. Nothing. Editorial jobs. A bunch pop up, but none are suitable. I don't think I'm ready to be managing editor of the *Financial Times* quite yet. I keep trying, with every different amalgamation of the words writing, editing, and freelance writer I can think of. Nada. I start feeling a bit panicky, and my search terms become increasingly generous. Assistant newsletter writer in a secondary school. Wigan County Council newsletter writer. Christmas travel information for Transport for London pamphlet writer. Nothing. Nothing. Big nothing. That feeling of dread from earlier crawls back, threatening my fragile stability, when Adam wanders back in and slumps in the chair opposite me, having presumably saved enough of the city from the undead to earn a break.

"Is this what it feels like to be you?" he asks glumly.

"Excuse me?"

"This feeling of emptiness. Men not wanting you because of your age. Being abandoned for someone younger."

I roll my eyes. Adam isn't mean. He just happens to

be as self-involved as the grandest of divas. Underneath that muscle, an inner Elizabeth Taylor is screaming, "It's all about me!"

"Adam, I know it must be weird to be the one getting knocked back, but she was a one-night stand. There's no need to cry about it."

"It's not that," he whines. "It's the whole ageing thing. I spent an hour this morning while you were out looking for wrinkles in the mirror. I think I found one. Look." He comes up to me and puts his face so close to mine that I can see his nostril hair billowing when he breathes.

"I can't see anything, Adam."

"Look!" he commands

I look again. "Oh, I guess maybe a tiny one. But that's normal at…" I trail off before adding "at your age."

Unfortunately, he deduces the missing words and looks thunderous. "It's alright for you. You've had several years to get used to wrinkles and rejection."

He realises about thirty seconds too late what he's said, and he tries to backtrack, but it's too late. It's been a tough morning; saying goodbye to posh omelettes and my tumbleweed existence, and my mantra about ignoring Adam's inner diva's ramblings fails me. A traitorous tear escapes and makes a bid for freedom down my cheek. I'm embarrassed, and I furiously wipe it away, but another one follows down the same track.

"Alex… Alex, I'm so sorry. I didn't mean it. I swear," Adam has that stricken look that women come to associate with a cornered man presented with a crying woman. He turns fuschia and ups the back peddling. "Come on. You know I didn't mean it."

I glare at him through my sodden eyelashes and say nothing.

"Alex… don't cry. How can I fix this? Do you want me to fetch your multipack of Mars bars?"

Damn, so he had spotted them hidden at the back of the cupboard. Slowly, the seeds of an idea start to germinate in my hungover, worried brain.

"No. But there is something else you *could* do…" I say cautiously. "Adam, how do you feel about… impersonation?"

He shrugs. "Go on."

I tell him all about my financial situation and about drunkenly applying for a job at *Ladditude*.

He listens carefully and then laughs, correctly guessing what I'm hinting at. "I can't pretend to be you. I think they'd figure it out. I don't barely speak English, let alone write it!"

"You're putting that on. Look, it's working from home! They never have to see me!" I protest. "You'd just need to do the Zoom interview. The rest can all be me."

"But…" he stammers.

Before he can come up with any negatives, I interject, "You just made me feel like Miss Bloody Havisham. This is the least you can do. You owe me. Also, at the rate things are going, I won't be able to afford to keep living here unless I get a new contract. You don't want to live with a stranger, do you?"

"Alex… I'd never get through the interview. I don't know anything about writing and all that shit you do."

I ignore the last bit. "I'll prep you," I plead. "And they have my portfolio. They'll be confident you can write."

"What if there's a test?"

"Well, then, I won't get the job, and I'll be in no worse shape than I am right now."

"Are you sure I can't just get you another Mars Bar multipack?" Adam pleads.

I glare.

"OK, OK. I'll do it. I'll go and talk crap about writing. How hard can it be? It's just making stuff up and remembering to use the spellchecker, right?"

"Adam Hunter. Welcome to the literati."

THREE

"OK. We're all prepped!" I announce cheerfully, steering Adam over to the kitchen table. He looks nervously at the waiting laptop, like a man approaching the scaffold.

"Are we going to get into trouble for doing this? Isn't this fraud? You know I'm too pretty for jail."

"Yes, I know. You mention that on a surprisingly frequent basis. Look. It's a Zoom interview for an online magazine. We're not talking about laundering money for the mafia. They'll never know. Anyway, you're the one who's always telling me to take risks," I tell him.

"I meant things like bungee jumping in New Zealand or staying out past 8pm. Not conning some magazine into thinking you're a bloke."

"It's a white lie. They really liked my samples. Anyway, why shouldn't I be an Agony Uncle? I can be just as dumb as any guy. All you need to do is stick with the plan; it'll be fine."

As Adam takes his seat, I position myself on the other side of the table with my trusty whiteboard and marker pens.

He still looks stricken, so I soften my tone slightly. I can't have him taking flight the second the phone is answered.

"Look," I say in my most soothing tones. "It'll be a thirty-minute video chat. Stick with the script, and remember to pull on your earlobe if you need input. You'll be absolutely fine."

I smile at him beseechingly, but he just grimaces slightly and takes on a somewhat greenish hue. Deep breaths. The room has turned from a scruffy Clapham kitchen into a gangster's den – all plots and secret signals. Suddenly, the laptop starts ringing with the incoming Zoom call. I keep my most reassuring smile plastered across my face, which I'm worried looks to others like a face from *The Shining*, and signal for Adam to answer. He does, with a nervous "hello", at least an octave higher than his normal pitch.

From my position by the whiteboard, I can just hear the tinny voices of a panel of men going through introductions and a summary of what they are looking for from their agony uncle. *Bloke's bloke… blah blah… but sensitive… strong writer… someone who spends more time in the pub than the theatre.* The expected spiel.

"Can you tell us a little about why you want to write for *Ladditude*?"

Adam visibly relaxes. This was one of the obvious questions we had rehearsed. An avid reader of *Ladditude*. He's a writer who keeps his finger on the pulse of men's issues. It trips off the tongue. Adam may not always be the most reliable flatmate, but it turns out he's an outstanding pet parrot.

"And we notice you've written for quite an unusually broad range of publications. How would you describe your interests?"

Adam fidgets and pulls his ear lobe. I spring into action, and my marker pen squeaks across the whiteboard.

"Pretty esoteric," I hold up.

"Er," Adam stalls, "pretty erotic." I drop the whiteboard and my trusty marker pen rolls under the table.

I hear a slightly nervous laugh from the laptop. "Erotic interests? In what way?"

At this point, Adam is pulling his earlobe pretty much down to his shoulder. The brief pause seems to last forever as I speed write 'just open about sex' on the board.

Adam lets go of his ear. "Just open-air sex," he tells the panel. I almost smash the whiteboard over his barely literate head.

There's definitely another nervous laugh from one of the panel and an agonising silence from the rest. Then one voice says decisively, "I like it. Exhibitionism. Dogging. Some of the sexual taboos people never want to talk about. You're an interesting man, Alex. One other question: We're looking for a talented writer but also someone who will connect with our readership. Tell me, what's the most laddish thing you've ever done?"

I freeze for a moment. I remember the hours I spent coaching Chris before his interviews in London, and one of the key things I kept stressing to him was the importance of connecting with the readership. Chris was – *is* – an immensely talented writer, but he occasionally comes across as a little patronising in his writing. We spent hours prepping, with me as chief cheerleader and supportive critic, getting him to change his tone from lecturer to equal.

Connecting with the readership. It's amazing how a single phrase can jolt you back down memory lane. I suddenly snap back to the present. I unstop the marker pen and desperately start scribbling, aware that leaving Adam to his own devices can never be a good thing. I'm writing almost before I know where I'm going, but it's too late. Before I even finish thinking of a story, Adam offers, "I once threw up on a nun."

How dare he improvise. I wave my arms at him in a little dance of rage.

"A nun? You were sick on a nun?" I hear one of the panellists ask.

"I was on a bus. And hungover. I *had* just got my GCSEs, so we'd had stuff to celebrate," Adam says by way of explanation.

Instead of being uncomfortably silent, the panel members are all laughing. They LIKE the mildly sacrilegious chunder story. Adam, always a crowd pleaser, follows up with a couple of stories you really shouldn't even tell your best mates down the pub, let alone in a job interview, but they seem to lap it up. A few more questions, and then the panel tells him that's it for now and they'll be in touch in a few days.

As the call ends, Adam leans back smugly in his chair, "I think I pretty much nailed that."

I feel more conflicted. "You told them Alex Taylor is into outdoor sex."

"I thought that's what you wrote on your dumb whiteboard," Adam protested.

"And you didn't even wait for my words before you launched into your nun tale."

"I was trying to, but you looked like a Basilisk had petrified you. I couldn't wait. And was it going to be better than my story?" he challenged.

Determined not to smile at his *Harry Potter* reference, I grumble, "Yes, as it happens – but it doesn't matter now. Do you think they really liked the answers?"

"Totally," says Adam breezily. "You didn't see their faces. One guy almost fell off his chair with the open-air sex bit."

Well, it's all done now. My name is either on their shortlist or a watchlist.

FOUR

I've been staring anxiously at my phone all week, willing it to be a call from *Ladditude*. For the first time in a long while, I'm hoping it's something other than an out-of-the-blue call from Chris. I'd consider that a major breakthrough if it wasn't so driven by necessity: I'm overdrawn by £1,000. I know *Ladditude* won't call, though. I just know it. After that farcical interview, I've about as much chance of getting that job as there is of Martin Scorsese directing a rom-com.

"Any news?" Adam wanders into the kitchen, looking hopeful. I shake my head.

I'd wanted to give him a hard time after the interview, but he looked so pleased with himself that I just didn't have it in me to berate him.

"Stop staring at it. You need to go and do something. You're focusing on it too much." Adam has a strange, slightly spiritual look, and I wonder if he found the article I'd tried to sell to *Zen Zumba* a few months ago. I'm pretty sure a few of the early drafts ended up scrunched into balls and thrown behind the sofa. It turns out to be surprisingly difficult to write about the power of yoga when you've never so much as tried to touch your toes.

"You need to go get laid or something," Adam continues, and I swiftly revise my opinion of him from 'zen' to 'constipated'.

He's right, though. About getting out in general, not about the sex. OK, maybe a bit about the sex. I think back to Chris. How well he knew my body, how he knew exactly how to touch me in ways that made me instantly melt. I could be having the worst day, and he would fold me into his arms, and it would all become instantly better. The security made the rejection-filled life of a writer that much more manageable, less sharp somehow. Even the 'thanks but no thanks' from *Zen Zumba* hurt that bit more.

I slam the door on my Chris reverie, grab my coat and wander out into the crisp autumnal day. I fully intend to go for a walk in the park and enjoy kicking up the blanket of burnt orange leaves – imagining myself lost in deep thought like a modern-day *Annie Hall*. Unfortunately, to get to the park, I have to wander down the high street, past so many enticing cafes full of warming cappuccino and fluffy pain au chocolat.

My willpower lasts about seven whole minutes, and then, almost of their own accord, I find my feet headed towards a little coffee shop. Before I know what I'm doing, I order a hot chocolate but manage to resist the blueberry muffin at a typical London price that could cover a decent evening meal in other parts of the country. My stomach grumbles at my resistance: Leaf kicking and deep thoughts are all well and good, but sadly, they're never going to compete with overpriced sugar on a fake antique Chesterfield.

I may have managed to avoid the exercise, but the unwanted thoughts creep in regardless of location or activity. Memories of Chris swirl and eddy, and the more I resist them, the more they become all-consuming. I pick up my phone and open Instagram, desperate for that swipe-induced dopamine hit to eradicate my thoughts. Seeing a post by Overheard Bumble, the Insta account of the popular dating app, catapults my thoughts back to the heady days post-break-up when I attempted to bury my emotions by dating up a storm. An error.

There was the date with Frank, the, it turns out, hugely religious guy who spent the entire date telling me he could only marry a strict Catholic. This was not listed on his profile, and I am not a strict Catholic by even the most charitable of definitions. Then there was Peter, the man who wasted my evening sobbing into a pint about his ex, who he was still paying rent for, as well as the occasional electricity bill. Then there was Simon, who had a chip on his shoulder about his height, who, despite claiming to be 6'3", was actually 5'6", which would have been fine if he hadn't been so resolutely furious about it. And then Doug, who was a bit of a know-it-all and thought he could do everything better than everyone – right down to leaning over the bar and pulling his own pint. Finally, the guy, Jonathan, who got the clock change thing wrong and turned up an hour early, only to go on a rant about women disrespecting men's time when I wasn't ready to leave – a rant which he didn't take back when a laughing Adam pointed out that it was his fault.

Worst of all, though, were the dates when everything felt amazing and electric, and I would melt into a first kiss like I've kissed them a thousand times. The ones where I was instantly connected to them and comfortable with them. I would be giddy all the way home, knowing with an unfamiliar certainty that I'd get a "safely home? I had such a great night – can't wait to see you again. x" text. The next morning, I'd wake up and look at my phone expectantly, knowing in my bones I'd have a sweet good morning message. But then boom. I was greeted only with the WhatsApp silhouette and no 'last seen' timestamp, meaning he'd blocked me, and I'm left to spend the rest of the week analysing with Bea over his clearly avoidant attachment style, his mother issues and his deep-seated fear of intimacy and commitment.

People say it's an ocean of available men out there, but we all know there's more plastic than fish in the sea at this point.

Feeling decidedly sorry for myself, I drain the rest of my hot chocolate and head home. Even the sugary warmth is not enough to exorcise the ghosts of bad dates past. I know this path of rumination only leads to bad things, but it's just so hard. With Chris, everything felt so perfect – so *right*; the chemistry was off the charts. I gave my heart and soul to that relationship, and it scares me. Even though I gave it my all, I still couldn't make it work. No matter what I sacrificed for him, be it attending his friend's birthday over mine when they fell on the same night or cancelling Bea, who was coming to stay because he had a big project at work, it just never seemed to be enough. He always seemed vaguely disappointed in me, like I was never quite living up to his expectations of perfection.

When I reach home and open the front door, Adam is practically jumping up and down with excitement. "Alex, Alex, Alex! Amazing news! About two minutes after you left, the house phone started ringing. I mean, I don't think it's ever rung before! At first, I thought it was the carbon monoxide alarm. I started opening windows and everything."

I roll my eyes. Adam's sense of drama can grate on a difficult day. "Is that the news? You've worked out that we have a house phone? And *I'm* the one who needs to get out more."

Adam continues, unfazed: "But then I followed the sound into the living room, and there it was, on that little table behind the armchair. This dusty old house phone! At first, I thought it might just be your parents or my parents because who even uses a house phone below the age of seventy? And then I thought it's probably just one of those dodgy scams…"

"Did your thoughts stretch at any point to picking up the phone?"

"They did. And it was them! It was *Ladditude*! They want me to start on Monday! I said I could. They said they loved my writing style and enjoyed how candid I was when it came to discussing sex and eroticism, and an open-minded, experimental, non-judgemental person is exactly what they want."

I gasp audibly. I never thought people do that outside the movies. But today, I manage it.

"I got the job!" I shriek.

"Well, *we* got the job!" Adam says. "They liked my eroticness! Maybe *I* could be a writer…"

"Writer? Adam Hunter, you have never so much as sent a single cogent or coherent text message in your life. I can't see you making it as a writer."

"Hmm. You said good writing is about communication, not grammar."

Great, *now* he remembers what I told him.

"Nah. Don't worry. It's your gig. But if you become famous, you better remember me generously. I've already been out to get us a celebratory bottle of Tesco's Finest sparkling wine."

An hour and a half a bottle of cheap sparkling wine later, I've composed my thank you speech for when I win the Best Agony Uncle of the Year award. Obviously, Adam hasn't found out any pertinent details from *Ladditude*, so once again, in my go-to pyjamas, I draft an enthusiastic email to Stephen Lippman, clarifying the salary details and the submission process. I also mention that I frequently travel so meetings are easier by phone. He replies swiftly (it is only 4pm), reassuring me that they don't mind being flexible as long as I get the work done, and as the Agony Uncle role is so self-contained, there's no expectation of my joining editorial meetings. Thank. God. I send an effusively grateful response and return to contemplating my new gig. Then, as if on cue to sap my joy, in pings an email from my appropriately cold-blooded managing editor at *Reptiles Monthly*.

Alex,

Your deadline was an hour ago. I expect to see the feature on the Sand Skink in thirty minutes.

Flora.

Damn. Back to reality. I get to work on finalising my compelling prose on the eating habits of the Sand Skink. It's kind of interesting, to be fair, if not something you'd want to read about while eating.

I'm polishing off the article when *Ladditude* sends over the first batch of correspondence they've received since advertising their new column in case I want to get a head start for Monday. Amongst the bodybuilding, erectile dysfunction, and fears of baldness, one email stands out:

I am 10 years old, and I'm kind of hating school. Since I was very small, I have always been bullied, but in the last few months, it's got a lot worse. My voice broke before anyone else's, and I didn't want to go to school at all, but my dad told me that it was a sign of being a man and that everyone would think I was really cool. They didn't, and the teasing is getting worse all the time. I saw Ladditude's *post about writing in with problems and stuff, so I thought I'd give it a bash. I really hate school – and nobody really understands. They say to just ignore the bullies, but that doesn't really work. If you ignore them, they hit you just the same.*
Thank you,
Troubled.

I frown as I read *Troubled*'s letter. Maybe I'm in over my head. I have no experience with voices breaking or anything that boys go through in puberty. I was sort of hoping to be advising from a (secret) female perspective on guys' various idiotic actions when it came to dating women. I decide to come back to *Troubled's* letter after I do some research. I move on to another.

Dear Alex,

I've been with my girlfriend for two years, and I really love her. The problem is her "best friend." It's a guy. I'm sure the problem could be my jealousy, as my girlfriend maintains, but I can't help feeling a little worried every time they're alone together. I'm really trying not to be that jealous, paranoid guy, but I feel like he deliberately provokes me. He flirts with her in front of me and tells her she looks beautiful all the time, and he knows her so well that even though she tries to hide it, I can tell he nails her birthday and Christmas gifts better than me. I just don't know what to do. Every time I bring it up, we argue, and I know if I were to give an ultimatum (yes, I know that's a terrible idea…), she would choose him anyway. I trust her completely… just not him.

Help! I don't want to lose her, but I can't put up with this forever.

Second in Love

Oh good, one I can answer.

Dear Second in Love,

That sounds tough. However, I think women have had to put up with their boyfriends having female friends and ex-girlfriends (and mistresses!) around for centuries, so I'm sure you can learn to trust and accept your girlfriend's version at face value. If you don't have trust, what is there? You say you trust her, but it takes two to tango, so there must be a small part of you that doesn't trust her if you're entertaining such thoughts. You don't own her. Come to terms with your jealousy, or move on.

Alex

I sit back, proud and a little drained from my masterful first response. Who knew dispensing wisdom could be so cathartic? I re-read my advice. Yes, it's good. I'm doing this girl a huge favour. I take a sip of tea and am just about to get to the next letter when Adam wanders in.

He sits down opposite me and stares at me, his slightly over-tanned features radiating smugness. "I've saved you," he announces, "yet again!"

"Saved me?" I ask. "From?"

"This time – from your impending spinsterhood."

I glance at him coldly, much like a western bush viper might consider a mouse. What has he done now? I suppress the absurd hope that, by some miracle, he has persuaded Chris to get in touch with me again.

"I've set you up on a date with Malcolm," he continues, with an expression of accomplishment that I find baffling.

"I don't want to go on a date with Malcolm," I mutter through gritted teeth. Adam's friend Malcolm is a complete troglodyte… he's the type of man that sends sane women running at speed for the nearest convent. Surely the last time he had a girlfriend was an after-school playdate? When Adam invited him here, he spent the evening drunkenly leering at me (despite my ardour-killing pyjamas). There is no way I'm going. None. I'd rather live on an island with only a palm tree aggressively dropping coconuts on me and an angry pelican for company.

Oblivious to my internal monologue, Adam continues, "You do. He's a nice guy who was just a bit drunk that time he came around. He's doing really well. He owns a two-bed flat in Battersea!"

I try to picture Adam in a Jane Austen-esque Mrs Bennet's bonnet.

"Look, he's around in Clapham later anyway, so he can pick you up at eight tonight. Remember, you promised your mum you would be more open-minded about dates. I'd hate to have to Facebook her with the truth…"

"ADAM!" I explode. "That is completely uncool of you." He looks unmoved, so I try a different tack. "I can't anyway. Even if I wanted to, which I don't, I have to get my first advice section sorted for *Ladditude*."

That catches his interest, and he strolls over to me and stands behind me, looking over my shoulder at the screen.

"Alex, you haven't sent that yet, have you?" He's reading my letter to *Second in Love*.

"Not yet, but it's good, isn't it?" I answer proudly.

"Good? It's horrific. No guy would write that to another guy who came to him in confidence asking for help!" He looks shocked enough for me to wonder if I should take him seriously. He ushers me out of my seat and starts pounding away at my keyboard.

"There!" he announces with a flourish. "Much better."

I reclaim my seat and read, correcting the proliferation of typos:

Dear Second in Love,
I totally get how you must be feeling right now, and I'm sorry. That really sucks. Without knowing your girlfriend,

it's hard to advise, but all I can say is that in my experience, honesty is the best policy, and communication is key. I think it's best to be truthful with her about your feelings. Explain that you love her and that you're feeling a bit threatened by this friendship, and ask if there are some compromises you can come up with. You could suggest you get to know him more so you feel less threatened, or you could do some double dating. If she doesn't meet you halfway, I'd genuinely reconsider the relationship, as it sounds like this is getting you down.

Yours,
Alex

"Wow!" I say, impressed. "That's actually pretty good. Why don't you treat relationships like that in real life?"

"Oh, I know what I'm supposed to do," Adam says. "It's just that women like a project they can fix. I'm happy to be that for them. Public service and all that jazz."

He continues, apparently immune to my ice dagger glare, "Speaking of projects… Malcolm. You should get changed. I know he's slightly batting above with you, but you should at least shower."

"Not. Going." I stand my ground, but Adam looks undeterred, pulling out his phone. "Are you texting Malcolm to tell him I can't make it?"

"Nope! Facebooked your mum. Told her she could stop fretting about your committed singleness. She's really pleased."

Ten minutes later, my phone pings. "That'll be her," Adam said, smiling.

I look down at my phone. Dammit. Text from Mum,

despite her loathing of 21st-century technology: "Alex. Adam.told.me.about.your.date!Your.father.and.I.are. over. the.moon!So.good.to.get.back.on.that.bicycle.again. after.Chris.Remember.your.hair.dear.A.quick.comb. never.hurt.anyone.and.also.be.careful.to.meet.publicly. in.case.he.is.a.sociopath."

I groan. Dammit. Also, interesting that advice about sociopaths is secondary to hair combing. I glare at Adam. Sometimes I hate him. Hate him.

"So!" he smiles brightly. "What are you going to wear?"

FIVE

An hour later, I'm back in the kitchen. In deliberate rejection of Mum's advice, my hair is carefully tousled à la "I've just fallen out of bed… a bed which, by the way, is frequented by ocean waves with the perfect amount of salt in," and a dress which I hope makes Malcolm think I am attractive and makes him want me, but doesn't in any way indicate that I may be dressing to impress or have any interest in him. It's a complicated balance. He is a lout, but I want to be very clear on having the upper hand.

Given the date was with Malcolm, I wasn't inclined to change out of my jeans and comfy sweater, but with the ever-present threat of Adam contacting my mother, I was grudgingly persuaded to make an effort.

To be fair, I started to get into the swing of things after about three outfits, enjoying twirling around in front of my mirror like Marilyn and feeling a bit princessy. I'm starting to feel excited about the concept of a man finding me desirable enough to want to have dinner with me until I remember that it's Malcolm. Still, though, maybe this is a sign that I'm finally ready to go on a real date. I make a mental note to download Hinge when I get home tonight. Adam has just put the kettle on when the doorbell rings. Usually, I value good time-keeping ability in a man, but not when it's something I'm about as excited as *Furcifer Labordi* Chameleons are about losing their virginity (thanks, *Reptiles Monthly*). I don't move, and Adam starts hissing, "Door!"

I studiously ignore him and stare at the kettle until he reluctantly gets up to answer the buzzer.

"Malcolm! Mate, come on in!" Adam reaches towards Malcolm and pulls him into a man hug. I can sense them meandering towards me, and I have never been so fascinated by my nails. Adam prods me in the ribs, and I jump. "Malcolm, you remember Alex?"

"How could I forget such beauty?" he murmurs, in what he probably thinks is a seductive manner, and I slightly die inside.

Malcolm is dressed like a student circa 1999 but shaped like a darts player circa 1989. Externally, I give a wry smile.

"Well! You two lovebirds, enjoy yourselves!" Adam simpers and bounds out of the kitchen.

"Shall we go?" I say to Malcolm, standing up awkwardly. I decide to make myself as physically and vocally unappealing as possible.

He makes a show of draping my coat around my shoulders and rushing around in front of me to open my own front door for me. In fairness, if I were the slightest bit interested in him, I'd probably be loving this. Maybe I'm being slightly too harsh. Then his eyes linger a distressingly long time on my cleavage, and I revert to my original dismay.

My expectations improve when we arrive at the restaurant. Malcolm's chosen an amazing French riverside restaurant, which I've always wanted to go to but could never afford in a million years. My stomach tenses as I wonder whether he will want to split the bill, but what with his faux chivalry and pomposity, that surely won't be the case?

When we step inside, Malcolm clicks his fingers and summons the maître d', "Garçon! My good man. The lady's coat?" My insides contract and I'm not sure I can survive the evening. A waiter smirks as he takes my coat and leads us to our table. It's far too intimate and secluded for my liking, and I suggest to the waiter that maybe we'd like a more central one.

"The gentleman specifically requested a quiet table, Madam. I'm afraid all our other tables are booked. It's a popular table, I assure you. Our most romantic, in fact."

I'm beginning to dislike the server.

Once seated, I take a moment to survey the restaurant. It is stunningly beautiful, but I really wish I was with pretty much anyone else… even my parents, who always take forty minutes to choose, having grilled the waiter over everything from the soup of the day to his marital status. I distract myself with the wine menu. Christ, it's expensive. I hand the wine list to Malcolm, thinking that if he's paying, he should at least get to set the bar. He selects one of the more expensive ones, and as the waiter goes to get it, I squirm. I'm starting to feel a bit bad. I don't like the guy, but he's clearly pulling out all the stops. The waiter comes back with the wine and takes our order, and I order the crab to start, followed by the halibut. Malcolm orders foie gras, followed by venison, and I feel my disgust beginning to rise again. "Foie Gras? Do you know how cruel that is?" I say with disdain, glad that I cancelled those lobsters and could retain the moral high ground.

"Tasty, though," he shrugs, and I suddenly don't care if tonight bankrupts him. I take a large sip of wine and look impassive.

"So, how are things?" he says like it's the start of a business meeting.

I give my best gallic shrug. "Oh, same old, same old."

He continues, "I heard about you and the ex. That's too bad! But good for me!"

I can't help it. I visibly shudder as he clinks the motionless glass in my hand.

Unfortunately, he takes this as sadness on my part rather than horror before he leans in lecherously and whispers, "I can think of a way to cheer you up."

I scream inside but confine myself to saying, "Yes, more of this," indicating the wine and taking several large gulps. Malcolm, misreading my every queue, seems to take this as an invitation to reach for my hand. His fingers curl possessively around mine just as my soul slowly curls into a ball. I snatch my hand back, and he looks temporarily taken aback but quickly rallies and decides to slide his arm around my waist instead. His fingers hover dangerously low. As he's leaning in to kiss me, he starts to slide his hand up my dress. With a mind of its own, my hand reaches up and slaps his hard. He looks stunned and pauses briefly before, unbelievably, putting his hand back on my leg and trying again. I slap it away again.

"No, no. I'm not a chew toy to slobber over. I'm sorry, but I'm going to make tracks." Before he can say anything, I've scraped my chair back and am fumbling around for a coat just as my crab arrives. I can feel dozens of eyes boring into my back, and I can hear Malcolm swearing, but I don't care. I run until I reach the street, stopping only briefly to grab my coat from the cloakroom, and then I dart out into the street. I pull out my phone and order an Uber I can't afford, quickly pulling my coat around my face lest the driver ask me concerned questions. He doesn't. I huff loudly. He keeps a dignified silence. I blow my nose. Three times – with an additional huff to be sure he can hear me. "You alright, miss?" The driver finally looks up.

Ten minutes later, I've just finished sharing the full account. He hasn't actually asked me anything, but he has nonetheless been updated on everything I deem essential background knowledge for my current situation. He doesn't say anything, which I take to mean he is rapt, but at that point, he interjects with, "You'd want to get a life, mate. Plenty more fish in the sea."

I dutifully launch into the reasons why fish stocks are actually pretty damn low, thank you very much. The driver looks unconvinced and just nods politely. I can't help but think he looks ever so slightly relieved when we reach my front door, but he seems cordial enough as he wishes me good night.

As I add a tip on the app, I feel the guilt pang over the mismanagement of my meagre resources.

I lurch into the sitting room, disconsolate, to find Adam sitting, slightly melodramatically, there in the semi-darkness – having muted a re-run of *You've Been Framed*. He has his thunderous indignation face on. *Shit*, I think. Malcolm must have texted him.

"Adam, wait!" I begin as he opens his mouth.

"I don't want to hear it, Alex. You at least owe Malcolm your half of the bill."

"What?" I ask, horrified. "I can't do that! You know I can't afford it."

"Too bad. I can't believe you just walked out because you didn't fancy him."

"But that's not why I left! He was…"

"You're meant to be the polite grown-up one. I'm going to bed. I'll send you his bank details tomorrow."

"Adam!" I'm aghast. "You have to hear my side!"

"Alex, all I know is that you never wanted to go on this date, and you sabotaged it. That's all I know." With the flair of a drama major at *Fame Academy*, Adam flounces out without even a backward glance at the fainting bridegrooms' compilation rolling across the screen.

I sink onto the sofa and have a lonely little moment as I unmute the TV, hoping I can take some solace in the misery of other people making an arse of themselves.

SIX

The next morning, when I eventually manage to work up the courage to extract myself from under my duvet mountain (mostly because I'm in desperate need of coffee), I'm hoping that Adam will have headed off on an early treasure hunt for giggly Gen Z-ers (morning jogs are now as much a hunting ground as late-night wine bars). Alas not.

When I shuffle into the kitchen, he's sitting at the kitchen table, scrolling the sports pages on his iPad and shaking his head while muttering unintelligible advice to various footballers. He glances up quickly and then stares very fixedly at the screen.

I bite the bullet. "Adam… I know he's your friend, but so am I, and we're family, so can I explain my side, please? Otherwise, this is going to make family Christmases incredibly awkward."

"Look, it's between him and you. But if you want to do the decent thing for someone you deserted, I've WhatsApped you his bank details. It's £110. Seems like you have expensive tastes. Seems a bit Kardashian –

ordering the most expensive thing on the menu and then flouncing out."

Ouch, to both the price and the comment. "Adam, can I explain my side, please?"

He makes a big display of yawning and stretching and then, faux reluctantly, says, "Go on then…"

To be fair to him, as I recount the evening, his expression changes, and he looks suitably horrified.

"I never understood why Malcolm was single until now…"

"You never understood?! He is awful. I kept trying to tell you that."

"I'm sorry. Forget about the money. I didn't know the full story. Malcolm's tale, as you can imagine, is pretty different. He said that he was the perfect gentleman but that you just were rude and abandoned him mid-meal – and called him vile and disgusting."

"Well, I did call him vile and disgusting…"

"But only after…" Adam interrupted. "There's no way you need to pay."

"No," I say. "I'm determined to transfer the money. I can't stop Malcolm from lying about the evening, but he doesn't get to say that I am cheap."

"Seriously, you shouldn't. Sorry, Alex, I thought he'd be a bit of a catch."

"Forget about it. But seriously? You thought he was a catch? Yeah, fair enough, he's not unattractive, but he sweats at room temperature. Sorry, that's unkind. I'm just… frustrated."

Adam, as usual, only picks up on the conversation's relevance to himself, and he looks momentarily stunned.

"I thought I was one of those metrosexual guys who could spot a great handsome guy a mile off."

"Oh, you're metrosexual, alright, but your good guydar is way off. I'm happy to give you a holiday from matchmaking and go back to Hinge. Definitely tell Malcolm he's getting his money, though. I'm not a freeloader."

I go and fill my coffee, head held high, but once I'm back in my room and have transferred the money, I feel sick. I've never been this far into my overdraft. I let myself have a few moments of unadulterated panic, and then I force myself to take ten deep breaths and focus. Currently, I can only afford one more month's rent, and that's taking the *Ladditude* money into account. I quickly fire up my laptop and get googling. Regardless of *Ladditude*, I have to find another job urgently.

As ever, the situation is pretty bleak. There are a couple of jobs that are way out of my league: politics editor for a broadsheet (I once got into a debate about proportional representation from the perspective of the media's unhealthy obsession with oversized breasts and butts, but that probably won't cut it) and senior copywriter for Musky Tobacco (hmm… salary is tempting… but who knew I had morals?). That's it. There's nothing else.

I turn off my computer and sit staring disconsolately at the wall when the doorbell rings.

I start to get up but then hear Adam talking to someone. Oddly, his voice seems to be unusually high-pitched.

"ALEX!" he summons me. I hesitantly walk towards the front door, and Adam is standing there with an indignant-looking Waitrose delivery man.

"Alex," he starts. "I'm going to give you the benefit of the doubt and assume that you didn't order £200 worth of fucking lobster?"

"I… I … I couldn't honestly say for sure. I mean, I did. But then I thought I cancelled it."

"For fuck's sake Alex. Ten dressed lobsters?"

"It was that chardonnay. The other day."

"The chardonnay ordered the lobster?"

"In a manner of speaking," I confirm.

I look at him beseechingly, and he rolls his eyes and turns to the delivery man. "Sorry for not believing you, mate. Didn't realise I was living with quite this level of lunacy." He wanders into the kitchen, leaving me to sign for and carry to the fridge all of my lobster-ey cargo.

As I stumble into the kitchen under the weight of my load, he is already crafting a 'hilarious' Instagram story about my antics. "Adam!" I hiss through a lobster. "Make sure my mother doesn't see that post!"

He's falling about laughing while I'm sacrificing Vienetta to make room for a more precious consignment. "I think the only solution is to have a party. We'll provide the lobster. Our friends can bring the booze."

"Oh, so it's 'we' now, is it?" I say, secretly glad that he's finding this amusing rather than idiotic.

I finish unloading the lobsters and slump into a seat opposite him.

"Why so glum?" he asks. "Come on, it's funny!"

"It's just… I'm a mess. I'm totally broke, and I really thought I cancelled the lobsters. I've basically spent most of my rent this month on a dinner I didn't eat and ten lobsters. This is not normal for a twenty-nine-year-old.

I'm also behind on *Ladditude* correspondence already, and I now have to find a new job to pay for these fucking lobsters."

"Right." Adam is in problem-solving mode already. "You get to work on some Agony Uncle stuff, but make sure I see it before it goes out to, you know, laddify it. I, meanwhile, will find you a job."

"A writing job," I interject.

"Any job that pays the bills at this point."

I nod sadly, and he gets to googling. I can't quite understand how all this has happened to me. When I left university, I was full of hopes and dreams, as well as actual writing talent. I was ambitious and motivated, and I felt like the world was my oyster. But rejection after rejection has eroded my confidence to such a level that even when I do find a remotely suitable job, I self-reject before they can even reject me. I mean, I still apply, but I don't even have a sliver of excitement or anticipation left when I hit the "apply" button anymore. When my cohort graduated, so many of us had the same dream, and slowly, everyone started taking temporary office jobs to supplement their income… then the temporary fell away. The next thing they knew, they were applying for promotions at Santander customer service. I was so proud that I was resolutely holding onto my dreams, even if I was writing about reptiles on occasion. And now I'm wondering how much more balanced my life might be if I'd chosen the office job route.

Adam brings me over a cup of tea and places it on the table in front of me, breaking my reverie. I log onto my *Ladditude* account and choose a letter.

Dear Alex,

This is a first for me. I've never written to any sort of Agony Uncle type thing before. I feel like a bit of a loser if I'm honest, but I was reading the sports pages and saw the advice column on the sidebar, so I thought I'd give it a read, and here we are.

Anyway, there's this girl at work who I really like. She's really friendly, and I think she's flirting with me, but I'm a terrible judge, so I just can't be sure. She's quite quiet generally, but she always seems a bit more animated when I'm around. I'm not sure if I'm sounding massively egotistical here.

The other day, we were talking in the kitchen, and she said we should have lunch sometime. I don't know if it's a friendly colleague thing or if she might actually like me. I am not experienced at asking people out in real life – I have mostly met previous partners on dating apps and sort of fallen into relationships. I really think this girl and I could have a thing here, but she's a colleague, so the potential for awkwardness is high if she says no.

Thanks for your help,
Ryan

I think he is so adorable, as I read his letter. He's definitely new to the world of Agony Uncles. He didn't even know he was supposed to come up with the standard sign-off like Confused from Hartlepool or something. I immediately start drafting a reply.

Dear Ryan,

Thanks for your letter. I understand how challenging dating apps can be. And I know how awkward a workplace romance can be, too. But, provided your HR policy allows, I think you're going to have to take a bit of a risk if you want to find out. After all, while in theory, the expectation is not always on you to take the initiative and do the asking out, in practice, it still often tends to be the case, I'm afraid.

I think it sounds like this woman likes you, but as you say, it's always hard to be sure. I'd suggest you take her up on the offer of lunch. You'll quickly determine whether or not she's interested, as she'll want you all to herself, or she'll open the invitation to other colleagues.

You seem like a guy who's happy to take things slowly, so I'd suggest only slightly pushing the boundaries of your comfort zone. Chug along at a pace comfortable to you, and it will soon become apparent how she feels. Maybe you're just the type that falls into relationships, and that's OK. Perhaps you'll fall into this one!

Fingers crossed for you.

Yours,

Alex

I prod Adam and get him to look at my latest.

He shakes his head dismissively and, once again, sits down to completely change my masterpiece.

Dear Ryan,

I feel your pain, man, but come on. A woman likes a man who can take charge in all areas of life. This girl clearly likes you. She's asked you to have lunch, for God's sake! If you don't pull yourself together, you're in danger of being masculated by her. She'll lose attraction quickly if she has to keep asking you out.

Follow up on that lunch invitation, and if things seem

positive, make a move! Maybe you can turn lunch into dinner...

Yours,
Alex

Before I can stop him, he's hit send, uploading the response to the system. "Adam! I don't think that's good advice. Not everyone is like you! Also, I think you mean emasculated."

He rolls his eyes, "Whatever. Needs to grow a pair."

"Adam!"

"Anyway, I've found you a job. Look at this."

My anger at his hideous advice dissipates, and I start reading over his shoulder.

Ghostwriter required by a small publishing agency to support a retired parliamentarian wishing to write about his life. Contract fees are limited, but free accommodation and subsistence are provided for the duration of the project. Looking for a talented writer to bring parliamentarian memories to life. CVs invited.

I look at Adam, uncertain. "It doesn't sound like it will pay well."

"Alex... I think we might have got to the point where we have to be honest with ourselves."

"What do you mean?" I say, slightly shrill.

"You either need to park the writing dream for a while and get a job, any job, that will pay the bills. Or you need to move in with this autobiography guy and at least have free rent so that anything you make from *Ladditude*, etc., is profit. You can't live off pot noodles bought with change found down the back of the sofa. Probably my change, by the way."

I stare at him glumly, and the fact that he is thinking along the same lines as my earlier thinking is depressing… it makes it more real, somehow.

"Move out though?"

"Temporarily," Adam says gently. "Look – rent in this place isn't easy even for me – super duper personal trainer to the stars. Well… that woman off *Eastenders*. And for you, it's a nightmare. This could work until things pick back up again."

"What if he's a weirdo?"

"Then you don't take the job, obviously. But that's the only thing I've found, so if it doesn't work out with this one, then you need to work in a bar or something. This situation isn't sustainable. But look at it this way: if you end up getting the job and moving out, at least we'll be throwing you one hell of a lobster-themed goodbye party."

"You're right," I mutter, defeated. "I'll call the publisher now."

SEVEN

One thing finally goes right. The publishers seem to think my CV is respectable enough, to my astonishment. They're more interested in my previous experience writing to deadlines than my weak grasp of UK politics. The editor I speak to, Carlos, almost apologetically, explains that the final decision sits with the politician. He gives me a number, saying cryptically, "His bark is worse than his bite."

Great. Nervously, I pick up the phone and dial the number.

"Yes, what?" a gruff voice loudly barks at me, and I almost drop my mobile.

"Uh, hi ... Mr Fenton... I'm Alex Taylor."

"It's Sir John Fenton, as a matter of fact. What do you want?"

"I... uh... I saw the ad in the newspaper... for a ghostwriter," I say.

"Oh, yes? Continue."

"Well, I, uh, spoke to your publishers, and they, er... gave me your number. I have a fair bit of experience writing for books and magazines."

Silence on the other end. I press on: "My degree is in... er... in English literature and film studies, from Warwick. I currently write freelance pieces, and I can show you a portfolio if you like."

Silence. Then, "Hmm. You sound very young. I was expecting someone more experienced."

I think about the early and unsustained success of *Galactic Unicorns*. "Er, I've had projects in the bestseller lists." Science fiction, under twelve, but he doesn't need to know that. "It'd be an honour to use this skill to cover a career I've always followed with interest."

"Oh?" the chill on the other end thaws slightly. "What in particular?"

Damn and fuck. I think of the most politics-ey thing I can say. "Well, your brave legislative programme for a start," I venture. He was a minister, so he must have had a legislative programme, right?

"Ahh, well. I suppose it's good to hear I'm not totally forgotten, even now in my dotage." The temperature is definitely thawing.

"I'm very committed. I'm fascinated by people and their stories, and I'd love to write about you," I blabber.

"Well..." I can sense him wavering. "I suppose there's no harm in meeting. You can bring this portfolio of yours. Have you got a pen? I'll give you my address."

I dutifully note down the address (he lives in Hampstead!), say my goodbyes, and promise to be at his house at "14:00 hours sharp" the following day.

I can't help but feel a frisson of excitement as I hang up. Maybe this could be my big break. If he already has a publisher, I could be a published politico! This could be my moment to shine. Not to mention the luxury of living in Hampstead. I can picture myself now, getting inspiration from a wintry, desolate heath, like a slightly more urban Emily Brontë.

Adam interrupts my thoughts, "I'd better come with you tomorrow. Make sure he's not some sort of psychopathic murderer in case you do end up moving in."

"What? I don't think I need a minder in Hampstead. He sounded pretty old, too."

"That's just how a psychopath would sound, to set a trap. Some spooky house, massive trees and thick walls in Hampstead. They'd never hear you scream."

I gulp.

"Besides," Adam adds cheerfully, "I've got the day off tomorrow and fancy an adventure."

EIGHT

I am thoughtfully munching through my porridge (69p for a whole bag that will last months! See? I am trying) the following morning when Adam breezes into the kitchen, whistling cheerfully.

"What's got you so happy?" I ask, both suspicious and slightly jealous.

"Met a girl last night. Called Jessica," he says, in a dreadful simpering tone I haven't heard before.

"Where is she?" I ask, looking around as if she's about to pop out of the pedal bin.

"Not here. I didn't take her home. I just chatted with her at the bar, and then we swapped numbers and made plans for this evening after we're back from meeting your psycho politician, Lord Fenton. She's amazing."

"Sir John," I automatically correct him. I'm impressed. Maybe Adam has finally found a girl he doesn't just see as a sex object.

"I can't wait to take her home…that body," he continues.

Maybe not.

"Well, I'll look forward to meeting her in the morning."

"You're not going to get all prudish and play lame music at top volume again, are you?"

"Shut up, please. I need to prepare for this interview."

I usher him away and get back to my portfolio. I've included a couple of my more interesting pieces over a slightly random career, a smattering of film reviews from my old film blog, and even managed to dig out a history of St Winifred's Castle I wrote for the National Trust four years ago. I throw in a few pieces from *Gardener's Weekly* for good measure. That seems like the sort of thing he'd be into, from a quick Google, although, to be honest, I couldn't find too much about him that in any way overlaps with *Galactic Unicorns* or *Reptiles Monthly*. He doesn't seem like someone who has much of a sense of childish wonderment, but we'll cross that bridge when we come to it.

Two hours of constant doubt later, and I'm off, zooming along the Northern Line to Hampstead with my self-appointed bodyguard. Adam is wearing a tie and has insisted I wear a dress and jacket, as "Lord Fenton's probably one of those old-fashioned old farts who won't like ripped jeans." I don't know where Adam's getting his ideas from lately.

"Shouldn't I be showing *Sir* John my real personality if we're to see if we'll work well together?" I'd protested.

"Steady on," Adam had replied before rummaging for my most sensible-looking shoes.

Anyway, it's too late now. We leave Hampstead Underground, and Adam pulls out his phone.

"It's right by those ponds on the heath!" he pronounces. "Hmm. Maybe we should have dressed more nautical."

"For God's sake, Adam. It's a pond, not the Atlantic. And he wants a writer, not a cabin boy."

When we arrive at the house, it's intimidatingly grand. A tall Victorian townhouse, on one of those tree-lined streets that could be from a Richard Curtis film. On closer inspection, the house in question looks like it's been less loved than its neighbours. Chipped and faded paintwork curls beneath crumbling window ledges, and uncontrolled ivy has taken over the façade. Inwardly, I thank Adam for insisting on coming with me and nervously approach the front door. It's got one of those ornate lion knockers, and I feel like I'm from another time when I give it a gentle rap. There's only deafening silence. After a few minutes, I try again, another light rap, nervous that Sir John is just slow to get there and if I knock too impatiently, I'll just irritate him. As usual, Adam has other ideas.

"Oh, let me!" Adam grasps the knocker and gives it three loud whacks.

After what seems like an age, the door opens, and a figure, presumably Sir John, emerges from the shadows. The hallway is definitely faded grandeur, but grandeur nonetheless. He glares at us briefly. "Alexandra?" he barks.

"Oh, call me Alex," I tell him. "This is my flatmate Adam. I hope it's OK that he's joining us. He can sit in another room during the interview if you prefer. I left a message with your housekeeper that he'd…"

"Yes, yes," Sir John snaps. "You'd better both come in. A circuit judge lives next door, by the way, if either of you are a fraudster or a hustler." With that warm welcome, he leads us past the elegant spiral staircase towards the sitting room, and I catch sight of a beautiful, albeit old-fashioned, kitchen with a massive island and a double Aga nestled along one wall. It's always been my dream to live in a house with an Aga. I prod Adam in the ribs and point to it.

"So?" He whispers. "You can't cook for shit. Watching *Grand Designs* and *Saturday Kitchen* has given you notions."

"I can still appreciate a good kitchen!" I hiss back.

Sir John guides us towards a worn-looking sofa and summons the housekeeper I'd briefly spoken to earlier.

Mrs Jenkins, a formidable-looking older woman, comes in and asks us if we want anything to drink. I ask for a cup of tea, milk, and no sugar. Adam requests a fresh lemonade. I look at him, aghast. "Adam, we're not at a restaurant. I think Mrs Jenkins means, "Did you want tea, coffee, or water," I say, glancing at Sir John to see how he reacts to his demanding guests.

"Oh no, it's quite alright," Mrs Jenkins interrupts. "I can easily whip up some fresh lemonade." She scuttles off, and Adam looks smug.

"Right," Sir John says, dispensing with small talk. "We'd better start with your portfolio."

I dutifully hand it to him, and he makes several "harrumph" noises while he ruffles through (too quickly, in my opinion). "You certainly have some very peculiar interests," he says.

Adam disloyally bursts out laughing, and I glare at him.

"I, er, do have significant experience of working with publishers. You'll see from my CV that I was a ghostwriter for Wilson's Media for four years, working on a book series."

Sir John doesn't look at me and continues shuffling through the paperwork. "Oh yes? And what was that series?"

Damn. "It was... er... speculative fiction rather than fact. Though there was quite a bit of research and getting to understand the... err... tone and detail. It was called, er, *Galactic*..."

I'm mercifully interrupted mid-answer by the arrival of the drinks. I gratefully take a sip of my tea, and Adam takes a huge glug of lemonade before gasping and spitting it out all over Sir John. He leaps up faster than I thought someone of his age could and exclaims, "What in the bloody hell, man!"

Adam is still gasping like a fish out of water, Mrs Jenkins looks stricken, Sir John appears thunderous, and I'm just frozen.

"Salt! Salt!" Adam eventually manages to splutter.

"What do you want with salt, boy?" Sir John asks, furious.

"Full of salt. Water. Please," Adam whimpers (in my opinion, slightly melodramatically).

Mrs Jenkins looks devastated. "Oh, the sugar... and the salt... were next to each other on the counter... and..." She rushes off to the kitchen for water. Sir John, however, has started guffawing. Huge, belly-rumbling laughs are rolling over his portly frame. Then Mrs Jenkins comes back with the rescue water, and even Adam manages a wry smile through his frantic sips of water.

Now that Sir John has laughed, albeit somewhat sadistically, at Adam's near-death choking, the ice is broken, and the rest of the meeting passes in a relatively happy blur. The secret, I discover, is to deflect from my CV by asking a few admiring questions about Sir John's career and even his childhood. He's actually had quite an impressive career, spanning several cabinet positions and influential roles in global summits I remember reading about in history class.

He looks at me earnestly at the end of his summary, "Well… you think there'll be enough to write a book?"

"Oh!" I'm slightly taken aback. "Yes, I think there's definitely enough in terms of content, but I do wonder if you need to add a bit of a personal touch for the adult years. You know, make it a little warmer, a little more human. The childhood bit is great; I just wonder about your family and friends during your adult years?" I trail off, suddenly noticing that there are no family pictures dotted around the sitting room or on the extravagant mantelpiece.

Sir John's expression clouds, and I immediately regret delving into such private territory.

"This is a political memoir, young lady. Not some kiss-and-tell. Anyway, in terms of family, it's just me now – so you'll need to find some other way for it to be 'more human'."

Mrs Jenkins' eyes betray her, and I suspect there is more to this than Sir John is letting on, but I decide against pushing further. For now.

Adam, as ever, is far less sensitive. "You can't just have no family! No cousins or siblings, or nieces or nephews? What happened to your parents?" Sir John's face darkens, but Adam, genuinely intrigued, pushes on. "A man like you… I refuse to believe you didn't have a handful of women on the go at all moments when you were younger. I know a fellow Don Quixote when I see one."

Slightly charmed, Sir John relaxes briefly. "Well, yes, I suppose when I was young, I was considered… rather a catch. There were, ahem, bedfellows." He looks perplexed and pointedly ignores Adam's attempt at a fistbump before continuing, "But anyway – the point is – this is about my career. That's the interesting bit. Not shenanigans when I was younger."

Mrs Jenkins blushes and starts aggressively plumping the cushions on one of the armchairs.

"Well Alexandra… Alex, I like you. And I like the cut of your young man's jib. If you want the job, it's yours. I don't particularly warm to some of your reptilian pieces, and you have terrible taste in film, but you can clearly write. I'll just have to train you in the correct voice."

I'm so delighted by this news that I choose to overlook the training and boyfriend comments. Adam does not, "Oh, John," he dispenses with formalities, "Alex isn't a bedfellow; she's my cousin."

Moving swiftly on, I accept Sir John's offer.

"Excellent news!" he seems genuinely pleased. "Can you start on Monday? As I said, I can't offer a lot. The writing fee has to come out of the publisher's advance, but you'll be able to live here rent-free until the project is finished."

I give Adam a sad glance. This means that's it for us. We won't be flatmates anymore. He gives me an encouraging nod, and I look at Sir John.

"Yes, please, I'd like to stay here."

I dread to think what my mother will make of this if she finds out. I can only imagine. Her beloved, hapless only daughter, staying with an ageing parliamentarian in Hampstead, whiling away the best part of her youth in a dishevelled mansion. It's like a North London *Sunset Boulevard*. Oh dear… or maybe something more Hitchcockian?

As Sir John ushers us out, I'm lost in thought, sad about leaving Clapham and even my dopey cousin. Despite all the times he's frustrated me with his cavalier attitude towards dating, his constant monopolising of the TV for any and every football match, and his telling tales on me to my mother, I'm really going to miss Adam. He really has been there through it all – he picked me up off the floor – literally, on occasion – after Chris broke my heart. He has encouraged me through every single job I've applied for, even if I clearly didn't stand a chance, and of course, he even stood in for me during the *Ladditude* interview. And he found me this opportunity, which is the only reason I'm not scurrying back home to live with my parents for a while, tail between my legs.

On the walk back to the Tube, I turn and express this to him. As sensitive as ever, he laughs, "I wouldn't worry about me. I am going to turn the flat into a sex palace."

I don't know why I bother.

NINE

Forty minutes later, we're back home. Adam goes to get ready for his date, and I sit down at the kitchen table, ready to solve more *Ladditude* problems and trying not to think about my imminent departure.

I open my mailbox and start scrolling through today's issues, deciding what to respond to publicly. Cheating, problems with the in-laws, erectile dysfunction, problems with the boss, flatmate problems, and money problems. All the usual. Then, I spot a response to my response. Beaming, I go to open it. It's not often that I get a thank you note for rebooting someone's life, thanks to my wise words. Not that I'm in it for the gratitude. But an outpouring of thanks is a nice top-up on the meagre writers' fee.

Except it's not thanks, by any definition.

It's that Ryan guy, who asked for advice about the girl he liked at work.

Alex (No Dear Alex, I immediately notice),
I took your advice about the girl I work with and went

for lunch with her. So far, so good. Except that, when the bill came, I tried to pay. She seemed reluctant, but armed with your confidence mantra, I pushed forward and insisted. I see in hindsight just how uncomfortable she was, but in the moment, I saw it as shyness, and I persevered. Then, based on your advice, I tried to "take control." I told her I liked her and asked her out. I have never seen anyone look so ambushed before. She talked about how she thought it was just a catch-up lunch between colleagues and couldn't understand how I'd read things so wrong. Then she practically ran out of the café. I'm pretty sure she's told multiple people at work already because of all the looks I'm getting and the giggling when I walk by. Sorry if this is ranty, but I'm so humiliated I think my confidence has lurched to zero... Appreciate it's pretty much on me – but wanted to let you know: sometimes things aren't as clear cut as your confident advice suggests.

Ryan

Arg. I can feel my scalp prickle in sympathy sweat. I feel awful. I know it wasn't my own advice – bloody Adam – but it was my responsibility. And Ryan thinks it was me. I'm the Agony Uncle. This is a disaster – I'm an amateur who's actually harming now.

Adam strolls out of his room in his pulling gear, whistling as if he and I hadn't been handing out deep complexes to the young men of London like they're sweets. I read Ryan's message out to him. I don't know what I'm expecting, but not the complete nonchalance and shrugged shoulders that I get. "So? He's just one person. And he says himself it's all on him – what was he expecting?"

"But..."

"Not every woman is gonna like you. He'll get over it. I wouldn't respond." With that, he strides through the door, off to meet the unlucky Jessica.

So much for support from my fellow saboteur.

I quickly start drafting a response to Ryan.

Dear Ryan,

I am so sorry that happened to you. I genuinely am. It's never my intention to give my readers bad advice, and I'm mortified that's happened on this occasion. You sound like a perceptive man. If you liked this person, then I'm guessing she's pretty decent. I suggest you send this girl an email explaining that you really liked her but misread her signals and that you're sorry. If she is any sort of reasonable person, she'll understand, be flattered, and stop gossiping about you. It will get better. People will move on to the next office scandal and forget all about it.

In the meantime, avoid the temptation of pulling away from dating just because of one bad experience. Otherwise, you really will set yourself back. Take another risk. I know you're from London – what about going to next Saturday night's Single Mingle in Soho? It's supposed to be a great night for singles, and lots of people meet good matches there. I've done some research, and they say that if you don't end up with a date out of it they give you free entry to the next one. I remember you said you were shy, and I wonder if this might help boost your confidence and get you used to talking to strangers? If you go, let me know how you get on.

Yours,
Alex

Actually, this Single Mingle thing sounds pretty cool. It's the sort of thing that Bea and I might buy a ticket for when drunk and then cancel when sober.

I go onto the website and look at the ticket prices again. The seed of a morally questionable idea is starting to form in my mind… What if I went as well, but solely as a mysterious stranger who meets Ryan and builds up his confidence? Would that be so weird? I'd just be another single person in the bar. I could meet him and flirt outrageously, then make my excuses – all having given him the boost to go out there and be himself with the other women. And, of course, if I happen to be swept off my feet by a handsome heart surgeon or a strapping fireman (very different, but in my view, the sexiest of professions), then it's a win all around. I could even go in disguise and with an enchanting pseudonym! I always loved a bit of improv at university.

I take a breath and click confirm on the ticket purchase, overly cheerful about waving goodbye to another £20.

As it happens, Adam saunters in not long after, on cloud nine and slightly drunk after his "most amazing date ever" with Jessica.

"Of course, you should go!" he slurs at me. "Everyone should find the sort of love I've found…"

Putting aside my deep desire to mock him for his newfound ridiculousness, I smile instead and determine that I won't be asking for a refund after all.

TEN

On the day of the Single Mingle, I'm bouncing between sheer dread at the thought of my stealth mission and exhilaration at the thought of meeting Ryan and playing matchmaker extraordinaire. I can't tell who is more excited about the reconnaissance mission – Adam or me. From the way he's talking, you'd think we were the hosts from *Love is Blind*. He's even offered to buy a ticket and "shadow" me, coming up with complex signalling suggestions for whether or not I'm doing a good job improving Ryan's confidence. I shut this suggestion down before he's even finished the sentence.

It's Adam's idea to go down the Russian royalty route. He's actually dated a Russian model (of course he has), so he gives me some helpful tips on things I should know if I have Russian ancestry or, you know, had ever actually set foot in the country. He also helps me choose the name Anastasia Edwards. "Very regal," he adds. I'm not 100% sure why I listen to him rather than becoming, say, Mary Addlestone from Peterborough, but all I can say is life has been pretty mundane recently. I am more open than usual to being influenced by Adam's particular brand of mischievous nonsense. I draw the line, however, when he tries to make me practise an affectation similar to an amateur production of *War and Peace.*

"No," I tell him firmly. "I will explain that I have been brought up in Knutsford and have my own accent." He grudgingly agrees, acknowledging that his most successful deceptions have always had kernels of truth in them. I ignore this particularly worrying little nugget of insight into Adam's inner workings and distract him by asking him about outfit choices.

"The less like you usually look, the better – glamorous and befitting a mysterious duchess," he says immediately.

"Adam…I'm supposed to be motivating him, not distracting him."

He looks perplexed and then concedes that perhaps the best approach is a flattering but classy royal blue midi dress with nude stilettos and a delicate clutch, along with my favourite sparkly Swarovski earrings – a 21st birthday present from Bea. I wonder aloud if I have now made myself look *too* glamorous. Still, Adam reminds me that Ryan is also more likely to have his confidence improved by having a flirtatious encounter with an elegant mystery woman than a tired old bag lady who looks like she slept in a hedge. There's something about his tone that implies this is more akin to how I usually look. I don't know where he gets this idea, but I'm not sure my self-esteem is up to probing.

He helps me with my hair and then, to my horror, insists that we do some power poses together while staring at our reflections in my bedroom mirror. He says he learned this from a Ted Talk. I've learned that it's usually quicker to agree and get the horror over with than to argue when it comes to Adam's eccentricities, so I quite literally grit my teeth and strike a pose. Maybe there's something in this power posing though, because looking at myself taking up space while dressed so elegantly, I really do start to feel a little bit more Anastasia Edwards and a little bit less Alex Taylor. I wander over to my dressing table, dig out my sexiest red lipstick, and smirk as I catch Adam still flexing in the mirror.

"Are you sure you don't want an escort?" he asks again.

"Quite sure, Adam, thank you. The last thing I need tonight is my cousin's assistance in flirting with this poor man. Or worse, you make him feel even *less* confident by jumping in and seducing every woman who he starts to speak to. I'll report back afterwards. It ends at midnight, so you'll probably still be up."

"Alright then, Cinderella. Go charm your Prince."

And I'm off.

ELEVEN

After the single mingle

I'm up at the crack of dawn the next morning, and the dubious bacon roll I bought at the station is doing queasy little pirouettes in my stomach on the train up to Chester. Why did I decide to subject myself to family time this weekend? And why did I add to the punishment by going for the 7:15am train from Euston, adding a lovely little hangover into the mix for fun? I never thought I was a masochist (I giggled awkwardly through all the 'sexy parts' in *Fifty Shades*), but maybe I need to reevaluate.

When I booked it two months ago, I imagined it seemed much more achievable. It had probably been one of those unicorn days where you wake up early on a Saturday morning and truly believe that the world is your oyster. I probably thought I'd meditate, do a yoga class, and vacuum the flat, all before 10am. The beginning of a new me, a me who rose with the sun and perfected the crow pose for all my yoga-loving InstaFans. I imagine I booked this train in a zen-like calm, exuding confidence in my own abilities.

Come to think of it; it's probably actually more likely that I went for this train time because it was forty quid cheaper or something.

The one good thing about the early train is that I was able to avoid too much scrutiny from Adam on my return home from the Single Mingle last night. I sauntered in just after midnight and Adam – as nosy as ever – was clearly waiting up for me, watching episodes of *Schitt's Creek* and sipping a beer. A couple of cold slices of pizza sat on the coffee table.

"How did it go?!" he demanded.

"Oh, you know, fine. He seemed nice. I flirted a little. I feel like I boosted his confidence a little. You know, exactly what we planned." I neglect to tell him about the number exchange or the slight fizzing feeling Ryan gave me.

"Anyway! Early train tomorrow! Better go to bed," I say, ignoring the worrying little niggle that I can't tell even the truth to someone who, by most measures, has the morality of an alley cat. I'll figure it out later.

Pulling my mind back to the present, I jam my laptop onto the tiny tray in front of me and fire it up. I have 4,000 words of scaly prose for *Reptiles Monthly* to get done by Sunday evening, but the bacon roll is still dancing, and my head is pounding. I decide the better life choice is just to loll in my seat and groan intermittently. I'll do the article on Sunday night.

I think back to the Single Mingle last night. Well, mostly back to meeting Ryan. I liked his half smile. Warm but ever so slightly tentative. Chris never did a half smile. He'd either be super serious or grinning like the Cheshire Cat. I miss that grin. I then remind myself that his serious mode was usually when he was pontificating about something he thought only he fully understood. And the grin was at its widest when he was laughing at his own jokes. Ryan, on the other hand, actually listened. He'd laughed at my jokes without that weird macho insecurity men seem to have when a woman is funny. That guy's love life will be fine, I think to myself. Not with me, obviously. That would be far too unprofessional, even for me.

The vibrations of the train must have lured me to sleep, but for once, luck is on my side, and I wake as we're pulling in. It was not like that awful time when I woke up in Holyhead at 1am and had to sleep on a bench on the platform until the trains started up again. I trudge off the train and find Mum waiting for me at the station with Scoop, our little collie-spaniel mix. As usual, she's immaculately dressed in her rural chic look: neat chequered slacks, Merino wool jumper, trim Barbour, and her hair is styled with an incredibly precise bob of brown-grey. She looks like she's stepped out of an advert in one of those country lifestyle mags from the doctor's surgery. Robust and healthy. My left hand instinctively tries to smooth down my own wilder hair, mussed from two hours of intermittent napping and the occasional half-hearted gesture towards my keyboard.

"Oh darling, you look terrible. Are you poorly?" she asks, simultaneously hugging, inspecting, and critiquing me.

"Oh, just an early start," I smile weakly, clambering into the jeep – like I said – right from the pages of *Country Life*.

My mother laughs shrilly. "Early, darling? Weren't you on the 7:15am? I thought you chose that train for a bit of a lie-in. I was out jogging at six, and your father had already taken Scoop for a walk." I say nothing.

We quickly escape the city traffic and start trundling along the Cheshire country roads. As with all trained interrogators, my mother's MO includes peppering seemingly inconsequential questions with deeper meaning into what seems to the untrained observer like basic maternal interest. Have I been very busy? (meaning I haven't phoned very often recently). Am I still coping with the cost of London? (Are financial struggles the reason I've turned up looking like a scarecrow that's been in a fight with a tractor). How is Adam? (Share some gossip, so Mum has the edge on his mother, Aunt Sheila). As we get more into the wilds, Mum's questions get heavier. She knows I can't escape and am now at the mercy of her conversational tentacles. The car's going too fast to hurl myself out, and we both know that I wouldn't survive in the countryside for more than an hour before being eaten by cows.

"Darling, Adam mentioned that date you went on the other day. What happened?"

My mother loves to let me know how often she and Adam talk, frequently commenting that she hears more from her nephew than from her daughter.

I mutter something about incompatibility, not wanting to be drawn. Mum glances at my slightly frayed jumper and asks suspiciously, "What did you wear?"

Oh yes, because the thing that ruined the date was my choice of top. Not the potential sleaziness of the male dating pool.

Mercifully, we reach the edge of Knutsford and pull into the drive of my parents' little cottage. It's pretty, one of those symmetrical, square little houses that looks like a kid's picture version of what a house should be. When my parents first bought it, they converted the rambling outbuilding next door into my mum's vet's surgery. The cars outside suggest Mum's deputy, Jenny, is having a busy morning.

"Looks like business is thriving!" I say generously, naively hoping that flattery will get me somewhere.

"Yes, darling. The benefits of a sensible career choice."

Evidently, it will not.

Dad, who I have never been more delighted to see, comes to the cottage door, hugs me and tells me I'm looking great. "My hero," I think smugly before noticing he doesn't have his glasses on. He is very shortsighted. Dammit.

"We're going to have brunch," Dad tells me excitedly, steering me to the kitchen, where, to my dismay, I can hear more bacon sizzling. Ever since he discovered brunch later in life, it's been one of Dad's favourite things. He has become a brunch evangelical. It can be unfortunate when he goes into extensive detail with friends and loved ones about the concept, the options available, and some of his culinary brunch adventures so far. For him, NASA boffins invented it in 2015, and he has become the self-appointed pioneer for the Northwest.

After a few menacing somersaults, my stomach feels settled, and I gratefully tuck into a pile of pancakes, bacon, and maple syrup. At the same time, my parents alternate between the latest Knutsford scandals and their CIA-level probing of life in London. For Dad, the questions are mostly tube lines, that damp patch in our flat's bathroom and what we're doing about it, and light pollution. Mum's are sharper-edged and involve more of an autopsy of my date with Malcolm, my long-term career plans, and when I will throw out my oldest, most comfortable clothes. I time my responses so I have a mouthful of pancake to murmur through until she gives up.

Despite all the questions, it is nice to be home. I anticipate a lunchtime snooze, curled up on the window nook in the little living room with a gloriously trashy novel. My mother, however, has other ideas. "Darling, I'm going to take you shopping. Treat you to some new clothes for your wardrobe." She glances meaningfully at my jumper once again.

"Oh, Mum, I don't need any clothes. I've got loads of nice stuff."

"I just decided I didn't want to wear any of that today," I add hastily as she gives me another disappointed once-over.

"I'm sure you do, darling," Mum lies, "but there are some lovely new clothes shops in Knutsford, designer and everything."

"Mother! I live in London. It's a global epicentre for fashion. It has like a thousand clothes shops. Why would I do my shopping in Knutsford?"

"I'll pay," Mum answers simply.

And we're off.

TWELVE

We leave Dad to his afternoon Pilates class. I don't know if this kicked (extended?) in at the same time as his brunchalism, but I think Dad is morphing into a millennial. I am considering buying him avocados in town.

As we wander into Knutsford centre, I dread to think what these "designer outlets" will offer. I imagine shooting jackets and tweed and a slight smell of rain-soaked gundog. I'm no fashion princess (to my mother's and Adam's dismay), but I still object to spending an afternoon being dressed up like Camilla Parker-Bowles. I shuffle, teenager-like, behind my mother, trying and failing to muster up some gratitude for her generous offer. She keeps trying to chivvy me along, making pronouncements like "The shops should have all the new season's looks!" to which I testily make witty responses, such as, "What season is that? Grouse season?" and chuckle at my own amusingness.

When I glance up from my huff to my eternal relief, it seems the shop does cater for the non-middle-aged farmer's wife crowd. Happily, Mum spots a client. Parent of a pet patient? She releases me to go in and browse by myself. There is a God. Inside, the relief fades. It's designer in the worst sense. Tiny dresses. Ridiculous sizes. Another of those places that seems to cater only for very wealthy pixies. I head further into the shop in search of apparel for actual human women.

As I look through the handkerchief-sized patches of sequins and taffeta, the shop door opens, and I hear a familiar voice. It can't be. It CAN'T. I peek nervously from behind the rack, and it is. It's Chris. Bloody evil ex-boyfriend Chris. And he's brought someone with him. A perfect blonde and petite pixie with a permanent "I've just stepped off a yacht in St. Tropez" tan, who looks like all the dresses in the shop were designed only for her. I'd start hyperventilating and demand a brown paper bag, except that it would give away my location. I adopt a crouch and scuttle further back into the shop.

"See, I told you we have a bit of the metropolis out here in the wilds," I hear Chris say to Pixie as she starts to browse.

There's no other way out. I'm five racks away from discovery, complete with a ratty jumper. Suddenly, I spy sanctuary. At the back of the shop, there's a curtain across a little changing room. I grab the first dress to hand and sneak up to the shop assistant in a half crouch. "Can I try this dress on?" I ask in a hoarse whisper. She looks in alarm at the mad bent-over crab woman in front of her, "Erm. Certainly… madam. There's a changing room just there."

In my new crazy crab woman mode, I nod and scuttle over to the curtain. Behind it, the space is tiny, but I'm safe and unseen. I can still hear them speaking like any loved-up, annoyingly glamorous young couple, going home to meet the parents for the first time. Must be serious, I think, as I curl over, my brain choosing to remind me how much I used to be in love. I picture Chris's lovely mum hugging this woman in welcome and offering her a freshly baked scone as his dad tries to explain the rules of cricket to her. Bad. Bad brain.

Furthering my quest to inflict as much misery upon myself as possible, I listen for scraps of conversation. Mostly, the pixie seems to be chatting about clothes, Knutsford, and where to go for lunch. I will hunger pangs on her.

The shop assistant's voice suddenly whispers through the curtain, "Madam, do you need a hand?" I realise the curtain stops at ankle height and that, from her perspective, I've just been standing motionless in the changing room.

"No, I'm fine, thank you," I croak.

Damn. I need to try the actual dress on. I look at what I selected. It is TINY. I swear I have scarves made of more material. But I can't continue standing still. The space is so small that as I pull my jumper off, my elbows graze the walls. Even the changing rooms are for stick insects. I take off my jeans. That should be enough ankle movement to keep her happy, I think. I then take the dress and mutter a little prayer before stretching it as far as I can and stepping in. One leg in. Winning so far.

I get the other one in and take a deep breath before trying to manoeuvre the ridiculous scrap up past my hips. This is a battle I'm going to lose, but at least the clothes assistant can tell I'm trying it on now. She can't miss the grunts of distress. It's really not budging past the hips. I try another deep breath and a bit of shimmying. Mid-shimmy, I hear a tearing sound. I panic and lose my grip, and the dress falls back to my ankles. I start to pull one leg out to inspect the damage, but the thing is like a noose around my ankles, and suddenly I'm stumbling.

There's a mad hop as I try to regain my balance, but the hop turns into a fall. The next thing I'm tumbling out through the curtain into the shop. There's a swirl of fabric and light and sound, and I reach desperately for the curtain, desperately flailing my arms around and trying to grasp anything that might help me regain my balance. I shouldn't have bothered. I hit the floor, catching my shoulder on a clothes rack on the way down and knocking it over. Time slows again, and there I am, flat on my back in my bra and knickers with the ripped dress around my ankles, drowning in a puddle of dresses from the fallen rack around me. I wish I could say that I'd followed my Aunt Sheila's advice and always made sure I had an attractive, matching set of underwear on in case I was in an accident and my clothes needed to be cut off by a handsome fireman, but I hadn't. The underwear style is more aligned with the tatty jumper than with an Agent Provocateur model, and I pledge myself that if I make it through this mortification, I will dress like a Victoria's Secret Angel – at a minimum – every day. Non-stop underwear thoughts cantering through my head, I just lie there, stunned, and stare up at the ceiling, paralysed by mortification as first, the concerned shop assistants appear, looking down at me in horror. Then, the Pixie. And then Chris.

It is the longest thirty seconds of my life. I become hyper-aware of everything. The Pixie's immaculately neat fringe. Her expression when she takes in my giant but comfy granny pants and my basic white cotton bra that has turned beige with use over time. The million micro-expressions that flash over Chris's face. The assistant helps me up as I muster every shred of dignity I have left before hiding behind the torn dress.

"Chris, how lovely to see you," I trill like we're reacquainting at a Soho book launch instead of during the most humiliating moment of my life so far.

"Are you... OK?" he asks. How familiar that expression is. I'd forgotten his ability to look so kind and concerned and so superior and condescending at the same time.

"Fine, fine," I say, hyper-cheerfully.

"Erm, this is Madeleine," he introduces the Pixie to me hesitantly – like putting a kitten in front of a slobbering rottweiler. I awkwardly shake her teeny, doll-like hand while using my left arm to keep the dress hanging over my body.

"Maddie, lovely to meet you. I'm Alex. I used to... I'm Chris's... We... I'm a friend of Chris's."

Her eyes widen in understanding. "It's Madeleine, please," she corrects me snippily. "So you're Alex? Oh. Chris has talked about you," she says, glancing at him. "Er, are you OK?"

By now, the three of us have pretty much entered into the mutual conspiracy that it's entirely normal to be holding a conversation in the middle of a clothes shop with a woman dressed only in tired underwear and clutching a ripped dress, the ex-lover that she sent more pleading text messages to than is acceptable, and his new… conquest.

However, we haven't drawn in the shop assistant. "Oh dear, let me help you back into the changing room," she says firmly, steering me back in before taking the remnants of the handkerchief dress.

I shout my goodbyes over my shoulder, and as soon as I hear the door sound their hurried exit, I slump against the dressing room wall. Oh, the humiliation. On the one hand, I've never been so mortified in my entire life. On the other, I can't wait to regale Adam and Bea with this tale.

Once I'm dressed and in a fit state to emerge, the prim shop assistant shows her softer side. She has a glass of water waiting and tells me not to worry about the dress; it can easily be repaired. Still, I can't help but notice the look of relief on her face as she waves the mad crab lady out of the door.

Out on the street, I'm relieved to see that Chris and Madeleine have disappeared, and Mum is coming out of the bakery with a couple of takeaway coffees for us.

"Darling, did you see anything you liked?" she calls.

I look at her wearily, "Mum, can we just go home?" Bafflingly, she seems to sense that today is not my day and says yes, we should probably make sure Dad hasn't pulled a muscle doing an extendable cobra fishcake or something.

The parental radar must sense that now is not the time to pry, so mercifully, we spend a peaceful afternoon sampling Dad's new twist on smashed avocado (he 'uniquely' adds chilli and is delighted with his ingenuity

– I best not let him go for brunch in literally any London establishment), reading, and playing Wordle. Mum has recently discovered Wordle, and her over-competitive nature means that Dad and I pretend we don't play when she's around, secretly sending our scores to each other later.

That evening, I head for a long-awaited catch-up in the pub with Bea. She's arrived before me and is frowning thoughtfully at her phone, brushing her red ringlets away from her eyes every few seconds. Bea's hair is her most prized possession – since the age of five, when she realised she had never seen a Disney princess with her hair tied back, she has insisted that it cascades around her shoulders. She's by no stretch a stereotypical princess in any other way, but she is adamant that her hair will never know the indignity of being scooped up into an elastic band. She has a table in the corner and, crumpled on the floor at her feet, appears to be some sort of mutant Muppet that makes Scoop look like Crufts Best in Show. She jumps to her feet when she sees me, and the warmth of her hug gives me a bit of a pang for how seldom I provoke that kind of delight. The Muppet's head moves, and I realise it is of the canine family – an indistinguishable sub-type and probably one of the most forlorn I've ever seen.

I sink gratefully onto the plush sofa beside her. She already has the wine poured and the salt and vinegar crisps open. God, I love this woman.

"What is that?" I ask, gesturing at the slobbering creature at my feet.

"Oh, Barley! We're not sure. We think he's part spaniel, part bulldog."

"Oh, I was only after species, to be honest."

"How dare you!" Bea asks in mock outrage. "Look how gorgeous he is."

"Yes…" I say doubtfully, watching him slobber on my handbag.

"Anyway, it's your mum's fault for getting me into animals." Bea's decision to work at an animal sanctuary stems from having been obsessed with unloved pets ever since she did work experience at my mum's practice.

"Anyway. You're looking scrawny, my love," she says, dusting crisp crumbs off her fluffy jumper.

"Oh, charming as ever, Bea! It's like my mum's here!"

"Well, besties are all about truth. Have you replaced me yet with your fancy city friends?"

"You know you can't be replaced. Believe me, I've tried!"

"Hmm, what about Megan?" Megan is one of the university friends I first moved to London with.

"Pregnant and moved to Harpenden for a garden and a second bedroom."

"Well, I'm glad and also sad. And no one else?" Bea asks, playing the jealous lover with aplomb.

"What about writery people – all drinking cocktails in some posh London bar and talking about literature?"

"Sadly not. Most writery people I only know from online. And they can barely club together for Ribena, let alone for cocktails. My closest gal pal is probably Adam."

"Ohh, him," she says, turning the corners of her mouth down. Then she giggles, the wine clearly having an effect already. "Awful. Great biceps. But awful. Yes, I would probably sleep with him after enough wine, but I'd need a shower afterwards."

I laugh. "Go for it. I'd love to have you in the family. But he brings as much good conversation as a Pot Noodle. No, that's unfair. He's alright. Just probably not boyfriend material for my best friend."

"I'm not sure I'd be after his conversation…"

"Anyway," she continues, "we need to find you a distraction after Chris."

I sigh in agreement and then, laughing, say, "Speaking of Chris…" and launch into the story from earlier about the clothes shop encounter with Chris and Madeleine.

She laughs along with me. "Oh God, I can't even imagine. You will have been nothing but queenly, I'm sure," she says loyally. "And I'm so pleased to hear you laughing about this," she adds in quiet afterthought.

She's right. It is a pretty big deal that I discovered Chris has a new girlfriend in the most embarrassing way, and I am laughing about it six hours later. Enjoying how impressed she is at my recovery, I tell her about Ryan and the normal London datey bits. I leave out the whole Dear Alex thing. As she seizes upon the lovely news, I feel sad and guilty that I'm keeping a secret from Bea. Still, I can't think of a single way to explain how I got from being slightly unconventional and a bit disorganised to somehow being the starring role in a self-created web of deceit. It's one thing talking to Adam about it; he's been there throughout the whole thing, but it's another telling Bea. She would never get involved in something like this. She's way too honest and just… straightforward. I couldn't bear to see her disappointed in me.

I indulge her in a few more details about Ryan before the guilt of the deception combined with the lie threatens to overflow. "Anyway, that's enough about my love life," I say abruptly, interrupting her musings about Ryan designing me a love nest to move into back here in Knutsford. I push my misadventures to the back of my mind and force the latest out of Bea about the young RSPCA officer she's been going "birding" with. By the time we finished off the rest of the wine and had another packet of crisps, I'd heard all about Alfie and their adventures. I can honestly say that I never knew the RSPCA was such a hotbed of flirting and lust. By the time I stagger home to bed, the world is put to rights, and I've sworn I'll come home more frequently, and Bea has promised to visit me (for me, not Adam, she promises tipsily).

The next morning, I wake to the wafting smell of bacon and coffee and praise the heavens once again for Dad. He greets me with a steaming mug and a bacon roll, already clad in Lululemon, handing it to me and telling me, "Must dash!" as he pirouettes out the door.

Generally, though, there seems to be some sort of unacknowledged understanding that I'm having a difficult time, so for the whole day, my parents are particularly lovely and don't bring up jobs, boyfriends, my impending baby-less future or even push on what happened in the disastrous twenty minutes I was left unsupervised in central Knutsford.

Instead, once Dad has returned, we spend the rest of the day in the garden, my mum and I drinking white wine spritzers and gossiping (my mother might like to publicly give the impression that she would rise above such idle speculation, but behind closed doors, she revels in gossip), while watching my dad tend to his tomato plants (you can't have a good brunch without tomatoes, apparently). I'm simultaneously enjoying listening to the latest village scandals while also thanking the heavens that London is much too populated to encourage much interest in the lives of your neighbours.

Apparently, Molly, the school librarian, has bounced back from her divorce in spectacular fashion and went on a romantic spur-of-the-moment trip to Florence with a man she met six weeks ago *on the line.*

My mother utters the phrase "on the line" in hushed tones as if we're in the 1950s and Molly has become pregnant out of wedlock at the hands of the local rapscallion. Good for Molly, I say. We end the evening in a local gastropub, my dad getting quite merry and telling me he loves me and my parents are proud of me "regardless of whether I have a boyfriend and even if I had to do a lifetime of *Reptiles Monthly.*" By this point, I've had a healthy amount of wine myself, so I just hug him and tell him I love him, too.

Sunday follows just as pleasantly, with my dad cooking a Sunday roast and sending me back to London with more leftovers than I can carry. Adam will be delighted. Despite how unexpectedly enjoyable the weekend has been, I'm still relieved to be left with my own thoughts on the train on the way home. As I sit quietly and force myself to work through the flashbacks, I'm so pleased that my reaction in the changing room wasn't because of Chris settling down with perfect Pixie Madeleine. I was only distraught because of the ridiculous embarrassment of flashing my granny pants to the world. When I think about it properly, as I stared at his face for that long minute while I lay prone in the jumpsuit aisle, none of the raw, soul-crushing feelings came back. Instead, I just saw his receding hairline, the slight podginess eroding his jawline, and that perplexed expression I had always hated. The one he reserved for anything that didn't fit into his very narrow view of the world. What I would have said was the worst thing possible only a couple of months ago had happened, but instead of being devastated, I felt liberated.

Just then, my phone beeps. It's Ryan. "No pressure, but just wondering if you'd like to follow up on that drink?"

I smile and type: "Sure :)."

I'm still high on joyfulness from Ryan's text when "I" (and I use the term loosely), get a message from him in a different format. And it's not addressed to Anastasia or even to the real me. It's addressed to Agony Alex. My stomach does so many backflips it seems to think it's trying out for an understudy role in Cirque du Soleil. Sweat beading attractively across my forehead, I open the email.

Dear Alex,

I just wanted to write to thank you for your advice. I went to the Single Mingle, and I actually met someone really nice and funny. Her name's Anastasia and we just clicked. We chatted for ages, and it felt quite natural. Usually, I would never have considered going to an event like that, but I'm glad I did. We're planning to go for a drink, so fingers crossed it all goes well.

Cheers,

R

Oh fuck, oh fuck, oh fuck. When I invariably have to let him down because he doesn't know my actual name, I am going to be the world's biggest bitch.

Hi Ryan, [Draft version]

That's awesome, mate. She sounds like a keeper. It sounds like you hit it off and don't have to worry – but a couple of tips:

Fancy candlelit restaurants may sound corny, but they never let you down

A rose is always romantic

When it comes to city breaks, you can't go wrong with Barcelona

Go get her!

Best of luck for the future

Alex

Hi Ryan, [Final version]

That's awesome, mate. Good for you – it sounds like getting out of your comfort zone was just the ticket.

It's great that things went well at the Single Mingle – and it's awesome to have confidence in yourself – but don't invest too much in one person right now. Remember, you don't know her from Adam! Keep that confidence in your own self-worth, and don't put too many eggs in one basket.

Best of luck for the future,

Alex

THIRTEEN

Ryan and I exchange a few texts over the next few days. All pretty light and friendly, but every time my phone pings, my tummy does a little flip; it's very distracting when I still have several thousand words to go on the finer points of crocodile care for my *Reptiles Monthly* deadline. I'm having an irritating internal battle between heart and brain, with my brain acting like a needy Pekingese puppy in its seemingly constant need to remind me that I am supposed to be helping Ryan with his confidence rather than getting carried away with images of handholding on the Embankment. Why do I do this? Why? The amount of times I've been down the aisle before a first date is just extraordinary. It's very impressive how I can coolly indulge in casual banter by text message, all the while running away to Happy Ever After in my mind. I firmly tell myself to stop fantasising, and we agree to a spring picnic on Wednesday evening.

For once, my mother would be proud of me. Granny pants and worn bra out the window (not literally – my neighbours think I'm strange enough). Best lingerie on, under a summer dress that I can actually fit over more than one leg. I even brush my hair. As I catch my reflection, I proudly think that I'm leaving the Knutsford Granny Pants Streaker behind. This is the glamorous me. Anastasia Edwards.

Adam pokes his head around the door as I'm putting the finishing touches to my make-up, looking suspicious.

"Where are you off to?"

"Oh, just off to see a friend!" I say non-committally. "Nowhere important. How's Jessica?" I ask, trying desperately to change the subject.

"Who?"

I sigh impatiently. "The girl from the other night. The one you didn't sleep with immediately. The one who could be *The One*."

"Oh, her!" he remembers. "Oh, nothing. Keeping things very casual. Why are you wearing make-up?" He shifts the conversation back to me.

"No reason, really – just thought it would help pull me out of the Chris doldrums."

I use the Chris card as I know that a) Adam will believe me, and b) he will run away as quickly as possible rather than risk opening the floodgates. I realise, too, that for the first time, it's a fib. I'm not in any doldrums. Instead, all I can remember is Chris's backhanded compliments about some of the outfits I chose to wear. "Ohhh, edgy," he'd laugh at some of my sartorial choices. Or when I'd try to dress up and think I looked quite glamorous, he'd say things like, "You look lovely, but is it really you?"

Fortunately, the fib is enough to satisfy Adam's nosiness.

"Oh right, lovely! Well, maybe you'll meet someone!" he says cheerfully before scarpering.

Ryan and I have agreed to meet outside St James's Park station at 6pm. He's already there, leaning against the fence – looking slightly nervous. Unlike slacker-me, he's been at work and is wearing a slimline blue shirt, sleeves rolled up, and some dark blue jeans. I notice that his arms are as nice as expected. Even better, one of them is holding a bag full of picnic-y goodness.

He leans and kisses me slightly awkwardly on the cheek. My face tingles. "You look beautiful, Anastasia," he smiles.

"Oh. Thank you. Where are we heading? The park?"

He looks shy all of a sudden, "Ah, it's a bit of a surprise. If you're OK with that? Nowhere dodgy," he adds.

I laugh, "It's OK. I don't think you're the serial killer type."

"This way." He makes a move towards taking my hand. Then he seems to get nervous, so I place mine in his (Anastasia would definitely be so bold), and he leads me on a complicated route involving detours through several small passageways before we emerge on a beautiful cherry blossom lined-street, with an imposing row of Victorian townhouses. It's the type of street I could never even dream of living on unless I manage to write several bestsellers. As my mother frequently reminds me through pursed lips, I'm more likely to end up renting half a hovel until they're "dead and gone", and I inherit the house. This is why I'm always served up as a cautionary tale illustrating my mother's perception of 'careers in the arts'.

Anyway, we wander down the beautiful street that I will be unlikely ever to call home. One of the houses is covered in scaffolding, and to my surprise, that's where we seem to be headed. Ryan leads me in through the magnificent entrance (well, it would be marvellous if it wasn't obstructed by netting), and he starts climbing the sweeping staircase. The building is in the throes of massive renovation; every room is a dusty building site, with ladders and random piles of bricks and planks of wood piled neatly in the corners of most rooms. The place is empty, and I'm beginning to get a little creeped out. After all, what do I know about this guy really? I really just exchanged a couple of anonymous agony uncle letters and then met him for all of ten minutes at a Singles Mingle.

Despite my inner reluctance, I continue following him. My brain whirs rapidly, berating itself for not telling Adam (or anyone) where I was going but also trying to plot the quickest escape route. We climb higher and higher in the building, and my palms get a little sweaty as my escape options diminish. Interestingly, I'm still worried about clammy hands not being very sexy despite my potentially impending murder.

I decide to come clean. "I'm starting to reevaluate my serial killer conclusion," I say nervously as he disappears up a final narrow staircase into what looks like an attic.

"Ryan, I'm going to be really disappointed if you ARE a serial killer."

We reach the attic, which is completely dark, and for a moment, I feel a wave of actual panic, as opposed to my faux, melodramatic, what-would-the-newspapers-write-about-me internal narrative. I'm about to actually make a run for it when suddenly I'm hit by a wall of light as Ryan opens a door out onto a huge roof terrace. I stop, transfixed, as my eyes drink everything in. Outside, there's a table set for two, complete with a red gingham tablecloth, a vase of daffodils, and two folding chairs. He puts the picnic bag down and starts unpacking. There's Chablis in a cooler bag and snack-type things like grapes, dips, bread, and olives. He then pulls out a container of the most delicious-looking salmon salad, followed by two slices of strawberry cheesecake. My heart feels just about to burst with the romance of it all. Like a kid in a sweetshop, my eyes flit from Ryan to the goodies to the amazing view across Westminster, stretching across to the river and beyond.

"This is amazing," I say, looking dreamily across at St Paul's Cathedral. "What is this place?"

He looks incredibly relieved, a shy smile in full beam. "It's my project. I'm an architect. We're converting it from flats back into a single house for some jet-setting billionaire. He wants a pool in the basement and a library, so it's all pretty exciting. I've kind of been smitten by this sun terrace since I first came; the views are just breathtaking.

"It's so peaceful," I sigh.

He chuckles, "You should have seen the place an hour ago. It was swarming with builders. I got a fair bit of teasing trying to set up for the picnic!"

I pull up a chair as he pours the wine. "Well, I love it."

I take a sip of wine and, at Ryan's invitation, help myself to some salad. For all of Ryan's quietness, he's surprisingly easy to talk to. He talks briefly about his plans for the conversion and how they're going to maximise the south-facing sun terrace. Then, shock of shocks, he stops talking about the project and asks me a question. I'm almost startled. It's a first. A guy who stops talking about themselves to proactively ask me a question, without me having to try and jump in on a vague tangent just so that I have the opportunity to say anything at all. With Ryan, though, that's pretty much how it continues. Without meaning to, I end up telling him the story of the Knutsford clothes shop debacle. He laughs loudly (such a pleasant laugh, I think dreamily), but he definitely gets the horror of it, too. Even I know mentioning exes at any length on a date is a no-no – so I skip over the closure the whole episode gave me and just play it for laughs.

"I'm not sure if listing all the undignified things that tend to happen to me is a good idea on a first date…"

"I wouldn't ever say you're undignified. I wasn't sure if you did just think I wanted more tips on breaking the ice."

"OK, well, balance me a bit," I say, teasing. "Tell me some of your past horrors."

In his quiet way, Ryan has a sly wit, making me laugh out loud with some of his more disastrous dates. Like the one with the girl who was so much shyer than him that pretty much the only time they spoke was to order their food and ask for the bill. Then there was the fellow architect who was just trying to get a job in his firm and asked lots of probing questions about the directors and what their interview styles were like. And then the woman who was actually married and was flagrantly cheating in order to make her husband jealous.

"Ha, these stories are really making me out to be a pretty good catch by comparison."

"You definitely are. So, why the name Anastasia?"

"Sorry?" I ask, momentarily confused as my brain relaxes into good food and wine.

"Why did your parents go for it?"

"Ooohh!" I think at speed, "My dad is Russian."

He lifts his eyebrows. "Really? But with Edwards?"

"Oh yes. They changed it. Because of the revolution." I cringe inwardly. I hate lying to him. I'm not particularly good at it, but he seems convinced.

"And then, when times changed, your dad decided to bring back a good old-fashioned Russian first name? Cool."

"Oh yes, he's big on that. Our house was a little slice of Russia as a kid." I warm to my theme.

"And you speak Russian?" he quizzes.

"My dad used to speak it to me when I was small, but I've forgotten most of it," I say, reddening and thinking of my dad pottering around his allotment in Knutsford, having never been to or even expressed an interest in going to Russia. The closest to Russia he's ever come to is a Dostoevsky collection he found in a charity shop.

"People always say that. I bet you haven't."

"Oh, believe me, I have," I insist before skilfully manoeuvring the conversation from Russia to my writing. I manage to make my job sound quite glamorous – even the *Reptiles Monthly* bit – and he seems so enthralled by the romance of it all that I find myself feeling quite smug about my job, which is a new and novel feeling. I tell him all about Adam, who he thinks sounds 'a character' and wants to meet, before confiding my fears about moving to Sir John's. He somehow manages to make it all sound very adventurous and exciting, and enthusiasm slowly replaces my trepidation.

Apart from the Anastasia interlude, the evening flows beautifully. There are a couple of moments where he says, "Anastasia," and I don't really respond, but he puts that down to me just "being a dreamy writer." We polish off the picnic and relax in front of the sunset, and as we finish the wine, I sigh contentedly.

He glances over from his chair, "You OK?"

I blush slightly, "Oh yes. Great. Thank you. I was just thinking that this has been one of my favourite evenings in London."

His face lights up in response, and his eyes hold mine for a few seconds longer than strictly necessary. This is definitely a moment. We are having a moment, I think excitedly. He leans towards me. I lean too, all caution forgotten. Damn, the camping chairs are an unromantic distance apart. I lean further, focused on his warm smile and bright eyes. Suddenly, my folding chair tips and starts to collapse. If the laws of my life so far were being applied, the chair would have pitched me into the table, and I'd have disappeared under a shower of leftover hummus and spilt olives. But for once, they don't seem to apply in this magical rooftop terrace world where I'm a charming and glamourous émigré. He gallantly leaps up, gently steadies me, and helps me out of the collapsing chair. I melt into him, and instead of another Charlie Chaplin moment, I'm kissing him against a perfect sunset.

***

Dear Alex,

Not really sure what to do here… I feel like I'm caught between my fiancée and my best friend. I'm getting married next summer, and my fiancée wants this really extravagant wedding on a beach on a tropical island in the Caribbean with fifty guests at the dinner. I've been working really hard to save for it, but on my salary, it's never going to happen. I managed to talk her down to twenty guests for dinner and the rest just for the drinks reception. She was pretty annoyed, but she eventually agreed.

The problem now is that my best friend is getting married in two months. We've been best friends since we were six. We went to school together, then to university… the whole lot. I'm his best man, and he wants a traditional, crazy Amsterdam weekend. I want to make sure he has a good send-off, and if that involves a couple of strip clubs and some weed, I'm OK with that. My fiancée, however, is the opposite of OK. She's partly annoyed about the strip clubs but mostly annoyed about the fact that I would dare spend money on something that isn't her dream wedding. But my mate will be spending loads of cash getting him and his wife to the Caribbean for our wedding next summer, and I know he'll organise the stag of my dreams. His fiancée is super chill, so she won't have a problem with him doing whatever for my stag. I hate to say it, but this is making me question marrying my fiancée. Ever since we got engaged, she's turned into the traditional bridezilla, and I just don't know how to handle it. She's starting to no longer act like the woman I fell in love with. Is this a permanent change?

What do I do? I love her, but I also care about my friend's wishes.

Cheers,
Stan

Dear Stan,

Wow, there's a lot going on here! I feel for you, man. A lot of women get caught up in the thrills of wedding planning. You say this behaviour is unusual for your fiancée... have you tried talking to her? Her dream wedding does sound very expensive. I have no idea what your financial situation is, but you mention not being able to afford what she wants, and I'd caution that it's not worth getting into financial trouble over a wedding. I think talk to her. If she is the woman you think she is, she may be upset at first, but ultimately, she will understand. If she's not, then walk away!

Yours,
Alex

***

FOURTEEN

I spend the rest of the weekend attempting to pack up my things for my Monday morning departure for Sir John Fenton's house. In reality, most of it is spent picking up objects, looking at them, and distractedly putting them back down again, all while humming Disney theme songs. Predictably, Adam walks into my room just as I'm singing "So This is Love" from Cinderella at the top of my voice.

"Have you been at the breakfast Baileys again?" he interrupts, destroying my rhythm.

"Whenever you get all Disney, it's usually that or some fantasy about Chris coming back and proposing on a starlit beach accompanied by a choir of small sea turtles or some such nonsense. Chris is an idiot. He's not even worth daydreaming about."

I deliberately haven't told Adam about my date with Ryan. I know even he wouldn't approve of me going on a date with him and would yell at me for not just briskly moving on to the next letter. He thinks I 'over-involve' myself in things that have nothing to do with me and then inadvertently make them worse. I have no idea what he means by that.

The alternative is even worse, however – that he would approve, and therefore lead me to question everything about my judgement.

"Nope, no Chris fantasies," I answer.

"Who then?" he asks suspiciously. Honestly. Allowing Adam to sense that there is gossip afoot is like feeding a gremlin after midnight. He turns from a relatively benign being into a crazed and bloodthirsty monster.

"I'm just happy," I answer, knowing that there's little chance of the gremlin believing me.

He doesn't.

"Rubbish. Last night, when I came home with Josie, you were being morose with a tub of ice cream about the idea of no longer living with me. Thanks for that, by the way. It somewhat ruined the mood. Anyway… What's with the Cinderella song?"

After a shared childhood and three years living together, Adam is well-versed in the Disney princess repertoire.

"I've decided to take a more positive view of this next step in my life. I'm going to become a published author, a leading – *the* leading – political biographer of British… political biographies!"

"I see." He looks unconvinced. "Does the UK leading political biographer of British political biographies still need four wheels to get her to her new des res? Or does she travel by her own hot air?"

"She requires the wheels."

"In that case, I'm off to pick it up now, so I hope you're packed and ready. I've only got the rental for a few hours."

Ever the sentimentalist, he strides out, and I hear the door shut moments later. Definitely crying beneath the strong man façade, I told myself. This day was always going to come eventually, I tell myself. It's been a great three years with Adam, and who knows, I might be back in a few months, but I need to try and see this as progress. It is amazing that I've found a job – a writing job – that gives me a free place to live. Many people would kill to be paid to write but instead work in a café during the day and write in the early hours. The fact that I'm able to make any sort of living doing this is an achievement. I think a lot of this self-recrimination comes from Chris being so critical of my progress compared to his. But it's not all about Chris. Not anymore.

With a sigh, I pull myself off the sofa and go to finish* packing.

*start

FIFTEEN

Two hours later, with a very excitable Adam (it's not every day he has the opportunity to drive a rental van), we are finally off to Sir John's. I take a drawn-out final glance at the flat's front door in the rearview mirror as it recedes into the distance and start to feel mournful again. I can't believe I never appreciated the beauty of the slightly cracked blue paint on the door or the way the hedgerow tilts somewhat to the left. My eyes almost start to fill as my home disappears from view for the last time.

"Oh, give over," Adam interrupts my reverie. "You're coming for dinner on Friday. That's in four days. I think you'll survive."

I glare at him through damp lashes and spend the rest of the drive looking out the window, vacillating between moping about our Clapham den and daydreaming about Ryan.

I'm caught up in a lovely fantasy of Ryan kissing me at the top of the Eiffel Tower when the van slows abruptly (Adam isn't as smooth a chauffeur as he would like us all to think), and we're pulling into the driveway of my new home.

I wasn't expecting bunting, a barbecue, and a Take That tribute band to welcome me, but Sir John's welcome, when he finally decides to open the door, is muted at best.

"Oh, you've come after all," he says, glancing pointedly at his watch in a tone that suggests he's pretty indifferent to my existence. It's only 11am. He sighs huffily,

"Well, I'm too old to assist with moving things, but I'll show you where to direct your movers."

"We are the movers!" I say, gesturing sheepishly to the collection of antique suitcases Adam is unloading from the car. "This is it."

If the suitcases were human, they would most closely resemble four very elderly, overweight and inebriated (but friendly) men who haven't made an effort with their outward appearances since England last won the World Cup. I can't remember exactly when that was, but from Adam's frequent mocking exclamations whenever England plays, I think it's been a long time. Even as I glance towards the cases, the eldest teeters drunkenly for a moment before collapsing backwards onto the drive (broken castors). It's not all bad, as it knocked a cobweb off one of the others as it fell.

Sir John looks for a moment like he's having second thoughts about me and the suitcase menagerie. Then, with a shake of his head and another (in my opinion) excessively dramatic sigh, he disappears inside. I drag two of the elderly brethren after him, praying they don't scrape, pull or knock any of his antique furniture as they trundle through. We go through the kitchen and turn right into another small hall. Through the open doors, I see a bedroom and a sun-filled but petite living room/

kitchen. Sir John directs me to the sitting room, where large French windows frame a mass of greenery so dense and wild it looks more like a scene from *Jurassic Park* than Hampstead.

There's beauty in the wilderness, though, and I look out as it stretches away, a brief untidy lawn disappearing into thickets of beech trees (not through choice, but I am a country girl, I notice these things) and great untamed bushes. As a view goes, it's already heads above Adam's living room vista of Londis and the bus stop. And a kitchen! Tiny and dated (I haven't seen orange tiles matched with fawn-coloured peeling wallpaper for a very long time), but it's mine and perfectly adequate for my culinary repertoire of pot noodles and toast. Maybe this isn't going to be so terrible after all.

"Are these rooms all mine?" I ask, thrilled.

I think Sir John prefers my premature homesickness to my rising excitement and looks faintly panicked. "Well, this sitting room and kitchen, that bedroom through there, and a small bathroom off the bedroom."

"They're quite small," he says, less apologetically and more in the hope of deflating my mood. "And they're very cold in winter," he adds triumphantly.

"They're lovely," I say, "and so quiet. Were these the servants' quarters?" (I've been a *Downton Abbey* fan for many years).

"They were the old kitchen stores and an office," Sir John replies. "We converted them to be the nanny's quarters back in 1972. For our daughter."

He falls quiet momentarily before barking that he's going back up to his library and will leave me to settle in and to call for him if anything else is needed (offered in a tone that suggested the "need" better qualify as life or death) and stomping out.

In the meantime, a sound resembling a small brass band trapped in a jungle gym heralds Adam, bringing the remaining three cases down the hall. He drops them with an exaggerated grunt on the living room floor before sprawling himself on the sofa and looking around, "Cor. Is this all for you? I thought it was just a room?"

I join the sprawl, finding the elderly floral couch mercifully well-sprung and comfy. "Did you just say 'Cor'?"

"It's being in a posh place like this. It brings out the working class in me."

"Oh yes," I reply sarcastically, "I'd forgotten your days as a barefoot urchin on the mean streets of Altrincham."

I look around properly. Everywhere, the decor is faded, which, given its 1970s vibe, is a mercy, but it's clean and private. My own living space as well as a bedroom. "It's not bad, is it? And no drunk lady-killing housemate with a revolving bedroom door."

"You'll miss me really," he responds.

And I will. Suddenly, the perkiness disappears.

Adam looks alarmed at the prospect of more waterworks, "You're not going to be far, though. You can phone me every day."

"Can I?" I say brightly.

Adam looks even more alarmed, "Well. Every other day. Maybe on a Wednesday and a Sunday. Non-gym days. And maybe text first in case I'm busy."

"Alright, alright. I'll make an appointment," I smile.

"And once you've made your dough and the tenancy comes back up for renewal, I can kick out your replacement, and you can move back in!"

"We'll see. I may have become too posh by then to slum it in Clapham with my cousin," I reply.

Adam helps me manoeuvre the elderly cohort of travel luggage into the bedroom. The avocado bathroom suite, complete with bidet (which I'm secretly quite excited about), looks like it was installed for the Queen's Silver Jubilee. However, it's scrupulously clean, and everything seems to work. There's one final door in the hall, with a jangle of keys behind it, which leads out onto the side path.

"Perfect," says Adam, trying the keys, "You've got your own entrance to smuggle as many men in as you want."

"Great," I reply, "I'll just call it the orgy door."

He looks horrified, which is more than slightly hypocritical, considering what I've had to grin and bear while living with him.

In the quiet after Adam leaves, I oscillate between contentment and lonely despair. My mood is pretty much dictated by my success rate in getting the TV working. After a lot of fiddling (how can a digital TV be so old?! How?), the BBC news theme finally blares out, and I flop down in relief.

SIXTEEN

Sir John has vaguely indicated that we should start work "after lunch", the next day, but nothing more precise than that. Around noon, I wander into the kitchen for some sandwiches (Mrs Jenkins has very kindly extended her full board service to me) and then attempt to navigate the main house with my brick of a laptop to track Sir John down.

Padding into the silent hall, I'm overawed by how big the place is. I wander through, feet silenced by the thick, fraying carpets. The place has definitely seen better days, but Mrs Jenkins does keep it spotless. I sing out "Sir John" occasionally as I search from room to room, like it's a Hide and Seek Senior Citizens Special. I hear a faint sound from a door on the first floor and wander towards it. "Sir John?" I call tentatively, pushing open the door and hoping against hope that I'm not about to walk in on him changing. It's the library (of course, he has a library), and I deduce that Sir John has nodded off because a small TV in the corner is blaring out *Home and Away*. As I walk in, there's a loud snort from the armchair in the corner as he wakes up.

"What IS this?" shouts an agitated Sir John. "WHAT IS IT?!" he bellows, as if the Australian teenagers on screen had invaded the library and were getting sand on his Dickens. Thus ensues a vacillating cacophony of bellowing about "their funny accents" and then switching, often in the same breath, to "Where's the dibber?"

"WHERE is that blasted dibber?"

I conclude he means the remote control and gesture to the side table by the chair. Blissfully, both antipodean drama and Sir John's bellowing fall silent.

I attempt a cheery, collegial tone. "Hello, Sir John. I think you suggested getting started this afternoon?"

He mutters and gestures towards the other armchair. I sit down and open my laptop, which causes a snide "I prefer paper and pen – call me old-fashioned," which I dutifully ignore. I try to look purposefully out of the window, in a thoughtful sort of way, while my laptop limps to attention.

"First things first," I say when it finally, grudgingly, agrees to open Word, in what I hope is my brightest but most businesslike tone, "Would you mind if I log into your WiFi first? What's the password?"

"My WHAT?" Sir John thunders. He looks at me with horror.

My bright and businesslike exterior falters slightly, "Your password…"

He continues to stare with a mixture of horror, confusion and disgust as if I'd just asked permission to fellate a Mariachi Band on top of his Georgian dining table.

By now, my voice has dwindled to a whisper, "You

know, WiFi so that I can connect to the internet. For research and emails and stuff."

"Oh. The INTERNET," Sir John says, as if it is my fault for using niche terms, "You won't find any of that nonsense here. I don't want lots of beeps and bops and hips and hops and what have you, and a bunch of overpaid Californians peering into my house through the computer machine. No. We don't have the internet here," he says triumphantly.

I gulp.

Noticing my distress, Sir John delightedly warms to his theme. "No, none of that. I believe there was one of those internet cafes on the high street. But then," he adds gleefully, "I think it became a small wine bar."

"But Sir John, I need the internet to do research for our work," I reason.

"Nonsense," he replies, heaving himself out of his armchair and walking over to a side table with eight huge stacks of paper on it. "That's all sorted. Each of these piles contains the most pertinent documents from the various ministerial posts I occupied. Obviously, these were just the junior minister posts. For my time as Secretary of State, there's the same again and then some. We still need to lay that out, but this is enough to get you going. No. Everything you'll need is here." He pats one of the towering stacks of yellowing paper and beams at my anguish.

It's going to be a long day.

SEVENTEEN

Ryan is waiting for me outside Hammersmith Tube station. He doesn't see me at first, which gives me the opportunity to take a moment to admire his loveliness. The gorgeous brown eyes and the rugged frame I've noticed before, but this time, in the early evening sunlight, I see just how attractively his hair curls. It's obviously important for me to notice these points so I can share them and build up his self-esteem. I definitely don't actually fancy him. I am selflessly bettering him for the benefit of womankind.

Before I can get too swoony, he spots me and waves tentatively. He heads over, simultaneously trying to gallantly take my rucksack and kiss me on the cheek, which results in me awkwardly becoming trapped in my bag strap and him kissing my nose. It's times like this that I wish I had an elegant little satchel, just containing a chic tablet, a book on French philosophy and an incredibly classy red lipstick. Instead, Ryan has to lug around a tired school backpack containing a tube of Pringles from a month and a half ago and a laptop that looks like it's connected to a Soviet satellite.

He doesn't complain, though, swinging it easily over his shoulder and starting down a small lane across from the station.

"So, are you finally going to tell me where we're going?" I ask.

He just laughs, "Wait and see."

Damnit, I think. This is the second surprise he's organised. My own creativity for dates usually just about stretches to finding the free dessert voucher for Pizza Express online. It's going to be hard to keep up if there is even a date three. *Date three?! I chide myself. Remember why you are doing this. This is a short-term mission, 'Anastasia'.*

I spend the walk running through all the places I've ever been in Hammersmith, and wondering if it could be one of those. The food in the Swan pub is pretty good; could we be going there? I've pretty much given up and am completely stumped as we turn into a quiet street, and Ryan announces proudly, "We're here!" He then leads me across the road to a sign reading *Russian Art and Culture – Special Exhibition*. "Surprise!" Ryan beams, albeit somewhat nervously.

"Ooooh," I say neutrally, my mind hamster scrabbling.

"It's an exhibition on Russian émigrés who moved to London – after the revolution," Ryan says, slightly hesitant and nervousness creeping back into his voice as he notices my confused expression. "I thought it might be interesting, given your family history. If you'd rather do something else, that's totally OK!" He manages to sound nonchalant enough, but his eyes give him away, and I'm touched by the effort he's clearly made.

"Oh! Cool! Yes, it is – definitely," my eyes light up, more from realisation than anything else – but hopefully, that's enough to convince him.

The exhibition is actually pretty interesting: photos of Tsarist aristocrats slumming in London boarding houses, tragic letters across Communist borders, etc., but it's hard to pitch the right level of interest when this is all part of your entirely fabricated family history. Should I look more mournful and less like a culture vulture visitor? I practise about a hundred different expressions as we browse through the exhibits. I temporarily lose Ryan to a display on Orthodox church-building in Britain and use the opportunity to surreptitiously check my phone for a reminder of when the blooming revolution actually happened. I can just about deal with the logistics of this white lie gone big, but the annoying pang of guilt in my stomach is gnawing at my nerves. It feels worse than that dodgy bacon roll the other week. I scroll frantically, but my phone's struggling to catch enough internet to run me through the entirety of 20th-century Russian history. Damnit. I look up, and Ryan is in animated conversation with an elderly man in a suit. He beckons me over. For a shy person, he certainly knows how to become confident at the most inopportune times. Guilt has turned my insides into a churning washing machine.

"Anastasia, this is Professor Ivanov. He's the curator here."

Another belly somersault.

Ryan continues, "Anastasia's family were émigrés too. They had to change their names!"

"Oh really?" the curator raises bushy eyebrows to look properly at me for the first time, "from what to what?"

Stomach somersaults reach Cirque du Soleil levels. "Oh, to Edwards," I reply – keeping my voice level.

"Interesting. So many people kept their family names as their one-link home. Your family must have had a particularly difficult time on arriving here," the curator pronounces sagely. "And what was their original name?"

Why? Why do my little white lies always grow like this? You would think I would learn.

I open and shut my mouth a couple of times in the hope that it comes up with an idea faster than my panicking brain. The third time open, and I pour out what I think are some Russian-sounding syllables. "Bar-row-sky," I tentatively pronounce.

"Barowski?" The Curator's pronunciation of my made-up surname is infinitely superior.

"Ah. Interesting. Barowski is an old name, more from Silesia than anywhere. Your family is Jewish, then."

My mouth, overconfident since the last save, opens with zero consultation with the brain: "Yes, that's right."

He directs us to a small exhibition on revolutionaries during the Russian Civil War before leaving us to it.

Ryan glances across at me, "So it's Anastasia Barowski! I feel very boring in comparison. My mum moved from Jamaica as a teenager, and my dad's great-granddad moved here from Sierra Leone, but no royalty or anything dramatic as far as I know."

I murmur something non-committal, cursing myself for now, having not just a fake name but an original fake name that the first fake name used to be. Not to mention having acquired a new religion. I briefly think about my parents' twenty years at Knutsford Methodist Church, not to mention the fact that Dad's love of brunch has a significant amount to do with its pork foundations.

As I look closer, the exhibition does turn out to be fascinating. In particular, a whole section on Russian émigrés and film-making brings up some of the old masters of European cinema that I hadn't thought about since university. But I can't shake off the pangs of guilt and the constant stress. Where did this dishonesty come from? I'm pretty sure I was a truthful kid, but now it just drips out when I part my lips. When did it start? I think about how much I had to stretch my CV even to get interviews. And then I recall how acerbic Chris could be if he thought I'd done something dumb. It just got easier to cover things up or tell a lie here or there. Yes, I did remember to do that. Yes, I knew that really. Yes, I thought that was funny. I just forgot to laugh. So career and Chris – that's when I started. Or is that just another lie – the easiest place to put the blame?

I deserve everything I get in this exhibition. Knowing my luck, I'll be called upon to sing the old Russian national anthem. Miraculously, though, luck is with me for once, and there's no further opportunity for me to probe my Romanov history.

It gets easier once we leave, and Ryan takes me to a little Thai place tucked away off King Street.

I peruse the menu. What to eat elegantly? I'm not known for my dainty eating when I'm hungry, and the stress of my wrong turn down some other family's memory lane has worked up an appetite.

Ryan glances over his menu, "You do like Thai, right? If you can't find anything, we could go somewhere else?"

"Oh yes, I love Thai, just trying to pick something new. I'm feeling adventurous," I say gaily.

Normally, my dates would take this as a cue to smugly take charge and show off their knowledge of Thai cuisine, dropping in their "gap yah" at an elephant sanctuary in Koh Samui. Ryan doesn't do this; he just offers to share. There's a funny, warm feeling somewhere in my chest that gets warmer. This is not the plan. What am I doing? I've gone so far along now that I've forgotten my original charitable purpose. But this is getting out of control. He thinks I'm called Anastasia Barowski. I've lied to him, and I'm creepily pretending to be some kind of blokey pen pal. Get a grip, woman; it's time to get back on mission. Make this your final date, end the mission on a positive note to boost his self-esteem, and then get out of there.

I assume my most judgy mindset. Once the waitress takes our order (I throw daintiness out the window and go for the spiciest curry), I plunge in.

Through a mouthful of prawn crackers, I demand: "So Ryan, what makes the ideal woman for you?"

He takes a cracker and chews thoughtfully. "I'm not sure 'ideal' is ever the best word, to be honest. Is anyone 'ideal' for anyone else? And if they were, that might be kind of dull, surely? I guess I'm looking for someone who's at least in sync. Who challenges me. And who makes me laugh, and who laughs with me."

Damn. That was an annoyingly unobjectionable answer. I wave it away with a cracker clasping hand,

"Yes, yes. But in appearance terms," I say, trying to be as objectionable as possible.

"Err," he swallows nervously. "I think you just have chemistry, or you don't. What about you?" he asks hesitantly.

I resist the obvious. "Ears."

He splutters. "Ears?"

"You can tell a lot about someone from their ears," I say simply.

"OK. Mine, for example. What can you tell me about mine?"

"You are… very creative… and… honest."

We're rescued from my ear analysis by the waitress depositing our dishes. I'm on high alert for bad table manners. Damn. He eats hungrily but neatly. Meanwhile, I've been overly ambitious on the chilli front and am practically choking through every bite.

Ryan looks worried. "Are you OK?"

"Fine," I rasp. "I (cough). Like it (cough). Spicy."

"Are you sure? Because we can swap if you like?"

I wave the offer away, opting not to speak because my throat has basically closed up. Again, an annoyingly kind offer.

Once I've established I'm not going to die from over-spicing, I decide to take a more direct approach to problem-finding. "So, what would you say your flaws are? Apart from being shy. If you had to choose something."

He looks at me thoughtfully, "You've got a very Paxman approach to dating this evening, Anastasia. Everything OK?"

"Oh, just making conversation," I answer, feeling my cheeks flush under his gaze.

"I'm not sure. You'd be better asking someone who knows me. Speaking of that, my housemates and I are thinking of having a barbecue next weekend. You could strap them in the interrogation chair instead if you want to get all my bad points." He smiles but looks a little nervous.

Oh no. Meeting friends. This isn't good. This can go no further.

"Next weekend? I'm not sure I can make that," I answer, feeling a wave of sadness as I think about my alternative plan – trying to hack Adam's Netflix account for a boxset binge on my phone (needs must when you are living sans broadband).

"Ah, OK. Sure?" He asks.

"Err, I'll check my diary and let you know tomorrow."

"No worries," Ryan manages a quick smile, but he looks disappointed, and my heart flips. This isn't good. It's the classic battle. My head knows that the reason I'm here is to boost Ryan's self-esteem after my original little agony uncle white lie. My heart, however, has other ideas. It's fluttering wildly in my chest every time he looks at me with those big brown eyes, and my stomach flips every time I catch a glimpse of his biceps rippling. My body is betraying me at every turn.

There's a bit of an awkward silence where poor Ryan is clearly trying to work out why I don't want to come to the barbecue, so I take the opportunity to try and convince myself I'm just having palpitations from too much coffee and then start talking about my new job with Sir John in quite a clinical, detached, job interview type fashion. Unfortunately, he looks genuinely interested and asks me a series of questions about my new lodgings and my new boss. He becomes genuinely concerned and compassionate when I tell him about Sir John's apparent reluctance to discuss his family history and my intuition that there's something there that he doesn't want to divulge. Ryan listens carefully and makes very gentle suggestions as to how I could build up Sir John's trust and take my time getting to know him in order to write the best account of his life.

He's effortlessly made me go from interview style to treating him like a confidante whose opinion I deeply depend upon. It's incredibly annoying. I quickly change tack. He is clearly perfect and completely flawless, so I feel I have no choice but to reveal my own deeply flawed self. I take a deep breath and begin my performance.

I survey the restaurant to choose a victim. It's a really cute couple, clearly deeply in love. I start snickering and gesture towards them, "They won't last a week!"

Ryan looks slightly startled. "What?"

"Them, over there. I give them a week. She looks like an airhead, and he looks so cocky."

"Right…"

Ryan is looking slightly puzzled. Good. I look down at my plate and scrape my finger through the sauce remnants. I bring my finger to my lips, making sure to smear some of the sauce on my chin. I make a loud smacking noise as I lick my fingers and make sure to have a good root around, picking at my back teeth. To my disgust, Ryan isn't watching! He's looking out of the window. I make a louder sucking noise, and he looks up. "You OK?"

"Fine, fine!" I say airily. "Just didn't want the sauce to go to waste!"

I then start spluttering on the last of the curry, and he swoops around to my side of the table, hands me my water, and rubs my back. "Let's get you home, I think," he says gently.

Oh, good, I think. He's finally had enough of me. I sit back, satisfied, as he asks the waiter for the bill. He insists on paying (which is simultaneously a source of guilt and profound relief) and then helps me with my coat. We walk slowly down the street towards the Tube station, and to my strange hybrid of disappointment/relief, he doesn't try to hold my hand. He's very quiet, and I quickly remember I'm supposed to be leaving him on a high.

"Thank you for a lovely date," I say. "You really are so kind and thoughtful."

He looks adorably bashful and gives me that lovely smile. I clench my teeth and forbid my brain from thinking romantic things.

We get to the station entrance, and I look up at him awkwardly. "Well... bye." My teeth-clenching trick isn't working anymore. I feel really, really sad at the thought of never seeing him again. I blink hard.

"Wait up," he says, interrupting the tragic love story unfolding in my head as he grabs my hand. "Let me at least escort you home."

"Oh... but you know... I'm living with Sir John... I don't think..." I trail off, mumbling.

"Not for that reason. Don't worry," Ryan says, looking embarrassed. I just want to make sure you get home safely, and I want to spend more time with you on the way. If that's OK."

Damn him for being so unbelievably cute.

He escorts me down to the platform, and during the three-minute wait, I am completely oblivious to the drunks stumbling and yelling on the platform, lost in my imaginings. I feel shy and strangely lacking in inspiration for conversation on the way back. Mainly because of that inner voice screaming, "The mission is over. Abort now."

I bat back the questions he continues to ask about me – I'm so sick of talking about Anastasia – and manage to keep the focus on his latest project at work. He's working on another chapel refurbishment, as well as the flat-to-house refurbishment that we picnicked at, and I can tell how much he loves it. Ryan's whole face becomes animated when he talks about it.

Too soon, though, we're back, and we're walking towards Sir John's. We pause in the driveway, and unbelievably for London, we can see the stars above us. Those traitors. Still holding my hand, he pulls me towards him, and I desperately try not to notice how toned he is. I know I'm starting to fall for him.

"Goodnight, Anastasia," he murmurs as he tucks a stray strand of hair behind my ear. He watches as I walk up the stairs to the front door, making sure I'm safely inside. As I turn the key in the lock, I ignore the increasingly prevalent feelings of guilt and let the butterflies take control.

EIGHTEEN

The next morning gets off to a good start with the discovery that Mrs Jenkins has purchased some more Coco Pops on my behalf. There was a lot of resistance to the alien cereal at first, but the other day, I caught Sir John secretly eschewing his porridge for them, so I'm pretty sure I have a new children's breakfast ally. I'm cheerfully watching the milk change colour with childish wonder when Sir John joins me at the kitchen table with a copy of *The Times*.

"Good morning, Alexandra."

"Morning, Sir John."

"I trust you had a nice evening?"

Is he... smirking slightly? Or am I just paranoid?

"It was lovely!" I answer. "I saw an exhibition on Russian émigrés who moved to London," I say, hoping Sir John will think I'm cultured and educated and, therefore, worthy of hearing his life's secrets.

"Harumph. With one of your bedfellows?"

I must have misheard. "I'm sorry?" I say, hopefully.

"Bedfellows! I saw you last night, scampering around with some young lad."

Chameleon-like, I quickly transition to the colour of my juice. "I… he's just a friend." I stammer. I can't move. My body is drained of all blood, except instead of draining with gravity, it's done some sort of anti-gravitational miracle drain and is all in my face. All of it.

"A friend!" Sir John *actually* cackles. "We didn't do that with friends in my day!"

"He's not a… bedfellow," I stammer. "Just some guy I have been on a few dates with." And am falling for, I silently add.

"Good Lord, girl! Don't go all prudish on my account. Before I was married, I had a "few dates" myself, you know. Three on the go at any one time. Kept things interesting, you know. Oh, Henley-on-Thames Young Conservatives were quite the party crowd in their day."

I have no idea what to say. I've never been speechless before.

Sir John continues, "Anyway, he looked like a nice young chap. Why don't you have him over for dinner if you want? I can see if he warrants my seal of approval." He has a mischievous twinkle in his eye. I am ninety-nine per cent sure he's winding me up – it seems a little soon for him to be taking this sort of paternal interest – but equally, I am sure he would follow through just for the joy of how awkward it would be – so I mumble something about it perhaps being a bit soon, and try to divert from this line of questioning.

"So, Sir John. Tell me about *your* bedfellows. I do have to write about them, after all."

He adjusts his braces, and there's definitely a smirk there this time.

"Oh! Well, quite a few, back in the day. I was a bit of a rake, you know, in my youth. Always with a girl on my arm. Cousin of a Windsor at one stage. And a semi-professional tennis player once. All this before I met Laura, of course."

"Scandalous!"

"Oh no, not really. A trifle roguish at best but never cruel and always discreet. Not like young people today – being utter rotters to one another. No, no…"

Sir John, lost in thought, stares down into the chocolatey swirls of his Coco Pops as if he can see his youthful reflection in the bottom of the bowl. "I was considered quite the catch in my youth."

"Were other men jealous?" I ask, fascinated by this insight.

"Oh, I wasn't the rooster. I was a pretty straightforward chap – a little bit mischievous. I think people appreciate that in a lawyer or a politician. My best friend Peter was much the same. Together, we were a force!"

I'm loving this side of Sir John; he's really opening up. He can't stop grinning, and I feel like it's been a while since anyone has taken such an interest.

"There was one instance when Peter and I first started in Chambers. We were helping out at an international law event at Lancaster House. A little too much of the free port, you know. Anyway, we ended up falling asleep in a very grand corridor somewhere away from the main event – pissed as newts. Woke at five in the morning, utterly bewildered. Tried to leave. And suddenly alarms, security guards – and an awful lot to try and explain while in the grip of a hangover."

"Ooh, you tearaways," I tease. "This is exactly the sort of thing for the book. Not just the policy and the politics. But the lovable rogue anecdotes. It's just what we need."

"Oh, I doubt anyone is much interested in that sort of thing. I was planning to focus more on the politics."

"Oh no, I really think the human-interest side is what will endear you to people. People want to know that you're relatable. They want anecdotes; the funnier, the better! We can pepper the politics with the personal. Trust me."

Sir John harrumphs – not quite convinced but not discounting my words entirely. I really am warming to him.

"So," I begin tentatively, "what was special about Laura? About Lady Fenton," I ask. "What made you fall for her?"

"Oh Laura," he looks wistful. "She was a beautiful creature. Everything you could want in a soulmate. In a partner. Fiercely bright, of course. Double Oxford first. Very glamorous, very challenging. Kept me on my toes. An amazing poker face. But when you cracked it, a dazzling smile. Quite serious at times, but very kind. I didn't stand a chance. I was utterly enchanted by her every move. She was the only woman who ever made me nervous before a date. I used to take her dancing every Friday. She loved jazz. She was a splendid dancer."

"And after that?"

"Well, we got married and had our daughter," Sir John replies slightly more gruffly.

"Tell me more about your daughter?" I probe gently, sensing the change in tone. Sir John hasn't mentioned his daughter since I moved in, and he referenced the former nanny's quarters, but now he seems to be shutting down.

"We're estranged," he answers abruptly.

I can see the shutters descending, but I need to maintain this openness, so I try to pivot back to Laura.

"Tell me more about being married to Lady Fenton. Was it wonderful?"

Sir John's face clouds. "Well. Life happened. Fate. Whatever you want to call it. Laura died young. Much too young." Sir John coughs and starts busying himself with the paper.

"Oh, I'm so sorry. So very sorry."

Sir John nods. He doesn't look angry, but I can tell the conversation is over. His face has darkened, and his features have visibly crumbled. He quickly folds *The Times*, pushes his chair back abruptly, and leaves the room.

I stare at him, feeling sad. I finish my Coco Pops in silence and wander back to my room to get ready to head back to the old flat for the day.

***

Dear Alex,

Advice needed. I'm torn. I'm seeing two beautiful ladies and have been for about five months now. I know it's kinda shitty, but whenever I try to end it with one of them, I just can't bring myself to make a decision. They're both really sweet, and they'd both be gutted. The first girl is amazing; she's smart and loves to travel. She's really on my wavelength as a fellow citizen of the world. The second is just the sweetest. Amazing chef, kind of crazy. She gets my sense of adventure. Both of them are gorgeous. How do I decide?

Craig

Craig,

Look at you. Aren't you the gentleman? Really nice to see how considerate you are about how travel girl and kooky chef will feel. They're lucky to have you. That, by the way, was sarcasm. I felt the need to clarify that as I'm not necessarily sure you'll get it despite the globetrotting intellect you bring to the table.

Are you sure these women will be as devastated as you think? Even once you tell them about that totally understandable accident where you've been accidentally two-timing them for almost half a year?

It might be, and you'll need to sit down for this, that instead of breaking down in tears, they high-five each other and disappear into the sunset in a Thelma *and* Louise *convertible, but without that bummer of a cliff. If anything, the question might not need to be how do YOU decide, but how you persuade either one of them to put up with your knobhead sexual incontinence a moment longer.*

If you are genuinely interested in a relationship, then ask yourself honestly which one you connect with more, and then think about a way to reboot your relationship monogamously and honestly. And then, if you're the praying kind of meathead, I'd light the bonfire of all church candles and start hoping she's in a forgiving mood.

All the best,
Alex

NINETEEN

I've never been so pleased to see Adam. I never appreciated all those Saturdays when he was engaging me in endless conversation about Spurs' mid-season performance or the latest flavour of protein shake. But now that I have my own space – it all feels empty and Adam-less.

I feel a bit strange as I get off the Tube at Clapham Common and walk the familiar route to the house. I really like Sir John's, but it's just not the same as living with one of my best friends. I miss Adam's silliness, our late-night chats over cups of tea and chocolate Penguin bars, and our wine-fuelled movie nights, introducing him to all those "ancient classics" that predate *Jurassic Park*. I reach the front door and root around in my bag for my keys before pausing. Should I be opening the door myself? Should I knock? I'm a guest now. I drop the keys back into my bag and ring the buzzer. No answer. I wait a couple of minutes and buzz again. Nothing. I pull my phone out of my bag and WhatsApp Adam. Last seen three hours ago. Hmm. Maybe he's been held up at work. Reluctantly, I reach for my keys and let myself in, thinking I'll just watch a bit of TV until Adam arrives.

Half an hour later I'm starting to get bored and a little annoyed. Finally, my phone pings: *Damn. I totally forgots. Went to pub. On way now. Will pick up pidzza.*

That sums up our friendship entirely. I'm all excited, and Adam completely forgets. Fortunately, I still had an episode of *Housewives of Eastbourne* to work through.

When I finally hear the key in the lock, I hastily turn off the TV, rearrange my features into an annoyed look, and cross my arms grumpily, trying to look at my most abandoned.

"Sorry, cuz! I am a bad person," Adam's words are slightly slurred.

"Hmm."

"Oh, come on… I've missssssed you." He jumps on the sofa and smothers me in a hug.

"Get offffff!" I scream, but secretly, I'm pleased. I give him a friendly shove, which sends him backwards over the arm of the chair. His squark of indignation dissipates any residual irritation as I dissolve into chuckles and help him to his feet.

"Ooops. Forgot pizza."

Irritation creeps back slightly.

"Ordering now!" He pulls out Deliveroo, keen to avoid enraging the dragon once again.

While we're waiting for the pizza, I tell Adam all about my conversations with Sir John.

"I knew it!" he crows. "I totally recognised a fellow hit with the ladies. It's all about the eyebrows."

I roll my eyes. "Anyway, he got really quiet when I

probed about his family. There's definitely something more there. He never talks about his daughter."

"Who knows," Adam shrugs, losing interest. "Let me tell you about my flatmate interviews."

"I don't want to hear. Too sad for me. I just assume I'm totally irreplaceable."

"Well, you're certainly unique… But, anyway, you DO want to hear. It's been hilarious."

"Oh," I perk up. "Go on then."

"Well, there was this one girl called Candice. She seemed great on paper. Then she turned up, and she was super hot! I thought I'd found the perfect flatmate. Then she says she recently was fired from work for gross misconduct. She had sex on the boss's desk… classic, right? Then she starts telling me about how she used to date a biker guy with a criminal record, and he wanted her back and stalked her sometimes."

"Wow! I'm assuming you said no?"

"Of course not – she was hot!"

I hit him with a pillow. "Even you aren't stupid enough to put sex above keeping your kneecaps. Who was next?"

"Then there was a French guy called Jean-Marc. Didn't like him."

"Why not?"

"Arrogant."

Knowing Adam as I do, I take this to mean that Jean-Marc was very attractive and would be unwanted competition for Adam's debauchery. "You know, Sir John had a wingman called Peter. Jean-Marc, with his gallic charm, could have helped you up your game!" I'm deliberately goading him here.

Adam glares at me, so I know I've hit the nail on the head.

"So, who did you go with?" I ask, ignoring his look.

"Some guy called Javier. Good job, likes the gym, friendly. Probably won't drunkenly order a bulk load of frozen seafood or cry on any of my dates until they run away."

"Ooh! He sounds great," I reply, ignoring the needling.

"Don't get too excited. He won't be interested in you. Oh… he may have a brother!"

"Actually…" I hesitate, not sure whether to tell Adam about Ryan or not.

He knows me too well, however, and he pounces. "You've met someone! Tell me everything immediately."

Reluctance bubbling over into excitement, I tell him everything… and I mean everything… That's one of the great things about Adam. He's so self-absorbed that he doesn't really bother to judge other people unless it directly affects him. I feel a slight pang of guilt at my ability to be completely honest with him when I can't be with Bea, but that's just a mark of how lovely Bea is. It's easier to confess to a fellow sinner than to a saint.

He reacts appropriately in all the right places and limits himself to simply shaking his head, wondering and saying, "You really do get yourself into some holes."

When I get to the bit about the barbecue, he demands that not only do I go, but he goes as my plus one.

"I can't go, Adam. He thinks my name is Anastasia, and my great-grandfather emigrated from Russia. I can't expand the lie and drag you in, too. Oh God, and his friends."

"I'm enjoying the irony of you living a lie after years of constant lectures about my treatment of women."

"Shut up. I'm not going. *We're* not going."

"We are," he says firmly. "It'll be fine. We'll work out a way to tell him the truth. Maybe get him drunk? That's what I did with Clarissa when I revealed after six dates that I didn't actually know her name and that she was saved in my phone as *hot girl*. She found it hilarious."

"He's not like you. He's sensitive. He'd be furious."

"Well, we have to do something. I genuinely haven't seen you this excited about anyone in a long time. We need to keep Ryan. You can't lose him over something so silly. Million times better than Chris."

Part of me really wants to go to the barbecue, but I just can't face telling Ryan the truth. He'll never understand.

"I just can't." My lip borders on a slight tremble, and Adam goes white with horror.

"No, no, no, no. It's fine. Don't cry." He hands me the corner of the blanket on the couch in lieu of any tissue. I resist both tears and that gross misappropriation of a sofa throw. "We're going to come up with a plan," Adam reassures as if he's boosting one of his personal training clients. "We're going to win this thing!"

TWENTY

The day of the barbecue comes around far too quickly. I spend an eternity going back and forth on my outfit choice and modelling things for Mrs Jenkins, and I still haven't completely decided. Mrs Jenkins, who seemed flattered to be asked, has immediately adopted a hybrid mother-best-friend persona and is eagerly advising me. We've narrowed it down to a chic navy shift dress, which I love but Mrs Jenkins thinks might be a bit much for a casual summer barbecue in the garden, or my lemon-yellow dress, which Mrs Jenkins favours but I worry might be too twee.

The problem, I explain to Sir John while holding court at the breakfast table, is that I can't choose a bag or shoes until I've decided on a dress. He looks distinctly uninterested, but I persevere with my theme until I wear him down to offer an opinion. He finally mutters, "I've always liked yellow... sunny colour," and returns to his paper. I can't help but notice he pulls it up a bit higher in front of his face, like people on the Tube who want to avoid any eye contact / having to give up their seats.

I might be overthinking this outfit choice.

Two hours later, clad in yellow and nude flats, I'm finally off. I've arranged to meet Adam at our old Clapham flat at 11am and travel to Ryan's house together, mainly so I can reinforce the fact that today my name is Anastasia, but also because I quite like the idea of arriving with an escort for moral support. I text him before I leave to make sure that he is a) awake and b) alone, and he replies to confirm that while only 50% of my questions are currently true, 100% will be by the time I arrive.

When he opens the door, I do a slight double take.

"Adam…" I say cautiously. "Where are you going?"

"To the barbecue?"

"Well, why then are you dressed in your 'attending a wedding' outfit?"

He's wearing an Oxford shirt with cufflinks, shiny black shoes, and suit trousers. Thank God I decided to meet him here so I could put a stop to this.

"It's in an old chapel. I'm being respectful," he answers, crossing his arms in a rather defiant fashion.

"You look like a used car salesman."

Adam looks sulky, so I try another tack. "Why don't you keep that lovely shirt but go a little more casual with the trousers and the shoes and lose the cufflinks?" I say in what I hope is a winning tone.

"I think I look great."

"You do look great! You look absolutely amazing. Very handsome. But maybe a little too formal for a casual afternoon barbecue?"

"Well, I only ever dress for personal training or dates…"

"Hmm. Imagine a date by the river on a sunny Sunday afternoon. That's the bit of the wardrobe to go for…"

After several minutes of gentle persuasion (on my part), met with stubborn resistance (on his), we agree to compromise, and he re-emerges wearing the Oxford shirt, minus the cufflinks, and wearing chinos and boat shoes. He still looks like he's attending a garden party at Buckingham Palace. Still, by this point, we're in danger of showing up unfashionably late, so each grabbing a couple of lobsters from my impulse purchase, along with a bottle of prosecco, we head for the Tube.

Twelve minutes later, we emerge at South Wimbledon.

"Right," I say, taking out my phone and opening CityMapper. "This way." Marching confidently ahead, the lobsters tucked under one arm and the prosecco under the other, I navigate us towards Ryan's flat.

"Is that it?" Adam says, *sotto voce*, as we approach.

"I think so!" I say excitedly. The place looks incredible. It's small, but even from here, I can see that it has beautiful little window arches and stained-glass windows set into the red brick. I've leapt ahead and am imagining an intimate wedding ceremony followed by a small reception for Ryan and my closest friends and family, the sun setting majestically in a smorgasbord of violet and honey-coloured sky, him kissing me gently as our loved ones cheer and my well cut diamond glitters in the fading light...In this fantasy I've obviously changed my name by deed poll to Anastasia Edwards, and all my friends and family have become willing conspirators.

"Alex! Alex!" Adam is rudely waving his hand right in front of my face, interrupting my reverie. "Good. You're back with us. Let's go in."

I've been so focused on getting Adam to dress less ridiculously and then transporting us and the lobsters safely and (relatively) on time to Wimbledon that I haven't had time to consider the enormity of the situation. I'm going to be a) introducing Adam and Ryan, b) maintaining the Anastasia lie in an alcohol-fuelled environment, and c) meeting Ryan's friends.

This is basically an announcement that we are on our way to becoming a couple. This is huge.

"Have I lost you again?" Adam's voice interrupts my thoughts, and I realise that we're standing on the doorstep, his finger poised on the doorbell.

"Sorry. Nervous. Remember, it's Anastasia," I hiss as he presses an index finger on the bell. I can hear the chimes echoing down the hallway and then the sound of footsteps on the approach. To my relief, it's Ryan himself who opens the door, casually clad in khaki shorts and a red polo shirt and clutching a beer. I glance pointedly at Adam's outfit, and he, in turn, stares pointedly at a spot on the wall.

"Anastasia… you look beautiful," he glances nervously at Adam as if checking it's OK to kiss me hello, the butterflies swooping back into residence as he releases me and turns to Adam. "You must be Anastasia's cousin, Adam. I've heard so much about you," he says slightly stiffly.

"All bad, I'm sure," Adam laughs in his 'charming' way and holds out his hand. "We brought lobster!"

"Oh yeah, wow," Ryan eyes the defrosted crustaceans slightly dubiously. "You shouldn't have, guys; really, most people just go for the Asda burgers."

Ryan relieves us of our lobsters, and we make our way down the hallway. There are two doors at the end, "One to each flat," Ryan explains, turning to Adam. "My university friends Jackson, his girlfriend Cecille and I bought this place about six years ago as a pet project and split it into two flats. They live in one, and I'm in the smaller one."

"Is it haunted?" asks Adam, whose interest in *Ghostbusters* long outlasted childhood.

"Er, not that I know of," laughs Ryan, Adam's charm seemingly melting Ryan's natural shyness. "But it was a complete disaster when we bought it. It had been disused since the 1980s. A fairly eccentric property developer used to own it. He bought it with the intention of renovating it and then selling it on, but he died before he could get started."

"And his spirit still roams the corridors today?" finishes Adam, sounding hopeful.

"Maybe. His daughter just never got around to doing anything with it. But she did want it to be something interesting like her dad had planned. It's just that architects are expensive, and she wasn't planning to stay in London. So she put it up for sale when she got some quotations about how much it would cost. It was on the market for quite some time before we bought it…an old chapel's not the easiest thing to shift. You get lots of people who are interested in having a nose around because of the novelty factor, but not many who want to do the work."

Adam looks as if he's about to drift off, but I am captivated. God, he's so handsome when he gets passionate about architecture stuff.

Awkwardly tucking one of the lobsters under his arm, he turns the key and leads us into his flat. It's stunningly beautiful, with little columns framing all the rooms and the light shining through the stained-glass window at the far end of the living room, casting everything in cobalt and red hues. He gives us the tour and starts gesturing to various architectural pieces left over from the building's original use before leaving us temporarily. At the same time, he goes to deposit our coats in his room and our marine life in the kitchen.

"Adam!" I hiss. "Stop looking like you're about to fall asleep."

"It's a bit bloody boring." He hisses back. "All this stained glass window, 1826, columns, shafts of light bollocks. It's a bit pretentious. He needs to throw a few more ghosts into his spiel."

"You're just jealous!" I mutter, turning my glare into an angelic smile as Ryan returns.

"Right! Let's go through to the courtyard and get started with the barbecue!"

"Would that be a traditional Tudor courtyard with hand-painted periwinkles?" Adam asks, with a slightly petulant glance in my direction. Sometimes, he really is a twelve-year-old. I elbow him in the ribs, and he dutifully falls into line and manages to muster some sincere-sounding admiring noises as we pass the old chapel font by the door to the garden.

The courtyard is sunny and warm after the cool of the chapel, and we are met by the sounds of frustrated swearing and four people gathered around a barbecue, seemingly struggling to get it started. Adam, in his manly element, leaps into action, barreling across to the stricken wannabe barbecuers and proclaiming something about briquettes and lighting fluid. I feel a small flush of pride at the brilliance of my contribution to the barbecue, i.e. Adam's pyromania, when it suddenly springs to life, and a regal-looking woman (wearing the most beautiful green summer dress) takes command of the tongs and throws on a round of sausages.

I can see Adam staring at her, and my stomach clenches. He absolutely cannot try and seduce Ryan's friends. Especially his coupled-up ones.

Ryan steers me over to the elegant barbecue queen and introduces me to her and the man standing next to her. "Anastasia, this is Cecille, and this is Jackson." He's like a whole new confident person around his friends, and I just stare at him for a bit until Adam rudely bounces over and waves a hand in front of my face.

Jackson is tall and quite well-built, with strawberry-blond hair and intense blue eyes. I offer my hand, but he pulls me into a friendly hug. "Anastasia! The Russian émigré! So pleased to finally meet you."

He has a warm, slow Canadian drawl. I remember Ryan telling me he moved from Vancouver ten years ago for university, fell for Cecille (and English architecture) and never left.

I offer my hand to Cecille, and she leans in to give me the most delicate of kisses on each cheek. "Lovely to meet you," she says in a beautiful French accent.

Ryan said she was Parisian, from one of those aristocratic French families who kept their heads and that she is a pretty big deal in conservation architecture. I feel immediately intimidated. No one would describe me as a big deal in anything, not even in the rarefied circles of reptile-keeping publications. I have a picture in my head that all Parisian women are stick thin, incredibly graceful, and sophisticated. That is pretty much the exact opposite of me. All of this is true of Cecille; she is breathtakingly beautiful. She has perfect olive skin and long dark hair that bounces perfectly off her shoulders in a way that I could never in a million years convince mine to behave. Her dark brown eyes are framed by the most Bambi-esque eyelashes imaginable, and I really, really want to hate her, except she seems so incredibly nice and self-assured that I can't. Damn her.

We talk for ages about London, the chapel, and Ryan. They are both genuinely lovely. As much as possible, I try to avoid the topics of Russian émigrés and my family. I glance nervously over to see how Adam is doing. He seems to be contentedly holding court with two women and working his way through the beers at quite a pace. Ryan ushers me in the direction of two other girls, who are standing at the food table, nibbling on Haribo and popcorn. These seem like more my kind of people. One has long brown hair and is wearing a slightly odd dress that looks like it's made of a grandmother's old curtains… all browns and yellows with a thick, somewhat woollen look, which she's paired with giant feathered earrings. The other one, with black hair, is dressed in slightly more standard barbecue attire – a short, flowery spaghetti strap dress and flip flops.

"Emma! You'll ruin your appetite," Ryan says chidingly to the non-curtain wearing one.

Did he say, Emma? Surely, she can't be Emma, as in his 'sister Emma'?

"Anastasia, this is my sister Emma, and this is her girlfriend, Mabel."

Oh my God. I am meeting his sister. He could have bloody well warned me.

"Emma! Hi! So lovely to meet you!" I say over-enthusiastically. "Mabel! Ryan's told me all about you both."

Mabel greets me warmly, but I can't help thinking Emma is a little more reserved. I was sure Ryan described her as bubbly and super friendly, but that could just be a slightly distorted sibling-esque view of the situation.

Ryan wanders off to oversee the barbecue, and I'm left making small talk with Emma and Mabel. "So, how did you guys meet?" I try.

There's a slight pause until it becomes clear to Mabel that she is pointlessly deferring to Emma and had better jump in. "Oh, we met at Emma's work, didn't we, Em?"

Emma nods, almost imperceptibly, so Mabel awkwardly continues, "I'm doing a postgrad in fashion, and Em runs menswear at Selfridges. I had to do some research for a paper I was writing on suits, power and the differences in men's fashion from baby boomers to millennial men. And Emma was just so helpful. I emailed her, telling her I got a First for my paper and offering to buy her a celebratory drink. The rest is history!"

Mabel is beaming, and I smile back at the cute story. Emma is still looking oddly poker-faced, and although the paranoid part of me wonders if it's me, my rational self tells me that maybe she's just in a bad mood, or she's less enthusiastic about Mabel than Mabel is about her or something. Just then, Adam bounds over, another almost empty bottle of Cobra in one hand and a sausage in a bun in the other.

"Ladies! A pleasure to meet you! I'm Adam. I used to live with this one. She's my cousin." He gestures, slightly tipsily, towards me, and I smile indulgently. Mabel and Emma both turn a million-watt smile in his direction, and my Emma-related paranoia comes clawing back.

"Very glad you could come. Thanks for the lobsters. This'll be the poshest barbecue I've been to," Emma says charmingly, and paranoia crawls up my spine. My lobsters, too. The absolute cheek.

"Hell, yeah. You can't have a barbecue without lobster." Adam replies casually. This from the man whose knowledge of seafood dining has never previously extended beyond Captain Birdseye's frozen fish fingers.

"So, are you also a Russian descendant, Adam?" Emma asks, the beginning of a less-than-friendly smile curling.

For once, thank God, Adam thinks quickly and comes up with the right response, "Oh God no, that's her dad's side. Anastasia's mum and my mum are sisters."

"Adam's a personal trainer – sometimes to the stars!" I say quickly, attempting to divert the conversation from Russia and to throw him a flattery bone by way of thanks.

Emma looks satisfied and suddenly more animated than she's been the whole time. She starts talking about healthy eating and peppering Adam with questions about personal training. Suddenly, they're off, all back-and-forth banter and tinkling laughs and cheering.

"I'm going to get another drink. Anyone want anything?" I ask, desperate to edge into the conversation.

"I'm good, thanks," Emma says shortly.

"No thanks! I'm still working on this Pimms!" Mabel adds.

"Another Cobra would be great!" chimes in Adam.

"Are you sure you shouldn't slow down a bit? You're on like your fifth beer already!" I say, half-jokingly.

"Alex, Alex, Alex… you're so judgy!" Adam slurs.

Emma looks at him strangely, and it takes me a moment to realise what he's said.

"Ha! He calls me Alex when he's drunk; Anastasia is a bit of a mouthful for him at the best of times!"

Emma is still looking at me with deep suspicion, and it doesn't help when Adam throws his arms around me and hiccoughs, "Yep! My lovely little flatmate Anasta-hic-lex. The flat's not the same without her. It's soooo much tidier." He cackles, and Mabel sportingly joins in.

I glare, disentangle myself and take my leave, deliberately not bringing Adam another beer.

Ryan spots me and puts his arm around me. I enjoy the heat from his sun-warmed skin over my shoulders as he pulls me closer.

"So, you're enjoying yourself?" he murmurs.

"Even more so now," I answer honestly.

"Did you get the chance to speak to my sister?"

"Oh yes, she seems lovely!" I say, a bit too perkily.

Ryan smiles. "Liar. It's OK. She's protective of all of the family, but especially me. I'm a bit accident-prone when it comes to relationships. Don't worry, it's nothing personal. To be honest, I wasn't expecting her here, but I think she wanted to do a bit of a recce on you."

"Oh, great. Well, I hope I'm making a good

impression." I try to sound nonchalant, but inwardly, I am cursing Adam's Alex slip-up. Of course, it would be in front of the protective sister during a reconnaissance mission.

"Don't worry about that. You've already made a pretty decent impression on me," he whispers into my ear. Despite the afternoon warmth, I get the nicest goosebumps as I lean closer to his chest.

I'm enjoying the moment when Adam launches over to melodramatically whisper: "HAVE YOU REALISED WE ARE WALKING ON DEAD PEOPLE?! WE ARE LITERALLY BARBECUEING BANGERS OVER A LOAD OF DEAD PEOPLE?!"

I groan. "Excuse me. I need to check on the toddler." Ryan laughs and releases me. I park a tipsy Adam on a perch by the wall.

"Do you think we should start to go a bit easier on the beers?" I ask in my sweetest, most indulgent babysitter voice.

Adam squints and studies me closely. "I reckon you're probably borderline now, so probs best to…"

"NOT me," I say slightly less sweetly through gritted teeth.

"Anyway, enough of your drinking habits. This place is seriously creepy. I've just realised. If that's a church, this must be a freaking graveyard. Dead people! All around!" he adds, still in a pitch several octaves higher than usual.

Jackson comes to the rescue. "Did I hear talk of graveyards?"

"Oh, nothing to worry about," I say dismissively, wishing, not for the first time, that I had normal friends to take to social functions. "Adam's got the idea in his head that because this is a chapel, he's partying in a cemetery. It doesn't bother me!" I add quickly, in case he thinks I am also liable to start shrieking uncontrollably.

Worried that's not quite enough of an explanation for my six-foot-one scaredy cat, I continue, "Adam had a… traumatic experience… in a church in Paris when he was five. He went on a tour of some catacombs and got lost for forty minutes. He's been terrified of that kind of thing ever since."

I pat Adam's arm reassuringly.

"I've never been to Paris," Adam hiccoughs unhelpfully.

"He's blocked it out," I explain, slightly digging my nails into his upper arm.

"Ah," Jackson smiles uncertainly. "Oh well, Adam – if it helps. This is a chapel, not a church. The land's not consecrated."

"Not consecrated! Unblessed graves?!" chirps Adam in alarm.

"Not blessed. No graves. No bodies," Jackson smiles and wanders off in search of burgers and, presumably, grown-up company.

I glare at Adam. "So much for good impressions," I whisper angrily.

"What! It was a legitimate concern. And, anyway, don't worry, I sorted out the whole Anastasia/Alex thing with Emma."

My heart shifts gears again. "I'd already sorted it… What did you say?"

"Well. She asked again."

"And…"

"And I said I call you Alex after Alex Ferguson. 'Cos you're so fricking bossy," Adam beams at his own cleverness. "It's all sorted."

Across the not-a-graveyard, Emma is studying me closely, and I know it's definitely not.

TWENTY-ONE

I must genuinely have aristocracy somewhere in my ancestry because I have adapted shamefully quickly to having a housekeeper around, keeping the kitchen stocked and the place clean and tidy. Not only does she do my laundry and change my sheets, but she also irons. Irons! She even irons things I've traditionally scoffed at my mother for, like socks. Somehow, when Mrs Jenkins does it, it's masterful. I now know I could never revert to Adam's Clapham lair, where you're more likely to find a stray three-year-old moth-eaten sock covered in cobwebs and dust balls and lodged under a sofa cushion than a sleekly ironed pristine one.

Perhaps the best benefit of Mrs Jenkins, though, is the massive fry-up she prepares for Sir John every Saturday, which she graciously now extends to me. It's become a particularly delicious routine to make my way to the kitchen at 10:30am to be greeted by the sizzling of bacon and the rich aroma of the coffee roast of the month. The weekly fry has the added benefit of putting Sir John in his mellowest (or least glowering) mood.

However, this Saturday, as I make my way to the kitchen, it's unusually silent, and rather than the delicious frying smells that coalesce with the coffee scent and summon me from my bedroom, there's just the bitter scent of burning. I open the door hesitantly, genuinely concerned that I'll find an unconscious Mrs Jenkins lying on the kitchen tiles, so I'm both relieved and concerned when I open the door, and she's not there at all. Instead, I'm greeted by the sight of Sir John, impeccably dressed and sitting in front of a stack of blackened toast.

I open my mouth to speak, but he intercepts.

"Mrs Jenkins has a cold," he says forlornly, picking up a piece of cremated bread and courageously trying to scrape off the blackened bit before realising it's actually more charcoal than bread and mournfully putting it back down. On the stove, there's a pot of congealed baked beans (How do you get baked beans wrong? How?! From a can! Even Adam can do that). I give thanks that he hasn't attempted any bacon or sausages. Yet.

I hear his stomach give a hungry whine of despair. Mine whinnies back. I interrupt their animated conversation to offer to try again with the toaster (a machine I suspect Sir John has never interacted with before).

"I've already used all the bread to make this." Sir John gestures sadly to the plate in front of him, which resembles a Borrower's funeral pyre more than an acceptable start to a Saturday.

"Coco Pops?" I venture.

"Gone! Gone yesterday," Sir John answers in grief. Both stomachs restart their chorus of anguish. I have no desire to start cooking for Sir John, who takes a delightfully critical approach to any fare presented to him.

I think of the great new love of my father's life. "Why don't we go out for brunch?" I suggest.

"Brunch?" Sir John doesn't have the energy to inject this with his usual level of incredulity and horror.

"You know. It's not quite breakfast…"

"I know what brunch is. I don't live in an attic," he snaps. "It's what lazy-do nothings who can't be bothered getting up at a decent time of day and have too much money to fritter away eat."

I somehow refrain from pointing out that turning up at 10:30am for your housekeeper to serve you breakfast is hardly going down the pit at dawn with nothing but water and a few soft pebbles to chew on.

"Well, it is a bit indulgent, but it's OK every once in a while. It'd give us the energy to crack on with a fair bit of writing today. In a way, the… er, 'toast' might not."

Sir John harrumphs, but in a way that suggests he is very open to persuading but needs to work through the charade of reluctance first.

With no food or coffee, I'm not prepared to indulge. "Well, if you don't want to, I might just pop out by myself and leave you to your toast."

"No, no," he responds quickly. "I suppose I'll try this brunch idea and see what the fuss is about." He sighs with the burden of the huge imposition I'm placing on him.

"Well, do you know any places around here?" I ask.

"There's a café on Harris Street I've been to before. I'm sure we can prevail upon them to come up with some sort of *brunch*." His weak, starved attempts to muster contempt are somewhat endearing. I admire his commitment.

"Right," I take charge. "Harris Street it is." It's not the most glowing endorsement, but it's definitely a step in the direction my stomach needs us to go. There's an agonising fifteen minutes as Sir John looks for his coat and makes us go room to room to check all the windows are closed, but finally, we're out and walking.

Sir John is a mercifully brisk walker – to the point I'm even struggling to catch up. Ten minutes later, and as I struggle for breath, we arrive at the café. It's not quite the rustic, shabby chic I have come to expect in my brunching spots. The front has a sign made of driftwood with "Christoff's" spray painted on in blue, and we're shown to our table by a woman with a ginormous nose ring and what looks like a series of genitalia designs in a tattoo sleeve down her left arm. The scent drifting from the next table suggests the young couple on it haven't been strangers to marijuana already this morning.

Over the gentle didgeridoo soundtrack playing as background music, I gently enquire, "Sir John, when exactly was the last time you came here?"

Sir John is studiously reading the menu. "I think it was 2009. 2008 perhaps."

"Hmmm. Is it possible it's changed hands since then?" I ask, absentmindedly playing with the ketchup dispenser – a plastic figurine of Queen Camilla dressed only in lingerie.

Sir John lowers his menu. "Possibly," he concedes, without even a hint of acknowledgement that he has suggested this place.

The menu itself offers quinoa waffles, kimchi-infused rice porridge and zucchini crepes. The next few minutes are absolute agony as Sir John demands information on each dish from me, as resident brunch expert, before snorting in exasperation as I give my best guess. I have now explained approximately twelve times that this isn't the typical kind of brunch I have. Still, I'm under no illusions that I am being held responsible for every element of this morning's adventure.

"Holy halloumi fritters," Sir John reads with distaste before giving me a meaningful glance. "I think I've underestimated just how much 'brunch' is a symptom of everything wrong with modern Britain."

"What about the veggie full English?" I ask as I fight to keep my hanger at bay. Sir John acknowledges that it is the closest thing to his breakfast expectations and "will have to do."

I call the waitress and give her my order. It takes Sir John a moment to stop reading the Latin motto encircling a flaming skull tattoo on her shoulder to give his. I shoot him a small warning glance in case he has any aspirations of voicing any tattoo-related opinions. Mercifully and uncharacteristically, he doesn't interrogate her. Probably the hunger.

"And what would you guys like to drink?" our waitress continues, oblivious to her near miss at having to justify her tastes in body art. "We're currently doing a two-for-one on Mesopotamian Mango Dawn juice. They have mango juice…"

"Two of those would be great," I interrupt as another pang reminds me of how ravenous I am. I never pass up a two-for-one on anything. I am truly my father's daughter.

The drinks arrive, complete with bamboo eco straws, and Sir John approaches his like nitroglycerin, giving it a cautious sniff, lifting out the straw and peering suspiciously at the floating fruit inside, stirring it and sniffing it again, before very tentatively taking a sip. I've already taken several huge gulps of mine. Whatever it is, it's delicious. Two sips in, and I already feel a million times better.

Sir John, for once, doesn't utter a word of complaint other than to mutter, "Probably full of sugar."

Such is the deliciousness of the drink that we've both finished by the time our veggie breakfasts appear. I'm left with the feeling of blissful contentment that I presume comes from finding a tasty way to imbibe so many vitamins in one go.

Even the waitress seems surprised at how well they have gone down, as we order two more.

Sir John is making short work of the halloumi on his plate. He takes another gulp of the juice, "I suppose I can see some of the rationale for why brunch has become so multvi… Uni… Multiversal."

As my stomach fills, I reach an almost Nivana-like place of contentment. "Multiversal isn't a word," I say, tackling the chilli mushrooms left on my plate.

Sir John harrumphs but otherwise doesn't react to my cheek, instead busily concentrating on chasing the last bit of tomato around his plate, his usual impeccable table manners slightly forgotten. "Well. I suppose you're the wordsmith," he says and then chuckles as though he's said something very witty.

The influx of food and healthy juice makes me feel almost dizzy. I take another large sip to steady myself.

Emboldened, I ask, "So, how are you enjoying the writing process, old bean?"

(Where the hell did 'old bean' come from – could the marijuana scent from the couple next to us be affecting us? Oh God, are we getting high on second-hand weed?)

My suspicions grow as Sir John chuckles in response. Dishing out the highest praise he can muster, he tells me, "You are far more tolerable than some of the wordy bores they first tried to foist on me." He takes a generous sip, "I suppose." He chuckles again.

By now, we've polished off both the breakfasts and our second round of juice.

"Waitress!" Sir John bellows. She drifts over and gives us a curious look.

I take over. "Can we order two more of the metropolitan…"

"Mesopotamian," Sir John corrects, stifling a tiny burp.

"Of the Mesopotamian magic mango drinks," I conclude.

The waitress raises an eyebrow. "The Mesopotamian Mango Dawns?" she asks drily.

"Yes," we both say simultaneously before giggling.

Who would have thought that brunch would bring us together so well?

"I admit," Sir John says, as our third round of mango magic arrives, "I'm almost glad Mrs Jennings has a cold."

"Jenkins."

"That's what I said. What about you? Are you enjoying the project? It's boring, isn't it?"

He holds up a hand before I answer, "It's alright. I know it is. No one wants to read about some old fart's time in government forty-odd years ago."

"They do! They do!" I say, banging on the table for emphasis. "But we have to have more personality. We have to get more of the personal sparkle in. I know you hate it."

"I do hate it," Sir John admits, but quietly, not with his usual bombast. "Does it really have to have all of that guff?"

"If you want it to sell…" I reply.

"Well, my accountants want it to sell," Sir John replies, almost sadly. "Ordinarily, I couldn't care less."

"Oh?" I hiccough.

He beckons me closer before continuing in a stage whisper as loud as his normal voice, "The coffers are depleted, old girl. I have a ministerial pension. And what's left of my parents' legacy. But it's all dwindling away."

"Oh dear."

"Dwindling, dwindling away," he sings, slightly unexpectedly. "Nothing to leave my daughter Ophelia."

"Well then," I say, banging the table again (it's now my favourite thing to do). "We're just going to have to make it a bestseller." I hiccough triumphantly.

"Hmmm. No family stuff."

"Surely your daughter won't mind," I reason, "If it's for the coffins?"

"She will." This time, he whispers for real. "We don't speak. Haven't for years. A card here. A phone call there. Nothing else."

"But you're lovely," I say, warmed by our brunch bonding. "You're a lovely old bean."

He waves the compliment away, knocking over the cheeky Queen dispenser. "It's very complicated." He has a slight slur to his voice this morning I notice; I begin to worry that the shock of Christoff's and Her Majesty's lingerie has given him a mild stroke.

"You have to tell me these things," I say in my most serious tone, becoming aware that I also have a slight slur. "As your ghostwriter, I'm like your lawyer or priest."

He nods seriously. "Very well. The truth is we were separated, Laura and I. It was a very… complicated time. Very stressful. For all of us. During that time, she had moved out. She was driving back to her new place after visiting our daughter, and… there was a car crash."

To my alarm, Sir John's eyes water.

"But Ophelia can't blame you for that!" I debate slapping the table once again but hold off.

"She thinks…" Sir John breaks off suddenly. "Oh, it was all a long time ago. That's quite enough for now. Even for my confessor," he says more decisively, draining the last of his juice.

I feel a warm wave of gratitude that he has confided so much. "Look. That's OK. We'll make it work. Just trust me." I reach across and pat his hand.

He hiccoughs in response and looks down with horror. I realise it's not his hand I'm patting but the busty brassiere of the plastic Camilla lying prone on the table.

I quickly pick up my empty glass. "Another?" I ask.

He nods and calls the waitress over.

"Can we have two final glasses?" I ask cheerily.

Her curious look has turned to one of mild alarm.

"OK, but you know these have quite a high percentage in them…"

"Percentage of mango?" I ask, confused.

"Percentage of vodka," says the waitress firmly.

"There's no vodka in these!" hiccoughs Sir John in horror.

"There are two shots of vodka in each drink," says the waitress, pointing to the menu. "I thought you knew that!"

"We didn't know that," I protest.

"Who serves vodka with breakfast?" asks Sir John indignantly. "What is this place? This is like Sodom and Canberra."

Suddenly, his bellow turns into a wheeze and then into a giggle.

"Drunk! Drunk, and the sun's not yet over the yardarm. This hasn't happened since my navy days."

I laugh, too, as the waitress shifts from foot to foot and mutters.

"Sir John, one more for the road?"

"One more for the road. Old bean," he agrees.

TWENTY-TWO

When we get in, all writing plans are set aside because Sir John decrees that he needs a nap and sways up the stairs, singing what sounds suspiciously like an ABBA medley.

I sigh and go and sit in the library anyway, in case alcohol-induced inspiration strikes. I stare at the piles of yellowing documents and wait, assuming it will strike dramatically. Nothing. It's all just minutes and letters from one CBE to another.

However, another positive to come from our wobble home is Sir John's slightly confused consent to reimburse me for any internet research I do for the book, so I happily connect the laptop to my phone's data. I'm a professional and savvy operator, so my first stop is Wikipedia. I recall from my hasty scans before the interview that it's a dry read. Name checks of a posh public school, Law at Oxford, some time as a barrister before becoming an MP in the late sixties. A succession of ministerial posts up to his retirement as Home Secretary in 1978. His personal life is similarly dry. Married an Honourable. One daughter. Loses wife in 1978. That's notable. He left politics the same year that he lost his wife.

I think about how he spoke about her to me. His eyes, his sad smile. A whole world gone. A few hasty sentences tapped out by some politics geek on Wikipedia fall so short of all of that happiness and grief. There's no way he is going to go anywhere near this with me yet, but it feels like an unavoidable watermark in any autobiography. I need to know more and so, the vodka giving me courage, I start a deeper trawl, plugging in Lady Fenton's name. I find several obituaries, and a beautiful black and white Press Association photo of her as a bride. She has fiercely intelligent eyes and the sort of poise that makes me straighten my back as I slump at the desk. There are some news stories too about Sir John's career, mentioning his wife, and one of those cringe interviews done at home with the family. I click through some pictures, and it's clear how amazing this house must have been in its heyday. Where now it's faded glamour, in these photos, it was just glamour.

I'm about to shut down the laptop and follow in Sir John's footsteps by going for my own nap, but then one final story catches my eye. It's a tabloid tale under the headline, "Is 'Family First' Home Secretary's Marriage Floundering?" It goes on to report a rumour that Sir John and Lady Fenton have separated, with a picture of Lady Fenton being comforted by her parents, Major General and Mrs Marchent.

"Neither the Conservative Party nor the Home Office has offered any comment. However, a reliable source in Westminster reports that the Fentons' thirty-four-year-old nanny, Jenny Hartley, has also recently left the family's employ."

I think about my unloved little nanny flat and Sir John's refusal to discuss his family life. So much for him opening up this morning with the euphemistic talk about separation. In the end, it's the oldest, most common explanation: the husband leaves his wife for a younger woman.

"Not your business, Alex," I chide myself. I'm an impartial, invisible ghostwriter. But I'm still surprised – there was something so pained and open about him whenever he spoke about his wife. It just doesn't make any sense. Maybe it's guilt? It would certainly explain why the daughter is estranged from him. It would be hard to deal with your father running off with your nanny and then your mother dying in the same year. I sigh. I feel like it's not my place to feel disappointed in Sir John – after all, I'm hardly a beacon of honesty and integrity myself at the moment – but I do feel a little disappointed that he could do this to Laura despite loving her so much. I wonder if he'll ever confide in me or if I'll ever find out what happened to the nanny. Probably not. Sometimes, it seems like it's one step forward, two steps back with us.

I'm pulled out of my pondering by a text from Adam inviting me to come round and meet his new flatmate, Javier. Great, I think, as if I'm not feeling sad enough, I need to meet Alex version 2.0 this evening. I consider writing a non-committal response but then catch myself. I quickly text back that I'll be over in the evening after an afternoon nap. The vodka is definitely taking its toll. Leaning occasionally on the wall for moral support, I make my way to my room, not even reacting to Adam's snarky text: "A nap at 1pm? You've been living with Sir John too long."

TWENTY-THREE

"Ah, memory lane," I smile wistfully as Adam welcomes me in.

"It's been two weeks, Alex." He rolls his eyes, leading me down the hall into the kitchen.

"And I reckon you've landed on your feet with that place."

"Maybe," I muse, still shocked by my post-drinking discovery.

"I see Sir John hasn't stymied your tendency to be tipsy by 2pm on a Saturday."

I straighten up and reply with dignity, "I may have had a fruit juice or two with some alcohol at brunch. With Sir John, I might add. Anyway, how did you know?"

"Hunch. And your jumper's on inside out."

"Oh." I start to mount a defence but freeze in my tracks as I see the most attractive man in the history of Clapham South and possibly the world.

Beautiful olive skin, thick curly black hair, muscles straining under his gloriously tight green t-shirt. I can hardly look away.

"Alex, meet your replacement, Javier! But with upgraded cooking skills! Javier, this is my cousin Alex."

"I... I'm Adam's cousin, Alex," I say unnecessarily.

"I just said that, Alex," Adam chips in helpfully.

Javier breaks into a gorgeous smile before giving me a huge hug. "Alex. The ALEX. I've heard so much about you. I love the room; thank goodness you left it to me! Coffee? You look in need of a good brew."

He heads over to a space-age-looking espresso machine as I commit the feel of his arms around me to memory.

Adam rudely brandishes a hand in front of my eyes. Pretending to look nonchalant and not at all in lust, I glance around the familiar yet suddenly unfamiliar kitchen. There are a number of shiny high-tech kitchen gadgets perched on the ageing 1970's Formica. It's as if the Starship Enterprise has suddenly docked at Milton Keynes motorway services. I'm pondering how the Milton Keyners would react to this, but Javier's muscles have a disconcerting habit of rippling as he moves around the kitchen to grab mugs and pour the coffee, and I decide to focus on them instead. To think all I had to do to get such a hunk in my bed was pull out of my lease.

The coffee is delicious, and I am almost revived. Just as I'm mumbling thanks, Javier takes me by the hands and solemnly kisses me on both cheeks. They burn as he solemnly wishes me goodbye before heading out. "Sorry to run so soon," he shouts from the hall. "Drinks with the boys."

Adam shouts his goodbyes, and I practically scream, "See you soon!" with the urgency of a besotted teenager at a Harry Styles concert.

Adam smiles smugly, "So... how's Ryan?"

My cheeks feel like they've gone several degrees hotter. "He's very well, thank you. He's out of the country."

"Figures... while the cat's away and all that."

"I don't know what you mean. I was just a bit startled. Javier wasn't what I was expecting. You've always hated the idea of sharing a house with competition."

"Come see your old room," I follow him to the back of the flat. I expect a pang of sadness when I see my scruffy little den, but it is totally unrecognisable. Every surface, every inch, is transformed. Thick purple velvet curtains have replaced my tired old blinds. An impeccably made bed lies somewhere under about twenty scatter cushions. Meanwhile, the bits of flaked plaster on the walls have been artfully concealed by pictures and posters, including a huge black and white print of a shirtless James Dean.

"Oh... that's interesting," I say hesitantly.

"Javier is great. He's a huge gym bunny – that's where we got talking. Amazing cook. Plus, he knows all of these gorgeous girls – they're always coming around."

"Humph. He sounds like the perfect flatmate," I say petulantly.

"And every other weekend, he visits his boyfriend in Manchester."

"Ah."

"That's right. Like you said, I didn't want any competition."

"Well, you've certainly found the perfect housemate," I mutter.

"Aww. You know you're irreplaceable. No one makes an omelette like you do."

I smile.

"No one would ever want to," he adds.

My smile fades, and I settle for a playful arm punch.

TWENTY-FOUR

Despite my short-lived daydream of having a passionate affair with Javier, I'm a little concerned about just how much I'm missing Ryan. I have it pretty badly. He's been in Copenhagen at some conservation architecture conference for what feels like several months (actually just several days), and there's a few more days to go until I get to jump him at Heathrow the way Martine McCutcheon's character in *Love Actually* did to Hugh Grant. I've had a fantasy of doing that since I first saw the movie when I was twelve, pretending to my friends that I was only appreciating it ironically. In my head, it will work out the same way, except possibly with fewer cameras. I'm also not sure whether you would actually be allowed to run towards the secure area that excitedly anymore or whether there's a high risk of being rugby-tackled by an overly enthusiastic (and armed) policeman. Maybe I'll just wait sedately until he makes it to my side of the barriers.

Just as I'm replaying my little airport reunion in my head, Sir John comes in, interrupting my reverie, with Mrs Jenkins pottering in behind, bearing our usual breakfast, plus some freshly baked croissants, orange juice, and a cafetière full of coffee on a heaving tray. She puts it down gently on the table, sets out the plates, unfolds Sir John's favoured paper, *The Times*, and pours us both a cup of coffee, stirring Sir John's milk in before quietly heading back into the kitchen. I watch her go, suddenly filled with societal guilt. When did this become the norm for me? I'm a member of the bloody Labour Party. I've always known I'm easily corruptible, but this is ridiculous. Still, I take a sip of coffee, and I feel the delicious aroma wafting into my nostrils and waking up my sleepy brain cells.

"Sir John…" I say tentatively.

"Harumph," he answers, not looking up from his article about The Duchess of Gloucester opening a bagel factory in Kidderminster.

Undeterred, I persevere anyway, summoning up the spirit of Che Guevara: "Maybe one day it would be nice if Mrs Jenkins had breakfast with us?"

That catches his attention briefly. "Mrs Jenkins is my help. She doesn't want to breakfast with us."

"You might be surprised!" I say brightly.

He glares at me. "Are you a Marxist?"

"Erm, no," I say hesitantly. I've never been 100% sure what being a Marxist actually entails, but I'm pretty sure the footwear is appalling, and Moscow's far too cold even for a spiritual home. "I just think it'd be nice to have everyone, erm, treated the same…"

His glare intensifies, and the spirit of Che Guevara wilts and flees. I decide to fight this battle another time, and Sir John moves on to reading some in-depth feature on town planning and the impact of zebra crossings on traffic flow. Resolved to push for equality, liberty and fraternity when Sir John's in a better mood (perhaps drunk on more mango punch), I let my mind drift lazily back to various romantic "return of Ryan" scenes. As if I've willed it, my phone pings just then with a message from him.

"Missing you so much! You'd love Copenhagen. Little Mermaid statue disappointingly small though xxx."

I start drafting one back, "Missing you too! Maybe next time I can be your conference plus one…" I blink at it a couple of times before changing it to "Missing you too! Yes, I've always wanted to visit. Can't wait to see you soon! Xxx."

Suggesting being his conference plus one might be a little much at this stage of our relationship.

"Maybe next time you could be my conference plus one… giant hotel room here, kind of lonely…" he texts back as if reading my mind.

I blush and am surprised Sir John can't feel the heat radiating from my face, but he seems oblivious, lost in what now looks like an article on Waitrose's restructuring problems. He's harrumphing testily and occasionally muttering "modernisation" and "nonsense!" under his breath.

I'm not sure how to reply to this one. It's not that I don't want to sleep with Ryan. I 100% do. Even the thought of it and I'm biting my lower lip involuntarily. The issue is, of course, that he doesn't know my name. Everything is based on my stupid lies. He wants to have sex with a Russian émigré's descendant called Anastasia. He does not want to have sex (or at least doesn't know he wants to) with a duplicitous woman named Alex, who lures innocent men into correspondence by posing as an Agony Uncle for a dodgy magazine and who is in no way related to the Romanovs. I'm going to have to tell him. It's gone too far. I can't sleep with someone on this basis. It's seedy and not in an acceptably sexy way.

I quickly text Adam, "Ryan sent a very suggestive text… what do I do?!"

"Fuck him. Obviously," comes the rapid response.

"He doesn't know my name!!!" I text back, scandalised.

"Meh. Hardly the first time it's been done."

Gah. He. Is. Infuriating.

I finish up the last of my bacon and go back to my room with the dregs of my coffee, pull out my laptop, and start crafting an explanatory email to Ryan. Surely, this is where a decade of wordsmithing will come in handy.

Half an hour later, I haven't got beyond the second sentence.

Dear Ryan,

There's something I need to tell you. My name is actually Alex, and I am actually the Agony Uncle at Ladditude.

No. Needs more build-up.

Dear Ryan,

One little thing that I hope you'll find funny. In the longer term…

Dream on, Alex.

Ryan,

I need you to know that I definitely have a lot of feelings for you before you read what I have to say. I've been caught up in a lie, and it's going to hurt you, but I never meant to. I need you to know I never meant to.

No, no, no. Some Agony Uncle I am. It's just… how did this even happen to me? How do I even start explaining this situation? Maybe the written word is too cowardly. Perhaps it's more of an in-person conversation anyway. Or a call?

I pick up my phone and consider exactly how that kind of call will go when it rings.

Adam.

"I'm not going to sleep with him when he doesn't know my name," I answer, saving time by foregoing pleasantries. I've learned that from Sir John.

"What? Oh right. Whatever. Like I said, I've slept with plenty of women without knowing their names. Anyway, not why I called."

"What's up then?" I say, irritated on behalf of all the nameless women with whom Adam has messed around.

"So, guess who just rocked up on a surprise visit?! Your parents!"

"Oh God! What seriously?! Why the hell are they there?"

"Your mum said something about a conference at some royal veterinary thing."

"They don't know I don't live there anymore! It'll totally freak them out. I am screwed. Screwed."

"It's OK. I told them Javier is your boyfriend, and you're at the shops."

"Oh God."

"It's fine! Javier is playing the role with aplomb. He said he's a thespian. Something about playing a robot in *Terminator the Musical*. He's been waiting in the wings for a moment like this since then."

"Strangely, that's not providing much comfort. Have they seen 'my' bedroom yet?"

"No, but it was a very near miss. Aunty Claire wanted to go there immediately, under the guise of 'putting her handbag out of the way', but clearly actually going to do a bit of reconnaissance on how much stuff Javier's moved in and whether he's sleeping over."

I groan.

"It's OK. I checkmated her and insisted on taking it in myself."

"Oh God. Hang on, she's calling."

I put him on hold. "Oh, hello, daughter-of-mine. Where are you? Guess what?! Dad and I are at your flat with Adam! We've met (sly pause) Javier… your… boyfriend. How did you get to the stage of your relationship where you go out and leave him here without mentioning him? When will you be back? Are you surprised? Are you free for dinner tonight? Dad and I thought we'd treat you to your favourite Italian place."

She takes a breath in the midst of her barrage of questions, and I jump in, "I'm shopping on Oxford Street." I lie too smoothly. "I'll be back in an hour," I add, quickly calculating that I can make myself presentable and get to Clapham at that time.

I'm currently still pyjama-clad. Sir John and I have developed a comfortable rapport where he "takes breakfast" in his suit and tie, and I eat breakfast in my sheep-patterned pyjamas. Neither of us has commented on the other's outfit, with the exception of Sir John raising a solitary eyebrow when first presented with the sheep.

"What are you doing on Oxford Street? You don't have any money."

"Buying new underwear," I say, hoping to embarrass her into silence.

No such luck, "Oooh! Not too racy, I hope. I hope you're not at that Ann Summers shop, Alexandra. If you need to do that to keep a man, then he's not worth it."

A text from Adam flashes up. "Take me off hold! Urgent!"

"Mum, I have a call waiting. Can I call you back?"

"Alex. I'm your mother... what could be more important?"

"It's *The Guardian*, Mum."

"Oh Alex, you must answer it. Remember to sound awake, dear."

She rings off before I can pull at that particular little thread, and I answer Adam, "What, what?"

His tone is hushed and weirdly echoing, and I'm struggling to make him out. "Where are you?"

"In your old wardrobe. I went in to remove any incriminating things from Javier's room while he was distracting your parents, but I heard them coming down the hallway and didn't think, so now I'm in the closet. I can hear Aunty Claire on the phone to you outside the door. What should I do?!"

"Stay quiet and put the phone on speaker so I can hear what they say," I instruct.

"OK," he whispers, and I hear a bit of shuffling and then the sound of the phone being placed on the bottom of the wardrobe before the bedroom door opens.

"Oh Javier... you're so funny!" my mother's tinkling laugh reaches me, and I can tell she's on full charm offensive. "Oh..." I hear her pause, which is unusual. "Alex has certainly changed things around here... I never knew she liked James Dean so much..."

Javier, the ham actor that he apparently is, jumps in, "Oh yes. She simply lusts after him. Well, he was such a handsome man."

I can picture Mum's confused expression, and I can hear my poor dad clearing his throat uncomfortably.

"Nice... cushions. They're new!" my mother says brightly, hoping to change direction. "And... so many of them."

"Oh, they're mine. I like to be propped up when I... sleep. They're lavender-scented!"

I cannot cope with this. My parents now think I'm a sex-crazed James Dean obsessive with very open-minded taste in men.

"So, Javier," I can hear my dad saying, "how did you and Alex meet? So odd that she's never mentioned you!" He sounds friendly, but I can sense a protective edge here.

Javier clearly has no such sense, "Oh, we met at a nightclub. She was totally ... what would you say? 'Sloshed'? Didn't remember my name the next morning."

What. The. Hell. I'm not sure what role Javier thinks he's playing, but it's definitely more Gaston than Prince Charming.

"Oh, err. I see." My poor dad. No father should have

to hear this about his daughter, especially if it could not be less true.

"So!" Mum jumps in cheerfully, "What do you do, Javier? For work and fun?"

Please not something sexual, I silently plead.

"I'm a trampolinist," he answers proudly.

"A… a trampolinist? Is that a… how do you, er…!" my mother says, trailing off in bafflement.

"Lots of ups and downs, I imagine," my father chips in with an attempt at humour.

"Well, it gives me the opportunity to meet lots of people." Javier continues, "For fun, I like to write haikus… and you know, the usual manly stuff, cage wrestling, falconry… the list is endless."

"Haikus?" my father asks. "What about?"

"Oh, the usual, man stuff. About my love of women. Of Alex, I mean. Only Alex, of course!"

"Oh… lovely," my mother says. "Can we hear it?"

"Of course," I hear Javier say, in a slightly higher register, "Right now? Er. Yes. It would be my pleasure."

There is a pause that stretches for an era before this little ode makes its way down the phone line:

Her breasts, my penis.
Hillocks of joy, passionate
Fumble. A quick end.

There's silence and then a large thump. My mother shrieks. "Adam! What were you doing in the closet?!"

There's a moment of muffled chaos down the phone, and then I hear a sheepish Adam, "I, err… Alex asked me to check that she hadn't left anything private lying around before you came back here."

"What do you mean private? I'm her mother, for goodness sake."

"You know, Aunty Claire, 'private'."

I silently curse him, but he continues, oblivious to my unspoken hex.

"Lucky I did. I had to remove a half-eaten pair of edible undies from the floor!" Adam adds, warming to his theme.

"They were delicious," Javier adds, completely unnecessarily.

I will kill them. Kill them both dead. I'm loathe to disconnect the call, but the longer I leave it to get there, the more damage can be done.

I decide to take an Uber so I can stay listening through my earphones.

"I think that's best left unsaid," I hear my dad interjecting.

There's silence from my mother, which is unusual and, in this situation, deeply worrying.

Oh. My. God. I will the car to drive faster, but the traffic lights all seem to have taken against me. Along with the entire universe, it would seem.

Adam is chiming in again. "Well, I think everything's been hidden away now, so I'll just…"

"Yes, thank you, Adam," my mother injects quickly. "Javier, lovely to finally meet you. Mr Taylor and I are just going to sit in the lounge until Alex arrives. Alone."

This is really bad. My poor parents. First, they're going to have to deal with what they've just heard, and then they'll have to deal with the fact that the rest of their lives will be spent visiting their only daughter through the Perspex window of a prison visitors' room after I've murdered Adam and Javier.

After what seems an eternity, the Uber pulls up outside the house, and I find myself wishing it wasn't quite there yet. I've spent so much time wanting to get there and put a stop to this charade that I haven't spared a thought for what to do when I actually arrive. It's not lost on me that I was in the middle of trying to fix the lie with Ryan when I was suddenly pulled into fixing the Sir John lie with my parents. I'm tired of deception being such a major feature of my life. Sure, I am a daydreamer and have a big imagination, but if I am really trying to point to Chris and launch my writing career as a source for my fragile relationship with the truth, then why am I still doing it? Why am I still lying?

I approach the door tentatively, but clearly, my mother has been waiting for my return because I see the sitting room curtains twitch before the door opens abruptly.

"Alexandra. There you are. Let's go to dinner."

Mum is already wearing her coat, with her handbag over her arm. This is not good.

"Come along, Graham!" she says, in tones more frantic than usual, as my poor dad struggles to tie up his shoes.

"I'm coming, Barbara," he says in the patient voice he's always used when my mother gets mildly hysterical.

They usher me along the street until we reach *Luigi's*, the local Italian restaurant my parents always favour when they come to London because it's family-run (if by family-run you mean an elderly man with an angry moustache bellowing at surly teenage waiters). Donatello, the jocular head waiter, bears down on us immediately like we're old friends. "Come in, come in! Lovely to see you." He greets us warmly, gives cheek kisses all around, despite Dad's best efforts at a handshake, and promises us the best table in the house. Fortunately, I know from experience that he doesn't have a clue who we are, and if he did, the welcome would probably be significantly less effusive. My parents still tip in shillings.

The best table in the house is apparently a wobbly one tucked in the corner behind the door to the kitchen. Still, there are candles, and most importantly, Donatello is pretty speedy at taking our wine order and ensuring its fast delivery to the table.

My parents, culinary pioneers that they are, settle for their usual order of margarita pizza. Donatello looks at me. "And for you, young *bellissima*, tonight, I recommend the octopus!" he proposes with a flourish. "You look like a young woman with a love for the adventurous, no?" Dad chokes on his wine, clearly having flashbacks to the earlier things he 'learned' about his daughter. This is going to be an awkward dinner.

"Oh, I… well. Thank you. Erm, maybe not octopus…" I mutter something I read about the octopus being smarter than a four-year-old child… "Er, I'll have the *scelta gamberoni*, please?"

Donatello looks disappointed I'm not taking his steer down the road of adventure, "You know, the prawns have feelings too!" he wanders off, chuckling merrily and leaving us to an awkward silence.

"Alexandra," my mother begins, "we've had quite an interesting afternoon, your father and I."

"Mum, I know... I have to..."

"Don't interrupt, dear. We have to make you aware of something. The thing is... I don't know how to tell you this, but..." Mum trails off, and Dad reaches over and puts his hand over mine.

"Love," Dad takes over, "we think Javier might not be quite right for you."

"We think he's LTG," Mum interrupts impatiently.

"LGBT," Dad corrects hesitantly. "Q," he adds after a momentary pause.

This is not what I expected at all, and I am not sure how to react. I decide to feign surprise.

"What?" I say, adopting a stricken expression. "Why?"

"Well, of course... we can't be sure. These things are very fluid these days. But you know. Um. Sometimes there's a vibe..." Dad trails off and focuses on taking a long gulp from his empty wine glass.

"What Dad's saying," Mum tags in, "is there was a lot that wasn't quite right about this afternoon. For starters, Javier seemed a little too fascinated by James Dean. I worry that he may be either confused or taking advantage. Perhaps he wants a passport. Or a bride to take home to Grandma. People can be very traditional in the Mediterranean." (Says the Women's Institute member from rural Cheshire). Choosing to pick my battles and leave the casual xenophobia for another day, I decide to come clean.

"OK. Mum, Dad. I have to tell you something."

For the next hour, I come clean with them about (almost) everything. I tell them about being totally broke, pretending to be an Agony Uncle, having to move in with Sir John, and becoming a ghostwriter. I leave out the bits about falling in love with Ryan and the Anastasia alter ego: There's a ceiling to my parents' coping abilities – and a two-hour limit on the table. When I finish, and I don't use this term lightly, they look absolutely thunderstruck.

"Alex, there seems to be an awful lot of deception in your life at the moment. Isn't it easier to just tell the truth?" Dad says gently.

Mum looks vaguely tearful and clearly incredulous. "Why didn't you tell us?! We would have helped you! What are they going to think at Rotary? That we couldn't be bothered to help our own daughter and to avoid the mean streets of London, she's entered into some sort of dubious arrangement with an elderly millionaire!"

"Mum, it's not dubious. He's a respectable parliamentarian! He used to be Home Secretary! And I'm pretty sure he's not a millionaire; otherwise, he wouldn't have to write this book!"

My protests fall on deaf ears: "Our daughter, Graham! Bankrupt and practically homeless. Doing goodness knows what to get by! Oh, we've failed. I bet Adam has told your Aunty Sheila! What will she think of me?"

We're starting to draw attention. Donatello's ears are wagging over his berating of a spotty young waiter. Fortunately, Dad, with years of experience dealing with my mum's temper, suggests that they might feel better if they meet Sir John and we all go out for lunch tomorrow. My mother takes to this idea immediately, and calms down enough to order tiramisu and coffee. She's positively cheerful again by the time she's downed the complementary limoncello Donatello brings across with the bill.

Safe in the knowledge I'm not planning to marry Javier and moderately reassured that I'm not prostituting myself to politicians, my parents head back to their hotel, and I go back to Sir John's, wondering how to broach the subject of a 'meet the parents' lunch. It's not exactly normal to have to meet your staff's parents.

I find him in the library when I get home, poring over an old photo album. He slams it shut as I walk in, and I'm too exhausted by the events of the day to push him on it.

"Sir John... I have a favour to ask," I start.

"Hmm. Do you usually ask your employers for favours so soon? What is it? If it's having someone over to stay, that's your business. But keep them away from breakfast. Poor Mrs Jenkins has enough to do with an extra mouth to feed already." Sir John hasn't ever shown noticeable concern for Mrs Jenkins's workload before, particularly when demanding seconds, but I let that slide.

"No, not that..."

"An extra day off? It seems a little soon, but alright, I suppose. You want a –"

I interrupt, sensing this could go on a bit. "No, no, nothing like that. I told my parents about moving in here and the new job, and they want to meet you, if that's OK? They've suggested lunch tomorrow," I add hesitantly.

"Well," Sir John ponders, "I suppose that would be acceptable. If Ophelia were living with an older gentleman, I think I would want to meet him and ensure all was above board."

"Thank you! They've suggested 12:30pm. I can book a local restaurant. Is that OK?"

"Yes, that's a perfectly acceptable time. And no need

for the restaurant. Mrs Jenkins can put a roast on. Ask her to make sure it's all the trimmings." Sir John decrees, apparently adopting a flexible approach to employer concern for Mrs Jenkins' workload.

"That sounds ideal. I'll let them know," I say. I text my parents and get my dad's usual technology-challenged response on his ancient mobile: "Thanks.Love.Looking.Forward.To.It.Night.night.Lovemumanddad."

I head to bed, relief mingling with the dread of asking Mrs Jenkins at 9:30pm on a Saturday to cook a Sunday roast dinner with all the trimmings for four for 12:30pm.

***

Dear Alex,

I have a great job here in the City. One of the top dogs in a fair-sized hedge fund. Nice flat and weekend place. Good range of cars. But I've got an opportunity to move to a much bigger global firm based in New York. Amazing opportunities, they'd provide me with a penthouse pretty central on Avenue of Americas. More ladder to climb as well. My concern is giving up being a big fish in a small pond, for a lake where I'll be a pike of as-yet unknown size.

Jerome.

"*A pike of as-yet-unknown size?" Seriously Jerome? What's the next stage above First World Problems? Because, mate, I think you've just levelled up. So, you're basically torn between being rich and important in London and rich and important in New York? Stop. You'll have readers weeping. Thanks for the extra colour about the two houses and the range of cars too by the way. Subtly done. You could just make a note of your bank balance at the bottom of your letter, just so we know exactly how well you're doing. Better yet, why don't you just slap your dick on the table so we can all stand around and admire it?*

On a serious note, Jerome (and by the way, I hope you're not pissed off by the first bit because I'm pretty sure you can afford a whole troupe of Serbian hitmen. This makes me wonder: What IS the collective noun for assassins? Troupe might be a bit too jolly. It sort of sounds like leotards might be involved too). Anyway, on a serious note, I'm interested in the total lack of any other considerations outside your career for the move. What about family? Friends? Partner? Where do any of the above fit in? And if they don't, why don't they? You're clearly doing well – but at what cost? This might be the opportunity to think not just about what you want out of the next stage of your career but what you want out of the next stage of your life. Think about it. If it's another shinny up the greasy pole that you really, really want... that's great. But if that's a distraction because other things don't go so well, then maybe now's the time to challenge yourself. Perhaps the real adventure isn't the next level in your job, but what's waiting outside your job?

If this advice was life-changing or, at minimum, helpful, then I'm more than happy for you to show your appreciation by gifting any handouts you choose from your "range of cars."

Yours, Alex

TWENTY-FIVE

The next morning, I'm up early, strangely excited for my parents to meet Sir John and for me to finally get to be honest about something. The sun is shining, and Mrs Jenkins has taken the request for a roast dinner in a few hours remarkably well. However, I ended up softening the request considerably to the point it seemed more like a plea to supervise me while I made the dinner.

At breakfast, Sir John is up and on his second cup of coffee, looking dapper in one of his less moth-eaten suits, but this time, he's wearing his favourite ancient tie and shiny silver cufflinks of little, tall ships.

"Sir John! You look very smart!" I exclaim. He clears his throat, glares at me and goes back to his paper. I hope he's a little more talkative with my parents. Fortunately, Mrs Jenkins is in a better mood, although as I start preparing the roast under her beady eye, her smile takes on a more rictus-grin quality.

"Have you ever peeled a potato before?" she asks cheerfully, having watched me wrestle with a Maris Piper for ten minutes and emerge the loser. I catch my breath and say slightly more aggressively than I should, "Yes. I think it's this thing that's the problem…"

"The potato peeler? Give it here, love." Mrs Jenkins takes over and ploughs through the potatoes like a root-vegetable version of *The Texas Chain Saw Massacre*. I am assigned next to peeling the carrots – which proves as challenging as their fat cousins and almost costs me my finger. Two of the carrots don't make it, thanks to spinning off the counter and disappearing under the fridge. Instead, Mrs Jenkins suggests it might be better for her to tackle them too, "now that I'm in the flow of peeling."

"Should I do something with the joint?" I ask, glancing at the oven.

"No!" Mrs Jenkins says a little too sharply. "I mean, no, no – let it be. What would be a big help is if you can, erm…"

"Make the gravy?"

"No, no. Count out the vegetables, dear. So, we know we've got the right amount for four people. I'll tell you what we need in terms of parsnips, cauliflower and the surviving carrots. You can make four piles."

"Are you sure this is a real task?" I ask suspiciously.

"Oh yes. Very helpful," says Mrs Jenkins soothingly.

The rest of the preparation goes smoothly – though for large chunks of it, I'm left sitting in a chair out of the way, counting things like the five-year-old Mrs Jenkins clearly thinks I am.

At 12:25pm, my parents arrive. It's a good start, as Sir John abhors anyone who doesn't abide by military precision. I can see they've also dressed to impress, my mum in a flowery dress, and my dad in his chinos, with a nice shirt and his loafers. Despite their reservations that he's a sinister sugar daddy, they manage to greet him warmly.

"Lovely to meet you, Sir John," Mum says in her speaking-to-Cheshire-gentry voice.

"A pleasure," says Sir John, smiling, and I can't help feeling relieved that he hasn't just said harumph.

Things noticeably relax when I show my parents my self-contained flat within the house – as far removed from a sugar baby's boudoir as you could get.

Two bottles of wine and four Sunday roasts later, miraculously, everyone seems to be getting on like a house on fire. So far, they've discussed agricultural politics (not something I could rise to join), their mutual love of the Lake District, and Sir John's clay pigeon shooting trophies. It's funny watching him talk to people he clearly considers adults, such as my parents, versus the way he deals with me and poor Mrs Jenkins, the help. I'm learning more about him from this lunch than I feel I have in weeks of living with him. We haven't delved into the personal at all since our accidentally alcohol-fuelled brunch. But still nothing too personal. He doesn't mention Laura or Ophelia, and my parents don't ask about family. Is he too ashamed? My mind can't help cycling back to this strange scandal in his past, but I don't like thinking badly of Sir John, particularly when he is going to so much trouble to welcome my parents.

"Shall we have pudding, then?" he asks, summoning poor Mrs Jenkins without waiting for an answer. We all nod, and Sir John decrees that we should all have an

Irish coffee to go with our desserts. The day has been an undeniable success, and the fact that I've managed to unravel this lie and tell my parents the truth has given me a bit of a boost at the prospect of coming clean to Ryan.

TWENTY-SIX

Mum and Dad leave at about 5pm, having established to their satisfaction that Sir John isn't a sociopathic sugar daddy. Or, possibly, having decided that even if he is, a detached house in Hampstead more than makes up for it and that their only daughter is a worthy sacrifice. I can already picture how the discussion would go: Dad tutting worriedly and Mum saying sternly, "Well, Graham, it's not like anyone else is claiming her from the shelf…"

Imaginary shudder-inducing conversations aside, I wave them off cheerfully and head inside to goad Sir John into helping with the washing up, which in his world involves transporting it to the kitchen to leave for Mrs Jenkins.

"Thank you for putting up with my parents," I say, deciding to go one step further than the norm and actually wash the plates.

Sir John, shamed into helping, gingerly picks up a tea towel, regarding it with suspicion and tentatively starting to pat at the first soaked plate as if it might explode.

"Oh, they seemed like fine people. Very fine people. Very normal. Not what I was expecting at all."

"Oh, thanks very much," I reply grumpily. "By the way, unless you're determined to remove the whole glaze, I think you can consider that plate dry."

"Yes, fine people. Nice to see you all together," Sir John mutters, much quieter than usual.

"Well, I do see them a fair bit anyway. They threaten to show up in London if I don't go back every eight weeks or so."

Sir John sighs. It's a very different sound from his normal snort of impatience.

"Is everything alright, Sir John?"

Glancing across, I see that the next plate is also being firmly dried into oblivion. I rescue it from him, put it in the cupboard, and then pat his hand encouragingly.

When he answers, his voice is different from that of the usual bombast: "Oh. Seeing you together today. With your parents. It made me think of my daughter. She's about your age, you know."

I curse inwardly. I know for a fact she's in her late forties, but I don't want to interrupt him.

"I can't think when we last sat down together as a family," he says, eyes looking suspiciously leaky.

I feel slightly panicked. It's like seeing a teacher on the verge of tears, but I find myself asking quietly, "Why, Sir John? Why don't you speak?"

Suddenly feeling brave, I ask, "Is it because of the nanny?"

He pauses for an excruciatingly long time. Have I gone too far? Am I waving goodbye to my contract? My heart is slamming in my chest, expecting him to erupt with fury.

Instead, he just picks up the next plate and starts drying. "How do you know about the nanny?" he asks, his voice almost a whisper.

"I've been using the internet to flesh out your story a bit, and I found a story from the eighties. It mentioned you and your wife separating. And the nanny moving out. It didn't take much to put two and two together."

For a moment, Sir John's face looks thunderous, but he takes a steadying breath. "Two and two don't always make four," he says sadly, clutching the plate to his chest.

I take it from him and put it away, deciding acting as normal as possible is the way forward. "I don't understand. Am I wrong about the nanny?"

"It was... complicated. Laura, my wife, was an extraordinary woman. She came from a typical upper-class world of privilege." He catches my slight eye twitch and adds. "Oh, I knew a lot of privilege too, although my father was a reverend, a younger brother, much poorer than hers. We were always ever so slightly cuckoos in the nest, my family. Anyway, despite the world she came from, Laura was always so different. So unexpected. She had a way of looking at people like she knew all their secrets, all their flaws, but never judged them. At the same time, she was inscrutable. You never knew for sure what she was thinking or what she would say next. I used to call her my mermaid. She was so ethereal." His eyes crinkle up, and he smiles.

"Then Jenny started as our nanny. She was the daughter of some neighbours of my parents back in

Sussex. And Laura was so different around her. She'd throw back her head and laugh. They'd both absolutely roar with laughter. Jenny would tease her; she'd say the most outrageous things to my perfect Laura. And Laura would giggle right back. They had a connection…and then they had more."

I am stunned, "But… I thought you and Jenny…"

"So did everyone else. It's the oldest cliché. The husband and the nanny. When Laura told me, I threw Jenny out. I was heartbroken. But I thought we could work through it. But Laura didn't seem to know what she wanted. We sent our daughter to my parents while we tried to work out what to do… and then Laura decided. It was twelve hours of arguing, but she finally made up her mind. She packed her bag and set off in her car to Jenny's. It was midnight, pouring with rain, and she was upset. Anyway, you can imagine the rest."

"That's when she crashed?" I ask, horrified and sad.

"Two policemen turned up on my doorstep."

"But I still don't understand about your daughter not speaking to you…"

"The muckrakers waste no time in Westminster," Sir John says bitterly. "Never underestimate the parliamentary gossip networks. They already knew Laura and I were having problems. The fact that I was taking time off and that we had sent our daughter away… all of that had made the rounds. Word got out that we were separating. Then throw in that our nanny had been fired, and everyone came up with the same equation you did."

I blush with embarrassment. "And that's what your daughter heard, too?"

"Later, when she was older, yes. More precisely, she heard the version that my heartbroken wife had packed her bags and fled the house from my temper when her car... when the crash..."

"Oh, Sir John, that's horrible. But why didn't you tell her the truth? You don't even *have* a temper!"

"Grief is a funny thing. It can make us thrash around desperately searching for answers and cling to the first narrative we come across. Even if we know deep down that it doesn't feel right. But I couldn't tell her the truth. All Ophelia had left of her mother were her memories. And the eighties were not kind for... that kind of relationship. I wasn't going to put Ophelia through that. I swore to her that I loved her mother and there was nothing between Jenny and me. But of course, the clues always led elsewhere. Ophelia went off to board at school, and eventually, she started spending more and more of her holidays at friends' houses. We'd have an awkward reunion every six months or so, but that became less and less frequent. Now we have a telephone call once in a blue moon, you know, Christmas, birthdays, Father's Day and the like, and that's about it."

"And that's why you stood down as a minister?"

"In any political career, you make enemies. This was exactly the ammunition they needed. My campaign motto, to make it even more ironic, had been 'family first'. My colleagues made it clear to me that the options were to step down quietly and they'd do their best to quash the rumour mill, which they managed after one or two shots across the bows from tabloids, or my enemies would have every assumed detail splashed across the papers. I couldn't risk that, for me or Ophelia."

Sir John looks old and frail, hunched in his chair. He glares at me fiercely, "None of this is for that damn book. This is confidential – between us."

"Of course, I won't use it for the book. But why not tell Ophelia now? Times have changed, and she's an adult; she'd understand."

"Too much time has passed. It's far too late."

"Of course, it's not. How can you say that?"

"You'd like me to mention this the next time she phones? By the way darling, your mother… your mother…" he swallows.

"Could you not ask to meet her? Tell her face-to-face?"

Sir John has had enough, "Sleeping dogs, old bean. Sleeping dogs. That's enough for now."

He starts to rise.

"Sir John," I grab his arm. "This is a terrible price to pay to keep a misunderstanding going. Do you really not want to take the chance?"

"I'm too old. I can't have this conversation now; it's all too painful."

I flail around for a solution, "A letter, then? You could put it all in a letter. Give her time to read and digest the truth. You can't wave goodbye to the relationship when you've done nothing wrong. It's crazy."

He pauses, "What kind of letter would that even be? It would be impossible to write."

"Of course, it wouldn't. I could help you. There's nothing you can't put in a letter," I add, thinking guiltily of the truth I need to disclose to Ryan.

He snaps, "I'll think about it. That's enough now. I'm tired."

He strides out of the kitchen but pauses at the door.

"Thank you regardless, Alex. Your parents are lucky to have you," he says gruffly before quickly disappearing upstairs. I stare after him. I feel terrible for jumping to the same conclusions as everyone else. I feel even worse that his lying has been to protect the people he loves, while mine has only ever been in my selfish interests. I study the peeling wallpaper for some time after he leaves, wondering how on earth I could have fallen so far.

TWENTY-SEVEN

Sir John studiously avoids me for the rest of the day. At one point, while I'm raiding the kitchen for Mrs Jenkins' scones, I hear his tentative tread on the stairs before the sound of a veritable scamper as he retreats upstairs. Presumably, he's terrified that I might try to force a family reunion on him in the fashion of a soapy Channel 5 reality TV show.

At breakfast the next day, the sizzling temptation of sausages lures Sir John from his hideout, but he does his very best to use this morning's *Times* as a shield. He shelters behind it to the point that he's almost camping while Mrs Jenkins potters around with the breakfast things.

"Have you had breakfast yourself yet, Mrs Jenkins?" I ask as she lays down a stack of pancakes and a few sides of bacon next to the heaped platter of sausages.

I see *The Times* quiver in irritation.

"Oh, I'm not a morning eater, to be honest, love."

"What about if I make you a coffee, and you grab a seat for a minute?" I ask.

More rustling.

"What for?" asks Mrs Jenkins suspiciously.

"Well, you made a lovely brekkie for us, so I thought it might be nice."

"I'm quite happy to have a coffee afterwards in the kitchen, thank you," said Mrs Jenkins firmly, heading over to the coffeemaker.

The rest of her kitchen bustling has a mildly hostile edge, and I'm relieved when she's finished and heads into the utility room to sort through Sir John's laundry.

The Times drawbridge briefly lowers to allow a brief "I told you so" glance from Sir John before sweeping up again.

I mutter and help myself to pancakes, ignoring a few indignant bangs and clatterings from Mrs Jenkins next door.

Eventually, the newspaper lowers once more. Sir John whispers conspiratorially, "I've decided. We'll attempt it."

"What?" I ask, concerned at what possible hair-brained scheme *we* might be about to attempt.

"The letter!" he hisses impatiently, glancing in the direction of the utility room in case Mrs Jenkins has her KGB ear pressed against the door.

"That's brilliant, Sir John!" I say excitedly.

"Keep your voice down," he warns grumpily, "An attempt. That's all. I'm not saying I'll post it. But we could attempt it."

When Mrs Jenkins is safely upstairs making Sir John's bed, I grab us a pen and a piece of paper. We spend some time staring at them both for a while.

"They're not going to move themselves, Sir John," I say.

"I know that," he says irritably, "You're the writer. What should I say?"

"Imagine Ophelia is here now. What would you want to say to her?"

Sir John coughs. "For a letter out of the blue, perhaps it would be better not to go straight into some of these things. This first letter perhaps could be on another topic…"

"Honesty, Sir John, take my word for it. That's the North Star for this." I inwardly wince at my own hypocrisy but press on: "Take my word for it. Maybe not from personal experience, but it's not enough anyway. But I'm absolutely certain: What this needs is authenticity, not politeness or small talk."

He gives me an appraising glance and frowns for a minute, "I'll dictate. You scribe."

I obediently pick up the pen, and Sir John begins, "Ophelia darling, Hoping this letter finds you well. After very careful consideration, I want to share something with you that may well be challenging and difficult. I do so in the hope it will aid your understanding of a painful time for all of us." He trails off, glancing at my expression.

"Why are you frowning?" he barks.

"It's getting there, but it's a bit businesslike. Yesterday, when you spoke about Laura, you were so open. I think that's what Ophelia needs to hear."

His frown deepens.

I try again, "Start with your daughter. What does she mean to you? You love her?"

"Well, she's my daughter. Of course, I love her," Sir

John whispers, dropping his volume in case Mrs Jenkins upstairs hears such a shocking revelation.

"Well, let's start with that."

"It's not my style," Sir John replies.

"I'm not suggesting little hearts on the letterhead. But now's not the time to hold back."

It takes several drafts and a lot more coffee, which I speedily make with a nervous eye out for Mrs Jenkins' return. Eventually we wrestle the letter into a form resembling less a terse police statement and more an honest and loving account in Sir John's own words.

Ophelia darling,

This is a painful letter to write, so please bear with me. I write now as I reflect on how difficult our relationship has been. I want to take a final chance to mend some bridges, and I hope you might, too.

There is a secret I have kept for far too long, and I bitterly regret the distance it has caused. I am sorry that it may shock you and even hurt you, yet I am sharing it now because I see no other way back for our relationship.

I know for a long time you've blamed me for betraying your mamma. Please believe me now when I tell you how much I loved her and that I would never have wished to hurt her or you. Our marriage indeed became complicated, and circumstances and prejudice meant your mother never had an opportunity to be true to herself. The truth is that over time, your mother's friendship with Jenny developed into something else. So, it is indeed true that Jenny had a role in the troubles of our marriage, but it was not in the way that you think.

We tried our best to work things out, and Mamma loved you so very, very much. She wanted to keep our home together for you as far as possible. We both did.

But then we lost her, and I couldn't bear any of this to change your memories of her. And why should it? She was a wonderful mother. Do you remember how she never read your bedtime stories from books? She always made them up. They were always so bizarre and fantastic and would have you roaring with laughter. You may wonder how she came up with them so spontaneously. The truth is that I'd often see her with a little pen and notebook, chewing the end of the pen and scribbling down ideas to keep you entertained on future evenings. She loved amazing and entertaining you with her tales.

And then we lost her. It was easier never to discuss what happened. First, you were too young to understand, and then even when you were older and started to pick up on the gossip about Jenny and me, it never felt right.

I'm sorry I wasn't brave enough to broach this then, and I'm ashamed that when our relationship started to deteriorate, I allowed it to. I hope this isn't too late to reach out.

Your dad

Sir John looks up, his face strained. "I still don't know. Is this the right thing to do?"

"Other than seeing her face-to-face…"

"Impossible," he says firmly.

"Then yes, if the other option is silence. She will never know the truth. You owe this to the two of you… the three of you, really."

He holds the letter one more time, his hands shaking slightly. Then he nods, picks up the pen, and starts to copy out the draft to send in his own hand.

***

Dear Alex,

This is a really awkward one. I'm your usual twenty-eight-year-old bloke. Except I haven't had a girlfriend for ages. I haven't dated for ages. And I think I might have fallen for another guy, a mate from my five-aside. I can't stop thinking about him. I don't think he feels the way I do. But this feeling is making me miserable. Should I tell him?

Help!
Ethan

Hi Ethan,
First of all, there's no 'usual bloke' like there's no 'usual woman'. I believe we're a mix of incredibly unique stuff and things every single one of us on this planet has in common.

I think yours was a brave letter to write, so thanks for sharing. Before we come onto your footballing mate, one thing that stands out to me is that nowhere in your letter do you use the word 'gay'. I wondered why. Some people are still not sure where they are on that pesky spectrum people talk about. Other people don't reckon they need labels because, after all, they're not a discounted tin of soup on a supermarket shelf. I wonder why not for you? The first step might well be taking a bit more time to think about how you feel about things and how you feel about guys and girls.

You don't need to have a definitive answer, but it can be helpful to go through the questions.

When it comes to speaking to this guy, it's hard to advise without knowing him or you. But I reckon a bit of caution is needed first. In an ideal world filled with birdsong and Man United permanently at the top of the table, anyone would just be flattered to be paid the compliment of being liked by someone else. We're not there yet (did you see Man United's performance last week? Dismal). And these things can backfire a bit or make a friendship a hell of a lot more complex. Given where you are in your journey of self-discovery (apologies, by the way, if that makes me sound like a hippy with joss sticks), there's also a risk that his reaction might complicate those final bits of the journey for you. You'll have a lot going on, and you'll feel pretty raw already without adding that to the mix. So why don't you take time first to decide more about yourself and what you're into, and talk it through with a friend you trust (ideally not a hot one who you fancy) and then after you've worked through that, maybe share it with your mate from football? See what they say – you may be able to pick up signals from there. Anyway, good luck mate.

Alex

TWENTY-EIGHT

It's finally the day Ryan is due home, and I feel extremely conflicted. I promised, immediately after our most recent goodnight kiss and therefore high on oxytocin, that I would meet him at the airport. Still, now I realise exactly how big a deal that is. Picking someone up at the airport is a bit of a milestone in a relationship, isn't it? I am so torn; simultaneously, I am very excited to see him and also nervous about what this might mean and what the day might hold.

The night before, I had laid out all my prep for the morning: my nicest make-up, a nice dress, etc., but looking at it all in the cold light of day, it feels wrong. With all the drama around Javier and my parents meeting Sir John, followed by helping Sir John craft his own letter, I never actually had time to think about the email *I* was meant to send to Ryan, revealing my true identity. And now he's in a plane hurtling back towards me, and it feels a little too late to have not done this already. All night, my brain was in overdrive, reminding me that this situation is immoral and wrong, and he thinks that my name is Anastasia. When I tried to quiet it, it ignored me entirely and just got louder. I decide that actually I will do everything I can to help me maintain my willpower, and I sadly hang my lovely dress back up and pull out an old and very faded pair of jeans, almost threadbare in places, and an old, oversized university jumper. I complement the look with the beige bra and granny knickers that made an appearance in front of Madeleine the Pixie, decide against make-up, and I'm ready.

During the whole journey to the airport, I'm thinking about how to tell him. I know I have to, but I don't even know where to begin or when the right time might be. Is it the second I see him? As we walk to the Tube? What about when we reach his house? I mean, can you imagine if I say it to him on the Tube and then he gets angry, or worse, upset, in the carriage in front of a load of confused and sleep-deprived tourists and solemn Londoners?

The lie just feels so big; I feel a pang, wishing I'd confided in Bea when this was in its infancy so she could currently act as my Jiminy Cricket. But I don't really need to hear it; I know Bea would tell me to do the right thing. I know that's what I should do, regardless of Adam somehow thinking I could play along with this for eternity and convince our families to play along.

As I enter the airport, I steel my nerves, resolute in my decision to do the right thing. Still, as soon as Ryan emerges from the mysterious one-way airport gates, he says nothing and just wraps me into what will probably go down in history as the best kiss that Arrivals has ever seen if they recorded such things (which they should).

"You look beautiful. I've missed you so much," Ryan murmurs in my ear between showering me with kisses, which, frankly, are becoming borderline public indecency, especially if he continues following that trail down my neck he seems so keen on. "I've missed you too," I whisper back. I can't believe he called me beautiful in this outfit. If I'd worn this to meet Chris, he probably would have pretended not to know me and then spent the entire journey home criticising me and telling me I was an embarrassment.

"Shall we go home?" Ryan says softly, jolting me back to the present. Electricity bolts through my body. He takes my hand in his and guides me to the Tube. During the whole journey from Heathrow to South Wimbledon, I'm completely distracted and only vaguely aware of all the stories he's telling me about his trip. "Uh-huh. Oh really? Sounds amazing!" become my trio of responses, my brain frantically trying to find a natural way to reveal to him that our whole relationship is built on a gaping chasm of lies. Not even being melodramatic.

The Northern line pulls into the station too quickly, and I still haven't managed to bring up my deception. Ryan grabs my hand and pulls me off the Tube with him, marching us up the escalator. I'm surprised we make it home, frankly. We breathlessly reach his flat, and no sooner than he's closed the door, he's pushed me up against it, alternating between kissing my lips and trailing kisses down my neck. This genuinely has to be the most electrifying experience of my life.

"WAIT!" I gasp.

He stops immediately and looks concerned.

"I…" I hesitate. "Do you think you really like *me*? Or do you just like the person you think I am?"

He looks concerned. "Anastasia, what's this about?"

"I just… I want to know what you like about me."

"Everything. I like your smile, the way you have an obscure film reference for every scenario, the way your hair catches the light, the way you laugh, your ancient old rucksack full of old receipts you seem to collect for no reason, the way you suddenly get nervous and laugh at inappropriate moments… everything."

"So not the fact that I'm a glamorous Russian émigré?"

He laughs. "No. I keep forgetting that part, to be honest."

"But I look awful!" I exclaim, desperately grasping at straws at this point.

"You always look beautiful to me."

I wonder if he'll feel the same when he sees the granny pants, but I know he will.

I hesitate. All those things he likes… that's the real me. Not stupid Anastasia. He gathers me into his arms again, and I melt. I promise I'll tell him soon.

He kisses me more deeply, and before I know it, he's lifted me and is carrying me towards his room. I lose track of the exact order of events after that, but I do know that three hours later, Chris never made me feel this desirable, this beautiful, this…safe.

Hormones make me want to express that last sentiment to Ryan, but he cuddles me into him and murmurs gently in my ear, "Shit, I forgot to tell you. I'm going to Mum and Dad's for lunch tomorrow, and they begged me to bring you. They want to meet this girl who's making me walk around with a stupid grin on my face all the time. Is that OK? I can totally get you out of it if you want."

Only a man would drop something as big as meeting the parents for the first time out of the blue the night before, and I go a bit cold. I was supposed to be stopping the lie, not expanding the web of deceit.

I start to answer before I really know what to say, but thankfully, he's fallen asleep before I can say anything too prematurely. I snuggle into his chest, and he sleepily curls his arm around me.

Half an hour later, though, Ryan is still slumbering peacefully, but I'm starting to freak out. I've just slept with a guy who doesn't know my name, and he wants me to meet his parents. Worse, I think I have fallen in love with a guy who doesn't know my name. There's absolutely no way I can see out of this that doesn't involve massive hurt. I either have to tell him, at which point he'll definitely be crushed and likely walk away, or I have to break up with him, walking away from the man who is possibly the love of my life.

I lie there, restlessly fidgeting and playing various scenarios back and forth in my mind, but I just can't think of anything. I need Bea.

TWENTY-NINE

I've ended up agreeing to meet his parents, mostly because of my inability to think of a way out of it. I insisted I had to go home and dress more appropriately, though, so I rushed off at the crack of dawn, avoiding any awkward moments in the morning and buying some precious private time to think. But I've come up with nothing. His parents are expecting me, or rather, Anastasia, and I can't think of a way out.

I commit to another layer of deception ruefully. While pacing back and forth in my room, I manage to scatter the contents of my entire wardrobe across the bedroom floor. There seems to be genuinely nothing suitable for visiting your boyfriend's family under a total pretence.

The summer sunshine beaming through makes all my dresses look worn and about a decade too young for me. After a lot of costume changes and exasperated sighs, I go for the most wholesome look, an ivory number with a blue iris pattern. "That's a little more Fulham parent visiting than Saturday night disco," I decide, chatting to myself nervously and straightening the hem in the mirror. To compensate for the ever so slightly twee cut of the dress, I choose to pin my hair up in a flirty style I pretty much invent from scratch, neat if a little odd. I survey the plant I've acquired for Ryan's mother one more time. It started as a sunflower but is looking like a steroid-pumped wilted daisy with every passing hour. My green-fingered attempts to restore it to its natural bloom have so far involved overwatering and putting a few dead leaves on the topsoil in the hope they may act as a shot of nutritious compost.

I take another look at myself in the mirror and start to have second thoughts. They're ended abruptly by the gentle toot of a horn outside. Ryan's as punctual as ever, damn.

After five minutes of speed rummaging to find the best footwear and bag, I rush out to him, flustered and hoping a winning smile can make up for keeping him waiting… again.

Ryan gets out of the car to kiss me hello. "You look great," he says before glancing at the flower. "Who's your friend?"

"It's for your mum." I clamber into the car and balance the plant on my lap. "It looked great in the store… but now it looks a bit like…"

"A triffid with the plague?" Ryan volunteers.

"Oh, it's a disaster," I panic. "Can we please stop somewhere so I can pick up something else? It looked great before, and I literally dug it up an hour ago. I mean… bought it."

"It'll be fine,' says Ryan, generously ignoring the obvious fact that I got it from Sir John's garden. "Mum loves an underdog and taking care of stuff. This can be her greatest challenge. And the pot's lovely."

"Maybe I could just get rid of the triffid and give her the pot?" I examine the gift as we drive along.

"That'd be reckless abandonment," says Ryan. "It'll be fine. It's really sweet you want to make a good impression, but Mum and Dad are really relaxed. They're going to love you. You don't have to try too hard."

"Oh, it's no trouble," I say, adjusting my hairpins.

"Well, you know you can be yourself," Ryan says, "and that means being comfortable. Including with your usual hairstyle."

Ignoring the tendrils of guilt encircling my stomach, I just point to my hair and say, "Don't you like this one?" somewhat defensively.

"Well, it probably looked great on Princess Margaret."

"Um, I wanted to look 'proper'," I say testily.

"You always look proper. But you don't have to worry. We're not going to Downton Abbey."

I tentatively remove all the hairpins, and my hair falls loose, but unfortunately, it falls loose in pretty much every direction rather than in a sexy, tumultuous fashion. "Crap, I look like a mad woman," I say in a panic, trying to finger-comb it into something decent.

I glance in the mirror again. "I've made it even worse," I wail. It looks like every strand has fallen out with the other, and they've all decided to pull in opposite directions.

"You look just great," Ryan assures me.

"I look like that woman out of Jane Eyre's attic," I cry, worrying that my appearance is punishing me for my horrific web of lies.

"Oh, I always preferred her to Jane," Ryan assures, his lips curling into a smile.

"Hmm." I've managed to corral my hair into something that looks more like a harassed woman in a storm, as an improvement over an escaped killer living in the woods.

As we get closer to Fulham, I can feel the butterflies of nervousness and the moths of guilt fluttering away together in my belly, having what feels like some sort of raucous party. The one thing worse than Ryan's family not liking me is them liking me when all along they're yet more people I'm dragging into my fraud.

The butterflies and moths start having midair collisions as we pull up in front of the house. It's a little redbrick terrace on a well-tended street – the sort of place a lot of normal families bought in the eighties but where only the extremely wealthy can afford now.

My knees feel wobbly as I climb out, awkwardly carrying the mutant sunflower.

Ryan's mum opens the door. A pretty woman with a soft Jamaican accent who barely comes up to Ryan's shoulder. She hugs me and looks far more delighted at the gift than the triffid deserves. "Call me Joy," she beams appropriately enough.

Inside, Ryan's dad shakes my hand. He's closer in height to Ryan, and he has Ryan's intense stare. Gareth is quieter than Joy but has a warm smile and leads us into the kitchen.

Joy insists on placing the triffid alongside some beautifully cultivated houseplants on the kitchen windowsill.

She pours us some generous glasses of wine, and I warm to her even more. "We've been pestering and pestering Ryan to get you over here," she chatters. "We've heard so much about you. Weeks we've been asking him, haven't we, Gareth?"

"Well, she's here now. Give the lad a break!" Gareth replies, handing me my glass.

"Well, it's lovely to meet you both," I say sincerely. They are both lovely. Joy is a bit of a wall of sound but seems happy to be teased about that by both Ryan and his father. Gareth has Ryan's dry sense of humour – he says less, but it's always funny when he does speak. He seems to sense I'm nervous and gives me a reassuring smile.

When we sit down to lunch, I feel Ryan's hand gently touch my own under the table. We break the ice with talk of weather and traffic from Hampstead to Fulham, and then I warm up and start telling them all about the ghostwriting job with Sir John. They tell us about how much the street has changed since they bought the house, then dilapidated, as a young family in the eighties. Unfortunately, however, what they find fascinating about me are the Russian roots Ryan has apparently told them all about. "Anastasia is such a lovely name," Joy says. "Is it after that poor lost princess?"

"Oh, I am, um…not entirely sure." The less I say on this topic, the better.

"Oh, I remember reading all about it," Joy nods sagely. "Horrible bit of history it was."

"You didn't read it. You watched the cartoon with the talking bat," Gareth teases.

Joy giggles, "Well, as good as."

We laugh and drink over lunch, and I decide I like them immensely. It means the butterflies are gone, but the moths have multiplied. Damn those moths of guilt.

Joy's carefully laid-out lunch table reminds me of my mum's immaculate approach to entertaining guests. All the best china gleamingly displayed. I'm going to have to be ultra unclutzy today.

"Joy, this all looks amazing! Thank you so much."

"Oh, no trouble at all," Joy beams again.

Ryan scrutinises his plate, "Mum, isn't this Grandma's china? I've never seen this out of the cupboard before."

Joy shushes him and serves, and I'm now even more terrified of breaking something.

Freakishly for me, my clumsiness remains pretty much under control for the whole lunch, and there are no further trips down the rabbit hole into family history. Instead, I just talk about Mum and Dad, my writing dreams, and moving to Hampstead. Actual truths instead of elaborate tales. It's amazing how easy digestion is when you're not spinning several novel-length fibs.

Ryan teases his parents and me. They happily take revenge with some of the usual embarrassing childhood stories: Ryan thinking every guy with a beard was Father Christmas as a four-year-old; his scream-inducing phobia of Big Bird from *Sesame Street*; being rescued by a fire crew in Hyde Park after over-ambitiously climbing to the top of a tree when he was eight and then being unable to get down.

"OK, OK, that's enough," Ryan pleads. He turns to me. "Your turn!"

So many anecdotes. Which one do I go for? Being taken to A&E with a chickpea stuck up my nose? Projectile vomiting onto the Virgin Mary in my school nativity (the pressures of being Sheep Number Three were too much for me). They don't seem suitable for the lunch table.

"OK, we'll give you some thinking time. But I'm not forgetting," says Ryan, "fair's fair."

"I'm sure my parents will tell you everything when you meet them!" I quip, and Ryan smiles at the prospect. The guilt moths now have an entire empire, as I realise sadly that he can never meet "Anastasia's" parents.

After lunch, Ryan and his dad do the washing up, which involves very noisily haphazardly stacking the dishwasher, while Joy invites me to sit in the little patio garden. It's a beautiful little sun trap where white walls hide behind trellises interwoven with pink roses.

"This is gorgeous," I tell Joy, meaning it.

She looks bashful, reaching to touch one of the budding roses. "It's one of the perks of having an empty nest. I tried to grow these years ago. But Ryan and his sister pretty much managed to squash every bloody one playing football. You met Emma?"

"Yes, at Ryan's barbecue. She's lovely."

"They've both turned out so well. We're very lucky." Joy pats my hand, "And I'm glad Ryan brought you here to meet us. You know this is only the second time he's done this. The other one was Harriet." Joy screws up her face. "Not such a nice first impression."

"Oh?" I prompt, torn between curiosity and a desire to avoid the awkwardness of conversations about exes with Ryan's mum.

"Oh, she was very hoity-toity. Fancy architecture student. Thought very highly of herself. All airs and graces.

Very glamorous and sophisticated. All stilettos and fancy eyeliner. Not like you at all."

I gulp my wine in surprise.

Joy looks mortified. "Oh, that's not what I meant. I just mean you don't have those fancy airs and graces. You seem lovely, down to earth, and honest."

I feel the guilt moths swell into ravens.

"She wasn't," Joy continues, "honest, I mean. I'm sure Ryan's told you. She led him quite a merry dance. Broke his heart when she went off with some other fella from their course."

I manage an understanding nod, all the time trying not to cry.

Thankfully, I'm saved from more of this conversation by Ryan and his dad coming out to join us. The rest of the afternoon is as lovely as the lunch, but all I can concentrate on are Joy's words. What am I doing? Silly, stupid lies; they'll have to come out eventually. And when they do, Ryan will be hurt all over again. I can't do that to him. It's time, I decide, to tell him the truth.

As Ryan drives me home, words of my draft confession churn through my mind. What to come clean about first? Faking an entire Soviet backstory or the fact that I've also been emailing him under the guise of an Agony Uncle? Which is the least bizarre? Which is the most forgivable?

Ryan glances over to me, "Strong and silent or bored and restless?"

"Sorry?" I say, jolted from my thoughts.

"Strong and silent or bored and restless?" he repeats. "That's what you asked me when we met at the singles night, and I was being a bit quiet."

I laugh despite myself. "Good memory. Sorry, I was just thinking."

He frowns, "Was this too soon? Meeting my parents and everything?"

"No! No, it was lovely. They are lovely. I'm just a bit tired."

"So, not too soon for parents?" Ryan persists. "You know how I feel about you?"

My heart pounds. How long have I waited for something like this from someone as amazing as Ryan? But all I can think is that he is talking about Anastasia. I respond with a distracted "hmmm" out loud.

Ryan glances again at me, saying much more sharply, "Well, I'd have thought the other night and wanting you to meet my folks would give you some clue."

"It does, it does," I say, suddenly tearing up, knowing I'm about to quash those feelings entirely. "I just…" I trail off. "Look, we're here."

Ryan pulls into Sir John's drive. I climb out, my knees practically knocking with nerves. Ryan slams his own door shut as he steps out. I can tell he's annoyed. His face is drawn.

He faces me, "If you don't feel the same…" he begins stiffly.

"I do. I really do," I say, desperately fighting back the threatening tears. "But I have to tell you, I have to tell you that…"

The front door opens, and Sir John barges up to us. I've never seen him move so quickly. He is waving at us with the enthusiasm of a cheerleader.

"There you are," he booms, grinning and ignoring

Ryan. "She called! I've been waiting for you all day!"

"Who called?" I ask, hastily wiping away the trace of tears with the heel of my hand.

"Ophelia!" Sir John practically shouts. "Ophelia called! Well, come on inside."

I glance from him to Ryan helplessly. "You better go with him," he sighs. Now, he's just looking sad. "I'll call you tomorrow."

"Come in, come in," Sir John herds me to the kitchen. I use the walk down the hall to regroup and surreptitiously dab at my tears.

THIRTY

By the time we sit down, I'm composed. "Ophelia called at 3pm this afternoon," Sir John chides, "I've been waiting to tell you this all day!"

"That's wonderful!" I gasp, forgetting my misery for a moment and getting swept up in Sir John's sheer joy. "What did she say? How did it go?"

"Well, it didn't go well at first…" Some of Sir John's exuberance wears off temporarily. "She didn't understand where this was coming from. Or why now." Sir John coughs and looks awkward at the memory.

"I guess that's understandable, right?" I say gently. "It is out of the blue, but we knew that. Were you able to explain a little more about why?"

"Eventually. She was a little peeved…"

"Peeved?" I probe.

"Furious then," Sir John concedes, blushing. "That something so big about her mother could be kept from her. And then she was sad for what it had meant for us. She had a lot of questions."

"Were you able to answer them all properly?"

"For the most part. It was difficult. But she wants to meet to talk more face-to-face," Sir John brightens. "She's coming to London next weekend."

It's easy to smile back; I'm so happy for him. "Where are you going to take her?"

"Certainly not to that opium den you dragged me to the other week," Sir John shoots back, returning to form. "I was thinking of Etienne's for lunch. It has some quiet booths."

Etienne's is one of the most exclusive eateries in Highgate. I consider Sir John's ever so slightly moth-eaten suits, all of them immaculately tailored originally, but that was back in the late seventies.

"If you're expecting company, we need to update your wardrobe a little," I say decisively.

"What's wrong with my wardrobe?" Sir John harrumphs. "Some of these suits are Savile Row, I'll have you know. They were bloody expensive."

"Yes, I'm sure you had to hand over a lot of shillings and groats or whatever the currency was back then. But fashion's moved on a bit. Even for retired parliamentarians."

"Hmmm. You're hardly one to talk," Sir John mutters sullenly.

"Meaning?"

"The other day, you came back with a pickled gherkin stuck to your coat."

I cough. Damn, that had been noticed after all. "Yes, well, that was a result of inefficient multitasking (eating junk food on the bus while trying to speed write the editor's intro for the June *Reptiles Monthly*), which you, as a man, can't possibly understand. Anyway, I'll make it as painless as possible."

"And I think I can get us a discount at Selfridges… like probably at least thirty per cent." I smile brightly, feeling unreasonably confident that Emma had followed through on her awkwardly agreed discount promise at the insistence of Ryan, regardless of her glacial aura.

Sir John's eyes light up at the thought of a discount. "Well, perhaps it would be good to have a little bit of a refresh. Tasteful mind, nothing youthful."

"Don't worry; we'll leave the skinny jeans and nose ring for another time. Trust me. We'll have you looking spiffy for next weekend."

Once Sir John has disappeared to bed, my mind turns back to Ryan, and a wave of sadness rushes back again. I send a long and slightly rambling text to him, telling him that I do like him. A lot… but there are things I need to explain. I ask if we can meet on Wednesday. Time slows to a crawl while I wait for a response. Just after midnight my phone beeps, and I dive at it.

Ryan has kept his reply to "Sure."

***

Dear Alex,
  Just, why?
  Descartes reborn.

Dear Fake Philosopher,
  Because.
  Yours,
  Alex, a compatriot in pseudo-intellectualism.

THIRTY-ONE

Fortunately, I have never had to take a tantrum-throwing toddler clothes shopping, but dragging Sir John out for a new suit has to come pretty close. Once over his bad temper at having to get on the Tube ("What do you MEAN you haven't ordered a car!"), his next wobble comes as we approach Selfridges, and he spies a mannequin wearing skinny jeans in the window. "Look," he gasps, pointing as if he's spied Dracula eating ducklings. He rounds on me. "You promised I wouldn't look foolish."

"Relax. That's just the ground floor. Their suits and formalwear are all upstairs."

It's still a long walk when we get inside. Sir John is adamant that he won't be seen dead in a "huddle," a phrase he repeats several times. I'm resigned to remaining confused about this until he points at the offending garment with a forefinger of outrage (it's had quite the airing this morning).

"That's a hoodie, Sir John. A hoodie. And it wasn't what I had in mind for Etienne's."

Upstairs, amid the soothing ambience of soft shoe

leather, tie silk and dignified knitwear, Sir John is much calmer. "Where do we start?" he whispers.

"This is where we get help," I whisper back.

"What? You didn't mention anything about reinforcements."

"You said it yourself. I don't know how to dress myself, let alone you." I collar a shop assistant, who looks reassuringly snooty. I explain we're looking for smart but not stuffy, and she instantly takes charge, recommending that we begin with some well-fitting shirts and then consider jumpers and chinos. I take a step back, relieved to have a professional in control.

Sir John appears mollified by her no-nonsense attitude and falls into line immediately, meekly accepting various garments and striding into the changing room without complaint. I see, with a bitter pang, that this place has proper changing rooms, not merely a prank curtain in a corner of shame from which people can tumble, underwear-clad, and flap about like a fish out of water in front of an ex and his new flame.

When Sir John emerges, the transformation is astounding. He looks years younger, thanks to the better-fitting apparel picked out by the assistant to match his eyes and complexion, as opposed to his previous haphazard approach to colour coordination.

"You look great!" I exclaim, restraining myself from giving the round of applause I so desperately want to, as I know that would lead to a large sulk.

The bloom of the moment is only slightly undermined when the assistant agrees, "Your granddaughter's right. You look lovely."

"She's not my granddaughter," he replies indignantly, heading back to the changing room. "We just live together."

That leaves the shop assistant and me standing in a very awkward silence for what feels like forever.

I break it with a nervous cough. "I'm his lodger," I tentatively start to explain.

She gives me a rigid smile that basically means, "I don't believe you, but it's none of my business. And even if I did believe you, this is still weird," but says nothing.

I try again, "I'm actually dating the brother of one of the managers here. Emma?"

The assistant's smile goes all the way to her eyes this time. "Oh, you're Ryan's girlfriend! Emma mentioned you. I think she added you to her friends and family discount the other week?"

I feel relieved. Not only have I escaped the suspicion of golddigger to an eighty-four-year-old sugar daddy, but Emma has also followed through on her discount promise. However, immediately after that first thought, another followed, pointing out how much that discount is on false pretences. Basically, as well as deluding people I care about, I'm branching into fraud. Receiving goods on false pretences.

"Emma's around here somewhere today," the assistant continues. "I think she's in the office catching up on emails. I'll let her know you've popped in."

"Oh, no need to trouble her," I say sincerely, thinking once again about that clothes fraud and the additional layer of guilt I've mined.

"Not a problem," the assistant insists. "I'll send her out." She disappears through a door behind the till.

"Great, thanks," I murmur weakly after her.

Sir John comes out of the changing room with the successful first tries. I grab his elbow.

"Sir John, look... Ryan's sister is going to pop out and say hello. She may not get my name right..." I start to whisper in a panic.

"For goodness sake, speak up, girl!" Sir John booms back. "I can't hear a word you're saying."

"I'm just saying she may call me..."

"Anastasia, hello." Too late. Ryan's sister is walking out from behind the till.

"Hi, Emma," I say quickly, "This is my landlord, Sir John Fenton. Sir John, Emma is Ryan's sister."

"Emma, how do you do?" Sir John says in his grandest and most courteous "meeting the constituents" voice.

"It's a pleasure to meet you, Sir John. Ryan mentioned you live in a beautiful part of Hampstead. How long have you been there now, Anastasia?"

My insides feel like they're being squeezed in a frozen fist with an iron grip. I wish she would stop saying my name. Surely, it's not necessary to keep doing it. It's not like she's a teacher and I'm one of twenty-eight unruly children.

"What's all this Anastasia business, Alex?" Sir John chortles.

The frozen fist clenches.

"Oh... I."

Emma looks confused, "I thought you always go by Anastasia?"

Sir John laughs again, "Alex, do you have delusions of being a lost Imperial princess?"

"Well, er… You know my ancestry…" My throat feels like it's narrowed to the diameter of a penny, and I can only manage a gurgle in lieu of the end of a sentence.

"Pretty close to that, isn't it?" Emma interjects. "Ryan told us about your family history, leaving the Crimea in the revolution."

As my mind flatlines, I emit another gurgle in response.

Sir John, however, has me covered and gives an even heartier laugh, "Yes, who could forget all those exotic Taylors, leaving their dachas to escape the Bolsheviks."

Seeing Emma's confusion, Sir John helpfully elaborates, "Alex's family are Cheshire through and through. Her parents were telling me all about it. You can trace both sides back to the 19th century; they were all just a few villages apart. Can't you Alex?" He turns to look at me. But the eyes I can really feel on me are Emma's. I keep my own on the floor as I feel a fiery blush sweep across my face. "That's only one branch of the family," I start to mutter, but trail off as my voice fails me altogether.

Emma is very still. "Alex. Taylor," she murmurs as if testing the sounds for the first time to see how well they go together. After a pause, she says, "Well, anyway, I'm going to leave you both to do some shopping. It was good to meet you, Sir John. Nice to see you… Alex." She turns and walks away.

Sir John, busily calculating 30% off his pile of potential purchases, asks absentmindedly.

"What was all that nonsense about Anastasia? What an odd girl."

"Nothing, Sir John. It doesn't matter," I answer, my face white.

THIRTY-TWO

While Sir John remains blissfully oblivious on the journey home, my entire body feels like a block of ice, and questions hurtle through my mind. What did Emma make of our encounter? How much of a big deal is it? Is it the sort of confusion you just clear up when you next meet up, or is it the sort of thing you phone your brother to warn him about? Even while I'm trying to calm myself, I know it's a big deal. I'm even lying to myself now. How can I get myself out of this one?

I scold myself. No. No more lies. That's what's got me in this mess in the first place. But all the same, it's not unreasonable to have generations of family in Chester cemeteries and just one line that branches out into Tsarist Russia, is it? That could explain everything. And as for the name, how likely is it that Emma would remember "Alex Taylor." But then I think back to how she was saying the name. It was like she was deliberately committing it to memory. I know it's time to come clean. I just hope I can get to Ryan before Emma does.

Meanwhile, Sir John happily holds court on the Tube, making loud speeches to a host of commuters who could not be less interested. I drift in and out as he drones on about the cost of clothes today and how much he once bought a suit for in Hong Kong in 1969. I can't help but smile occasionally; his joy is infectious.

Oh God, though, If Emma says the name "Alex Taylor" to Ryan...It's not likely that Ryan would have mentioned his correspondence with an Agony Uncle to his sister, is it? Even if he did, Emma would not remember his name, which is unlikely. But then, why did it look like a lightbulb had gone on when Sir John said it? My brain spirals on and on, and before I know where I am, I've ruminated the entire journey away.

Later, as I start getting ready to meet Ryan, I continue my internal debate. I keep remembering how suspicious Emma looked. I apply my make-up as I ponder the degree of suspicion. Is it "This woman is lying to my brother" or is it "She's exaggerated her life story to seem more interesting; that's vaguely pitiful but in a lovely way." I hope against hope that it's the latter. That's possibly the kind of thing you could laugh about around the table at Christmas... just another bizarre family anecdote.

As I straighten my hair and choose my nicest, least Alexy shoes, I reason that I'm not *such* a bad person. I *was* planning to tell Ryan. It was literally on the tip of my tongue on Saturday before Sir John interrupted me. And now I'm telling him this evening instead, which was my next possible opportunity.

On the Tube to meet him, I practise my speech. I mutter through the lines – the sincere lines – about how much I liked his letter. How bad I felt when the advice went wrong. How I just wanted to make it better but then ended up falling for him, and how I'd never do something like this again.

I know he'll be shocked at first, and I'll need to give him time to cool down. But this couldn't be the end… surely not?

On the walk from the Tube station to the wine bar, I continue to rehearse. I go through all the things I love about Ryan. Yes, love, I suddenly realise, feeling a pang at the memory of all the sweet things he's done and said. As I get closer to the bar, my shoes feel heavier and heavier, and my legs have turned boneless. I stop to take a deep breath and brace myself. It's going to be scary and difficult. A painful confession. Painful for him, too. But I can do this. We'll be better for it in the long run.

I take a deep breath and walk into the bar. He's already in a booth at the back, looking despondently into a glass of red. He hasn't ordered me one, which is unlike him. He looks up, and with one glance at his face, I can tell he already knows.

I slide into the seat opposite him, knees almost knocking. He doesn't even glance up from his drink, but I can see his jaw clenched, the fingers of one hand drumming an angry beat on the table edge.

"Hello… Alex," he says. The lack of tone in his voice is worse than if he sounded angry.

"Ryan…" I begin.

"Is this you?" he interrupts. He shoves his mobile across the table. The screen is open on one of my – in the guise of Agony Uncle – emails to him.

I swallow and reach for his hand, but he moves it quickly away. "Yes," I say, looking down.

All my arguments, my narrative about this came to be, have just evaporated.

He nods and looks down, staring fixedly at his phone.

"It's a long story, but…" I begin, but he cuts me off.

"All this time, you've been emailing me as him," Ryan says, more a statement than a question. His voice is clipped, tight.

"Yes."

"And letting me email you – about Anastasia. About personal stuff."

"Yes."

He laughs hollowly, but there's no humour in it, just fury and humiliation.

"I know how stupid and weird it all seems," I say, starting to tear up.

He looks up properly for the first time, but I almost wish he hadn't. His eyes are glacial. "It's not stupid and weird. It's much more than that. It's dishonest. It's lies on top of lies. It's creepy and invasive. And it's a betrayal. And I just mindlessly believed you! All my instincts told me that it was weird for a writer to have no social media presence and that, surely, you'd use it to promote yourself, but you know what? I didn't even Google you. I just trusted. What a fool. And not only did you let me waste my time taking you on dates, you slept with me! You met my friends and family! You completely humiliated me. And for what? Was this some sort of game?"

I start to choke up, "I know. I was going to tell you anyway tonight. And last Saturday, after we visited your parents, I was going to tell you... and then Sir John interrupted."

"After I'd already brought you into my parents' home – with your fake identity – and let you make a fool of all of us? After we'd already been dating for three months? Then you were planning to tell me you're a made-up person?"

"I'm not! I'm not made up. Everything else about me was real. Just the stupid name and the family stuff."

"And the fact that I wrote to you, and I thought you had written back in confidence. To a totally different person." Ryan's voice is low, but it feels like it drips with hate. "Emma was right to be suspicious. She knew from that barbecue... there was something." Ryan looks like his own eyes are tearing up, "I wish I'd listened now rather than just telling her to stop being difficult about someone I love. Loved."

"Ryan, I..."

"And what was all this for? Some article for that magazine?"

"No! Of course not! I didn't mean for any of this to happen; it all just ran on ahead. I only meant to help you at first at the singles night because I felt so terrible for the bad advice, but then you were so lovely I said yes to a date. And then ended up really liking you. And all the stupid lies just got bigger because I couldn't tell you my actual name... and then I just didn't know what to do next."

Ryan gulps his wine and slams down the glass. "So that's why you came to the singles night. Because I was so pathetic, you thought you might need to pretend to be interested in me to improve my self-esteem. Well, that worked out well."

"Not pathetic. I just wanted to boost your confidence. That's all."

I have never felt so wretched in all my long, rich career of stupidity. I think about the other "worst" moments of my life. The moment Chris didn't take me to a family party because he was ashamed of my lack of success. The moment he wouldn't introduce me to the editor of *The Guardian* because he wasn't confident that he could endorse me as a writer. The moment he broke my heart. The moment I realised he'd moved on. Nothing compares to this. I'd repeat any of those moments again and again if it meant I could spare Ryan this pain.

Ryan is silent. He's still seething with fury. I can't bear it.

"I would have told you," I try, "but I didn't want to lose you. And I couldn't see any other way out. I knew it was weird. It was creepy. That's why I've been torturing myself for weeks."

"Wow. Thanks so much. It was really good of you to feel so guilty about making a total moron out of me." Ryan is giving no quarter. The most painful thing is his refusal to look at me, but when his eyes occasionally flick up, it's even worse. They're icy with disdain.

I take a breath and start to tell him everything in a rush, from applying for the job as an Agony Uncle for extra cash to first seeing him at the bar. To how amazing the first date was, and how I was falling for him. The times I'd tried to tell him but failed.

"I wasn't cheating on you. I wasn't laughing at you. It was just stupid. You know how I get myself into stupid situations and make them worse," I'm crying now. "This was one of those."

He stays hunched over his drink. "This isn't some funny little accident we can laugh about. You've been lying to me since we first met. You know what that means to me. What trust means to me."

I choke back tears, "Yes. I do."

"It's the one thing I needed. The most important thing to me."

"I know… and I promise, no more stupid stuff. No more lies. I'm not lying when I say how I feel about you…"

"That's the problem," he interrupts. "There's no way to say what's honest and what's not. Not anymore. As stupid as this stuff all was, that's what this has cost us. That's what kills it."

"Kills it?" I ask weakly.

He runs his hand over his face wearily. "Yes, kills it. We've been together for three months. And for 100% of that time, I've been the idiot going out with a made-up person. I don't think we can go anywhere else from here."

I nod. I can hardly argue. I've brought all of this on myself. After a few more minutes in silence, I try again, "But… all the stuff I told you. Not the stupid name and stupid ancestor stuff. All the rest about Chris and my work and what I love. All the important stuff – that was true, that was real."

Ryan doesn't look up. He's focusing entirely on his empty glass. He shrugs his shoulders. "Sorry. It feels a bit too late for that."

I try to stem my tears. I can't blame him for any of this, but the pain is horrible. The guilt makes it twenty times worse. It feels like there are 100 miles between us across the table… the guy who would take my hand and laugh at all my stupid antics might as well be carved in marble now. He's drawn so far away. And it's all my fault. This is worse than when Chris broke my heart. At least then, I had some self-righteousness, some sense of pride, and knew I was the injured party.

His voice rises, "I just find this unbelievable. Not only did you do this, but you thought we would just be able to carry on when you told me. Did you think we'd laugh about it? Did you?"

"Yes. No. I don't know. I just… I didn't think," I say, defeated, slumping my head into my hands.

"Yes, well, that's true. You didn't think. That might be the first truthful thing you've ever said to me."

We sit like that for what feels like forever, him staring down at the table, me leaning forward into my hands and occasionally peeking through my fingers to make sure he hasn't suddenly softened. He hasn't. I feel the blood pumping in my ears as I will him to say something else, anything to break the torturous silence.

He finally does, and I wish he hadn't.

"Goodbye Alex."

He says it almost gently before standing up and slowly walking out. I carry on sitting there in the booth as the early summer light fades and everything turns to shadows.

THIRTY-THREE

I've drafted 672 apology messages to Ryan and sent about twenty of them. He's read all of them and responded to none. I've spent most of the day stalking him on WhatsApp, feeling a spark of hope every time he comes online, swiftly followed by what feels like a punch in the stomach every time he goes offline without responding. I keep replaying the other night in my head, and I just can't think of a way to fix things. He's right. I did lie to him and totally betrayed him. How could he ever trust me again? I wouldn't trust me. I don't trust me.

I phone Bea; she answers quickly:

"You don't sound so good, my lovely."

"I'm not," I tell her, "I'm a crazy, mean, compulsive liar and messed up super-screw-up."

"Well, this I know," says Bea soothingly. "Come on. Shock me."

I tell her everything – the full truth rather than the sanitised, normal version I'd shared up to now.

When I finish, there's a pause before Bea says loyally, "Well, I'm still waiting to be shocked. OK – you've got yourself into a tangle, and it's led to a few people being let down. You've not killed anyone, have you?"

"No, but…"

"Well, you know I'd help you with the body if you did. Look… it's not going to be easy – but give him time. It wouldn't have hurt so much if he wasn't serious?"

"I don't think he's serious any more. It was Anastasia he cared about…"

"You made up a name and a bit of a family tree. It's random. It's not great. But everything else was all you. He liked the cringe jokes, right? He liked the chat unless you were having an out-of-body experience. That was Alex, not Anastasia. And all this talk of what a terrible person you are… well, it kind of makes it all about you. You need to make it more about him."

"How did you become so wise?"

"I think about what you would do – and then I reverse it."

"Bea!"

"I'm kidding. Look. Hold on in there. Be patient. You're no better or worse than anyone else. You just have a knack for adding a hell of a lot of extra drama. Some of that's always been you. And it's one of the reasons that I love you. Some of it…"

I sense Bea hesitate. "Go on, Bea, you can say anything at this point. I need to hear it."

"Some of it got a lot worse when you were with Chris and when you moved to London. I'm just saying I think you started practising not quite being yourself when you were with him. And that was long enough for a hell of a lot of practice…"

I think momentarily about all the times I plastered on a smile or thought through what Chris would want me to say before I said it in front of him. "I can't blame my ex being a dick for me being a dick to someone else."

"No. It's not about blame, but just thinking through some of how you ended up here. Remember, 'here' is not at the end of the world. Lots can be done about this. And if you need a break, you can escape here anytime. You know you're always welcome at Chez B."

Two hours later, and after a mix of straight talking and some pity down the phone, we finally hang up, and I reflect on everything Bea said. I knew she didn't ever like Chris, but she had never said she thought I'd changed when I was with him. I sit for a while and try to think deep thoughts. None come. There's a tentative knock on my flat door, and I shuffle over in my slippers and sheep pyjamas. It's Mrs Jenkins.

"I brought you some coffee, dear. It might perk you up a bit before the tea today."

Sir John was on the verge of cancelling the afternoon tea with Ophelia due to nerves, so last night, I promised him that I would go along with Adam and sit at a nearby table for moral support. I am currently regretting that promise.

"There are some lovely poached eggs waiting for you downstairs," Mrs Jenkins continues.

I catch sight of myself in the mirror and suddenly understand the anxiety in her tone. I look horrific. I haven't slept properly in days, and it shows. I have giant dark circles under my eyes that no amount of make-up is going to hide, my sheep pyjamas have more stains than sheep currently, and my skin is red and blotchy. Sunday's mascara is trailed across my cheek like a snail trail, and I have acne that I haven't seen since my teenage years. But I don't care because I will never find true love again, and I am going to die alone like Bridget Jones always feared. Except there will be no Mark Darcy to save me. So, it doesn't really matter what I look like.

I eventually stumble downstairs half an hour later, finally compelled into action by the thought of what Adam will say if I turn up in my current condition. After thirty minutes of scrubbing, I still look much the same. I've been stained by sadness, I think melodramatically. That's a good line, I ponder; I should store that away for that novel I'm never going to write. To my surprise, Adam is sitting at the kitchen table with Sir John, making short work of the poached eggs I'd been promised and gossiping away. Sir John is laughing heartily, and I watch them fondly for a while before I realise they are laughing at my expense.

"And then I fell out of the wardrobe! You should have seen her mother's face."

"Alexandra definitely appears to get herself into fixes," Sir John is saying. "And her interests…Since this latest drama, she has been spending all her free time watching some cartoon about monster Italian-American tortoises wandering around doing mixed martial arts."

It takes Adam a moment to process this. "*Teenage Mutant Hero Turtles*? Oh yes, eighties cartoons are her go-to after a break-up. Apparently, after Chris, she worked her way through all of *Thundercats* in one weekend."

"Thunder…?" Sir John queries.

Before more betrayal and an agonising explanation of science fiction animation, I march in, holding my head as high as I can. "I don't think Sir John needs any more boring details about my life…"

The pair at least have the decency to look sheepish as I head over to join them at the table, glaring at my now almost empty plate of eggs. Sir John even makes a show of standing and pulling out my chair before retreating behind his newspaper.

Usually, I would roll my eyes at this, but the events of this week have just been too much, and I give my most baleful glare. Adam has the sense to look uncomfortable, as he should, given he knows me best. When Sir John does peer over his newspaper, he seems so stricken that I can't help but feel a little guilty. I know this is a big day for him. He pats me awkwardly on the wrist and mutters very quietly, "Young woman, these things do all come out in the wash. Fear not."

I give him a weak smile: "I know. Let's focus on getting you through today." He nods, pulls out his favourite red silk handkerchief, and thrusts it awkwardly at me before retreating behind his newspaper, harrumphing all the way. After my non-breakfast, as Mrs Jenkins starts washing up, Adam and Sir John simultaneously almost magically seem to dematerialise. I collect the plates and wander through to the kitchen to lend a hand. Mrs Jenkins gives me a long look.

"Now, lovey, I don't know what's going on, and you don't have to tell me. But if I know anything, it can only be a silly man that's got you in this state. I know I might not look it, but I know a thing or two about men, and all I can tell you is that sometimes they reappear when you least expect it. They're not all very good at handling emotion, and sometimes they run away, so you just have to be patient."

I sniffle, and despite the slightly 1950's housewife "let him come to you" style advice, I know she means well. If this was an ordinary situation, I might even take some heart from it, but this is unchartered territory. No dating manual covers how to get a guy back after you've lied so much and so bizarrely. Instagram advice influencers don't go into this.

Last night, when I'd exhausted my *Turtles* binge, I went down the dark rabbit warren of posting anonymised versions of my crimes in relationship forums. As expected, the response was not good. In fact, it indicated that in the hierarchy of crimes, I was somewhere between that woman who put a cat in the bin and punching a nun. There's nothing like already sinking into the swamp of self-pity and then inviting online trolls to dissect your sins and pass sentences. My favourite responses include someone telling me I deserved to be alone and should be ashamed forever. Another contributor called me the Moriarty of relationships. In his own way, Adam was more helpful, but only in that he distracted me with ludicrous suggestions along the lines of going over there naked but for a trench coat or taking pole dancing classes. It wasn't clear whether these were tactics that had worked for him or on him, and I didn't have the stomach to clarify at that time in the morning.

After I've applied some make-up, I'm beginning to feel human enough to face this afternoon tea. With the emotional support of Mrs Jenkins, I meet Adam and Sir John to get ready to go out. I have to say, they both brush up well. I take full credit for Sir John's attire (although I obviously wish we'd gone to another store). Still, I'm pleasantly surprised that Adam took my instructions seriously and is wearing his interview shirt again. It's much more appropriate this time.

"Right," I say quietly. Shall we go?"

Sir John goes a bit pale, and I notice a slight tremble in his hands as he leans on the table to get up. For the first time, he looks frail to me. Temporarily distracted from my own dilemma, I rush over and pat him reassuringly on the arm.

"It will be totally fine, Sir John. Totally fine. You're going to have a lovely afternoon. If Ophelia didn't want to have a relationship with you, she wouldn't be coming. I promise. Just take it nice and slowly."

He only grunts in acknowledgement. Mrs Jenkins comes to the door to wave us all off, and we walk in silence towards Etienne's like we're walking to the gallows, each apparently lost in our respective thoughts.

THIRTY-FOUR

When we're around the corner from the restaurant, we split, Adam and I lingering behind for five minutes so that we can surreptitiously arrive separately from Sir John. When we decide enough time has elapsed, we head in. Adam, in full surveillance mode, immediately puts the maître d's guard up by asking to sit two tables away from Sir John, who I can see is seated at a lovely window table opposite an elegantly dressed woman in her late forties who could only be Ophelia.

"Sir," he starts, "we don't usually accommodate such requests."

"It's fine!" I say too hastily, only making us seem more stalkerish. "Sir John asked me to."

"I'll just go and let him know you're here then?" he offers, clearly not believing me for a moment.

"No!" I say several octaves higher than usual. "You can't!"

Adam launches into the story about Ophelia and Sir John's reunion until, thankfully, he changes tack and trails off to "Look, mate. Any table is fine. We're just here for discreet moral support."

The maître d' looks unconvinced but dutifully ushers us towards a table in hearing range of Sir John. I glance at Adam gratefully and then realise that he still has his sunglasses on. "Adam," I hiss. "What the hell are you doing? You've still got your sunglasses on."

"Um. Yes. We're on an undercover mission. Duh…"

"And who exactly are you undercover from?"

"Ophelia… obviously."

"The same Ophelia who has never met you and has zero idea what you look like? That Ophelia?"

"Yes," he says defensively, crossing his arms grumpily.

"The Ophelia who wouldn't have paid any attention to a guy she doesn't know but who probably would clock a man wearing shades indoors on a cloudy day?"

"OK, Alex, that's great. I respect your opinion. However, Sir John and I are mates now, so it's very likely that I will meet her officially months from now, and I don't want her to recognise me and then have to explain the whole situation. We aren't all as comfortable with deception as you are."

"Wow," I say, taking my seat. "Just wow." I pull the menu in front of my face so he can't see how much that last line stung. Adam pulls down the menu.

"Sorry. That was harsh."

"It was."

"I'm sorry. Genuinely sorry. Look, it will be OK. Ryan loves you. He doesn't love your name. He loves you. What's that Shakespeare quote you love so much?"

"A rose by any other name would smell as sweet," I supply automatically.

"Exactly! See, it will all work out in the end."

"Adam. That line is from *Romeo and Juliet*."

"And?"

God, he is so dumb sometimes. "They both die in the end? Not exactly what I'd call 'working out'."

He waves his hand dismissively. "Minor matter. You two aren't dumb teenagers."

I roll my eyes at him and study my menu. It's £12.50 for a bowl of porridge. Adam beckons the waiter over. "Prosecco, please!" Glancing over at me, he says, "I assume this is on Sir John, as we're his wingmen?" I look at Adam in abject horror, so he adds, "Better make that two" to the waiter.

I glance over at Sir John and cringe slightly. The conversation seems friendly but stilted. Sir John fidgets constantly with his cufflinks. On the other side of the table, I can see Ophelia twisting and twirling a little silver bracelet. I listen hard and can hear snippets about the weather, train delays and how Hampstead has changed. After they order – slightly more freely than the two of us over in economy class – Ophelia gets up to use the bathroom. I take the opportunity to go over to Sir John for a bit of a pep talk.

He grips my wrist when I get there. "Alex! This is terrible. I've gone to ground. I have more in common with Mrs Jenkins than my own daughter!"

"It's not that, Sir John," I say patiently, ignoring the slight to poor Mrs Jenkins. "It's just a really weird situation. It's bound to be stilted. It's difficult to make small talk. I really think a couple of drinks and a bit of time will really help. It will help you both relax."

He opens his mouth to argue, but I catch sight of

Ophelia returning out of the corner of my eye and scuttle back to the table.

"Stealthy," Adam mutters, clearly still aggrieved about the sunglasses. "Definitely didn't look suspicious at all."

To my delighted horror, Sir John summons the waiter (admittedly with a totally inappropriate click of his fingers) and asks for a wine list.

"See," Adam beams, "he's doing alright. Back to you, now we've got that sorted."

"I wouldn't say it's completely sorted. They're talking about Italian wines – not opening up about feelings. But if you are feeling like you're on a roll… what am I actually going to do about Ryan?"

"Honestly, I don't have an easy answer. It's a new one even for me. Look. In the worst case, you can learn and walk away from it. And you'll still be fine. I promise."

"I don't think I will, though. I know I said this about Chris, but I really love Ryan."

"You did say that about Chris. And also, that junior doctor when you dislocated your shoulder…"

"I was on a high from the laughing gas that time. It hardly counts. What's your point?"

"I just mean you've said yourself, you've been through this, and you've come out of it again. It will happen again. The falling in love, I mean."

"The only reason I'm not a total wreck right now is that I'm still holding out hope."

"Well, that's cool. Just not too much. You've kind of got to be open to moving on, too. Just in case… you know… things don't completely work out. You can see

Ryan's point of view. Your whole relationship is built on a lie. He's kind of humiliated."

"You've changed your tune. You were literally just saying that it would work out, and he loved me, not my name."

"Alex. I don't know what you want me to say. It's a very odd situation. Would I care if a girl lied about her name? No. But I'm only looking for casual stuff. Ryan's clearly looking for something a hell of a lot more serious. And maybe when you're in that mindset, things like honesty matter more."

He says this last part dismissively as if he can't ever imagine honesty mattering all that much.

I can feel the tears prickling behind my eyes again, so I take a large sip of my prosecco. The waiter comes over again at that point, so I order more prosecco and the afternoon tea for two. The prosecco will help me stomach the bill.

I tune into Sir John's table again. It sounds like it's going a lot better. I've heard at least two chuckles on his part, a few giggles and one bigger laugh from her. They seem to be talking about their old dog – a temperamental old lurcher I've seen in photos. "And then!" he chuckles, "Remember when he would pull the bedsheets from next door and drag them into our garden."

"And we always just thought they were ours, and they'd blown off the line," Ophelia adds.

"We added quite a few items of linen to our collection thanks to old Toby," Sir John chuckles, sounding almost tipsy at this point. He clearly enjoys having a fresh audience and moves on to one of his favourite parliamentary anecdotes. Ophelia patiently sits through a particularly rambling one and even has the grace to chuckle through the denouement. "It's very difficult to storm off when one's trousers have fallen down! We all had to wait until he'd gone in search of new braces before we could start laughing!"

They both laugh, and I feel like my heart might explode with pleasure. But immediately after the chuckles, awkward silences resume while they struggle for more recollections.

He does need to get onto the serious issues, though, at some point. Sir John gets up to go to the toilet, and I send Adam to follow him in and encourage him to get onto the deep and meaningful stuff. Adam resists, at first, something about men not being able to make eye contact in toilets but grudgingly goes when I tell him it's his chance to do some undercover work.

He takes it very seriously – too seriously – tipping his shades lower on his nose and making exaggerated glances to the left and right over the lenses. He also seems to be staying as close to the wall as possible and going around the long way to avoid Ophelia's table. Definitely a result of watching too much *Spooks* rather than any actual spying aptitude. I notice the waiter eyeing him suspiciously before coming over to me.

"Your boyfriend… does he need help finding the washrooms?"

"Oh! Not my boyfriend, he's my cousin. Actually, I am seeing someone at the moment. Sort of. I mean, we've had a fight, and I don't really know what to do, but I am definitely in love with him, and I need to fix it," I explain.

"Right. Your cousin… is he OK?" the waiter says patiently.

"Oh. Yeah, he's fine."

"It's just that he was crawling along the walls and doing odd little peeking around the pillars movements?"

"He's an actor," I say pompously. "On the West End!" I embellish.

The waiter looks suitably impressed, so I continue. "It's a new murder mystery. He's a detective."

"Is it a comedy?" the waiter asks, laughing at his own joke, and I downgrade 'impressed' to 'caustic'. "I must admit I don't recognise him."

"Oh," I airily explain, "he's the understudy, to be honest. But he'll be appearing in *Casualty* soon."

The waiter politely tries to arrange his face to look as impressed as possible and wanders off as Adam arrives back. "Let's not leave him a tip," I say, motioning towards the departing waiter's back.

Adam just shrugs, used to my eccentricities at this point.

"So?"

"Well, I told him that he should get onto the personal stuff before too long."

"And?"

"He nodded."

"And?"

"Genuinely no idea what you want me to say."

"Did the two of you exchange any thoughts on how it's going?"

"No. It was a public toilet, not a radio phone-in."

Exasperated, I sigh pointedly and glance over at Sir

John's table again. Sir John is building to something. His face is red, and his eyes are shiny. Ophelia is looking down, playing with her bracelet.

Adam is still wittering on about the awkwardness of conversations – but by straining, I can hear snippets of their conversation. "Genuinely thought it for the best…love you very much… your mother's happiness… paramount … broke my heart…"

I watch as Ophelia's lip starts to quiver, and I know that tears are on their way. Sir John, typically, seems totally taken by surprise and almost doesn't seem to notice she's quietly crying until tears are rolling freely down her cheeks. To my absolute joy, he gently reaches over and takes one of her hands in both of his. I look away, embarrassed at intruding on such a tender moment.

My own eyes fill with tears. "Adam," I whisper, "look at them. Reconciliation is possible, even after so much hurt and so many years! There's still hope."

Adam has very self-consciously pushed his sunglasses further up his nose.

"I know it's not like this. Not like them. But I'm going to speak to Ryan tonight. I'm going to go to his flat and just talk to him. I'll just wait outside until he comes home."

"Alex. Wait outside his home? Isn't that a tiny bit bunny-boiler territory? What would Agony Alex say about this?"

"Don't mention Agony bloody Alex to me," I groan.

"But still, what would he say?" Adam persists.

"Probably some guff about how I need to give him some time and space and then respectfully *ask* him if he wants to talk. How, after everything I've done, I do not get to impose my will on him."

"Seems wise..." Adam suggests tentatively.

I'm about to respond, but we're interrupted by the arrival of the waiter. "More prosecco, madam? Sir?"

I consider more Dutch courage but opt instead for being sensible, "I think we've had enough, thank you. Just the bill, please."

"Ah yes, you wouldn't want a hangover for your week of rehearsals," he smiles at Adam.

Adam looks baffled.

I kick Adam sharply. "Yes! I mentioned your new play to the waiter."

His face darkens. "My new what?"

"Oh, Adam. I know you're just the understudy, but the West End is West End. You're going to have to get used to celebrity!" I say, looking at him imploringly.

"Right. Yes. That's it. Can we get the bill, please?" He looks very tetchy.

Adam seems to be sulking over his undercover alias but grumpily asks how we invoice Sir John.

"We're not invoicing Sir John," I hiss.

"But he wanted us to come here," Adam whines.

"Yes, but we could have had soup and tonic water... Nobody made us reach for prosecco."

Adam gives a dramatic sigh that a West End understudy *would* have been proud of and pulls out his credit card. I reach for mine in the hope Sir John might cover the food at least. Or that the credit card company is so incredulous as to my spending habits they decide just to write me off.

Adam is still sulking when we get outside.

"Understudy? Understudy! You could have at least made me the star. Or even better – not made up the whole story in the first place."

"What's wrong?" I say innocently.

"I just mean, you have just spent hours – no, days – telling me about how lying has ruined your life, and you will only tell the truth from now on, and now you've made me into this actor – not even the main star – in a detective play in the bloody West End. How the hell do you get all of this garbage out so quickly? Don't you worry that you won't know what the truth is anymore?"

"You're the one who went undercover," I protest. "Ducking and diving around the restaurant like James Bond or a dying crab."

"Alright. Fair point. Maybe the waiter did rumble me. Though I reckon I was fairly subtle."

"You were not subtle," I snap back, heading in the direction of Sir John's house.

"OK, OK, that one's on me. But I just think it may be time for Truth Week. Or even Truth Decade. No fibs. No matter how weird stuff is. Only honesty."

I stop mid-stride. It's not said meanly, but Adam's words hit home. In a big way. How much lying comes as second nature to me.

After such a moment of profundity, Adam looks almost awkward. "Anyway, I'm going to head off. Apparently, I have lines to learn for my big new career. What I said... it was just my two-pennyworth. I just think Truth Week would play better, though... in terms of getting things back on track..."

I nod and give him a wave as he wanders back to the Tube.

Suddenly, I feel tired and sad. I perch on the restaurant's garden wall and, for a moment, can see a horrible montage of every silly and unnecessary fib I've ever told spool through my brain. I allow myself the smallest of sobs.

Suddenly, I hear a loud cough and look up. It's the waiter. I'm not his biggest fan, but I'm pleased that another human has come to check that I'm OK. I look up at him, trying to smile weakly, with the panda eyes that are becoming my stock style.

He looks at me for a moment, "Madam. This wall isn't for patrons. Would you mind?" He hands me a napkin and then turns abruptly on his heel and heads back into the restaurant. I'm so taken aback that it prompts another sob into my newly acquired napkin.

An older man wanders past with a little dog at this point and gently asks if I'm OK. This small grain of humanity makes it all the worse. All I can do is nod numbly and reach out a hand towards the puppy, investigating my handbag on the floor. He comes up inquisitively and gently licks my hand. I smile and already feel calmed as I stroke him. All is better with the world. The puppy looks at me with his cheerful brown eyes and simultaneously cocks his leg and pees on my favourite handbag, a twenty-fifth birthday present from my parents. My smile fades along with the world's rightness, and the poor old man apologises profusely before hurrying away.

THIRTY-FIVE

I'm sitting quietly on my bed, listening to one of Spotify's carefully curated lists for the broken-hearted, when my phone pings. I don't even lunge for it this time; there's no way it could be Ryan, so what's even the point? I pick it up morosely, and my breath catches in my throat. The name 'Chris Westwick' is on the screen. I take a breath and open his message.

Hey Alex. It was weird seeing you the other day... with Madeleine in the store. I haven't been able to stop thinking about you. Can we get a drink? xx"

I stare. This is pretty much the last thing I expected. I'd have been less shocked by a message from Ryan than this. I pick up the phone, read the message, and put it down again. Repeatedly.

I phone Bea.

"Do *not* go!" She cautions. "Under no circumstances should you go."

"But..."

"No."

There's a long pause.

"You're going to meet him, aren't you?" she sighs.

"Yes, but…I'll be on my guard."

"But why Alex? Why? He was so awful to you. You don't want him. You're just heartbroken."

"Bea, maybe it will give me closure."

"Nonsense! That is a stupid North American pop psychology term. It means nothing, and you never get closure anyway. Life isn't about closure… it's about learning from the past and moving forward."

I know she's right, but I'm not strong enough. "I'm going, Bea. I'm sorry."

I end the call, and I know she's going to worry. But she'll also be there to pick up the pieces. I just know that I have to do this. Once I see him, I'll know.

I tell Chris I can meet him, and he suggests tonight at 8pm. Not much time to think about it is probably good. I message back, "OK." and flop back on my bed. It's awful knowing you're making a mistake and still going ahead and doing it anyway.

It's bizarre. I have dreamed about this moment for so long, and now that it's happening, I just feel a bit numb and wish it was Ryan instead. Maybe Chris has changed, I tell myself. Perhaps I'll be surprised.

I still haven't shaken my funk when I head to meet Chris, and I don't feel nervous so much as I feel nothing when I see him sitting at a corner table in the bar, having already ordered me a drink. I guess that's my answer. He stands up to greet me and moves to kiss my cheek, but I move my face, and he ends up kissing my ear instead. Ever confident, he styles it out. He gestures to the seat opposite him, and I sit down, not feeling anything except that I wish he were Ryan.

"I won't beat around the bush here," Chris starts.

"You never did…" I nervously try to make a joke.

"I made a mistake. All those women I dated after you…it was a huge mistake. I just…it's just that everything was getting so serious with us. I knew you expected me to propose. And I just wasn't ready."

"Chris… we were together for five years. If you weren't ready by then…"

"Yes, five years. Five years when all my friends were out dating multiple women, experiencing dating apps, and going on holiday together and hooking up with random girls. I missed all that."

The old Alex would have lapped all of that up. Not anymore, though.

"Right, I get it. So, you tried the dating apps, hooked up with some randoms, and you've now realised that it's not all fun and games and that, actually, you spend more time wondering why you've been ghosted than you do going out for brunch on a Sunday morning with an attractive new conquest? And in that mindset, you miss good old Alex, who was always there and always reliable?"

"Babe, come on. I'm trying to apologise here. I miss you. I love you. I want us to try again."

"I'm not your babe. So you're telling me you want to marry me? Is it over with Madeleine?"

He visibly pales. "Let's not be too hasty. Let's just get to know each other again and see what happens."

I stare at him evenly. "Chris. I don't want to marry you. I'm not your 'babe'; I'm not getting back together with you just because you've had a chance to sleep around, and now you miss the person who put up with all your shit. I'm not some fallback option. And by the sounds of it, you haven't even ended things with Madeleine."

"I mean, you're being a bit dramatic here. I broke up with you. It's hardly a crime. And now I'm trying to be honest and say I made a mistake, and you're acting like a prima donna. You're making me think that ending things was the right thing to do. You're being crazy."

The old Alex would have exploded or cried when he called me crazy. Not Alex version 2.0, though. I stand up.

"Chris, for almost our entire relationship, you were an arsehole. You were cruel and rude, and you undermined me. You were embarrassed by me, and you took credit for my ideas. You took more from me than you gave…for *years*. You never made me feel safe. You made jokes about keeping me on my toes, but they weren't jokes, were they? We're done. You and me, we're done."

I stand up and turn on my heel, for the first leaving him speechless. I'm sure he'll fashion this into some sort of self-serving narrative for his friends, but I don't care. Nothing he does has any power over me anymore.

I text Adam and tell him that I've just seen Chris and that I'm coming over. He opens the door and immediately presents me with a glass of wine, ushering me to the couch. I'm absolutely certain that alcohol is the exact wrong thing to do right now, but I take a sip regardless, too tired to start training my willpower now.

"So… what happened?" he asks softly. "You, OK?"

"Surprisingly, yes," I answer. As I recount what happened, I stand up and start pacing around the sitting room, warming to my theme as Adam starts convulsing with laughter.

"Amazing," he pronounces when I've finished. "Simply amazing. I never liked him anyway."

Exhausted from my performance, I collapse on the couch and put my head in my hands. "It just made me realise what I lost in Ryan…when I was sitting there telling Chris how awful he was, I could only think about how Ryan is everything Chris isn't."

"Seriously, Alex, he's just a guy. There are plenty of us around. He's nothing special." He pats me gently on the back.

He tops up my wineglass and puts on *When Harry Met Sally*, which is one of my all-time favourite films. Adam absolutely loathes it and never managed to sit through it once the entire time we lived together. He's clearly making a gargantuan effort. Despite it all, I'm lucky. I have Bea, I have Adam. I can get through this. As Bea said, I just need to keep moving forward.

THIRTY-SIX

The next day, I wake up curled up into a small ball on the sofa. I have a moment of blissful ignorance as to the events of the previous few hours before the hangover punches me in the stomach. Eventually Adam slinks in, sitting on the couch beside me and firing up his PlayStation.

"I am dead," I tell him.

"When's the funeral? I hope it's not up to me to tell your mum."

"No, I'll tell her. It's the least I can do. Oh Christ, my head," I sigh.

"You ok?"

"Yes, just thinking."

"Thinking… and with a hangover, too," Adam looks alarmed. "What about?"

"The meaning of life," I say, somewhat dramatically.

"That's deep! Not surprising after Chris-gate. Want me to get you some breakfast?"

I'm tempted but want to get back for the full scoop on Sir John's lunch with Ophelia. I can tell I'm a new Alex because I pause before summoning an Uber on my phone, remembering my penniless existence, and head for the Tube instead.

I head in as Sir John is having brunch, and he looks up hopefully before I say, "No. Ryan hasn't forgiven me. I fell asleep at Adam's."

He looks momentarily subdued before excitedly filling in the gaps over his lunch with Ophelia yesterday.

I'm genuinely really happy for Sir John after his family reunion, but there's a slightly sour bit of me that reckons the one thing more annoying than him stomping around in a grump is his sudden sunny and whistling phase.

Later that day, I grab some breakfast and almost choke on a strawberry, thanks to Sir John randomly slapping me on the back with a cheery, "Old bean. Did I mention Ophelia is coming down to spend the day? More to talk about. I'm afraid we'll have to push writing back a bit."

Back in the nanny flat, I've been able to construct a private den of misery away from any cheerful whistling or Mrs Jenkins' endless cleaning. There's a pizza box on the floor and several discarded piles of comfort clothes strewn across the living room. Sweatpants, Sir John's dreaded nemesis – hoodies, my penguin pyjamas that have always been my go-to when I've been under the weather. None of these clothes would live up to the dress code of a motorway services McDonald's, but their soft fabric and non-judgemental elasticated waistbands are the closest thing I can get to a hug and a bit of understanding. I'm not sure why a hovel is more comforting than order at times like this. But it definitely is, I think, as I push an old empty bottle of very bad chardonnay out of the way of the telly so that I can indulge in another four hours of mindless comfort TV.

After four hours spent in the company of the *Gilmore Girls*, sailing through lunch because I don't have the emotional energy to get up from the sofa (I call this my self-pity diet), there's a knock on my living room door.

I brace myself for a lecture on tidiness from Mrs Jenkins and call her in. But it's not Mrs Jenkins. It's Ophelia, holding two mugs of tea. I sit up in alarm, "Sorry. I thought you were Mrs Jenkins," I mumble in confusion. Being interrupted during a four-hour self-pity orgy is like being woken suddenly from a nap – it takes you a while to begin interacting properly with fellow humans again.

Damn, this is a horrible first impression. She probably thinks I'm some sort of homeless hustler who's tricked her way into her father's home. I shake her hand and invite her to sit on the armchair after hastily removing the sheep pyjamas off its back. She sits down with the hesitancy of someone putting their arm in a badger's set but is far too polite to say anything. I can hardly blame her.

"I'm so sorry to interrupt you," she says, glancing about.

"Oh no," I say, "I'm just doing some tidying."

Tidying? That's like Dr Frankenstein telling visitors they're interrupting his medical ethics meeting. "You know how it sometimes has to get worse before it gets better," I explain, elegantly nudging the pizza box under the coffee table with my foot.

"Oh yes, I'm just the same," Ophelia nods too enthusiastically for it to be at all credible.

"Well, I won't keep you from tidying (she gulps a little with the effort of making that sound sincere), but I just wanted to come and say thank you so much for encouraging my dad to get in touch with me. I really mean it. You seem to have changed his entire outlook on life. He brunches now, I hear."

I feel a wave of relief that we're not going down the 'Why in God's name have you moved in with my eighty-odd-year-old father' route.

"Oh, I didn't really do anything."

She waves that aside. "I know my dad. Better than he thinks I do, for all the time we've not spent together. I know this didn't come from him. But in the last twenty-four hours, I've learned things I didn't know. That I probably never would have done." She pauses, and I realise with horror that she's fighting back tears. Doesn't she know this is a Sanctuary of Heightened Emotion, and anyone else expressing a single emotion could tip me into the cavernous abyss at any time?

"Anyway, I don't know why I'm beating about the bush. I wondered, why did you push my dad to do it? I'm curious. Is it for the book? A better story?"

In my current state of self-involvement, I hadn't even thought of that. "It would be a better story," I admit. "And an honest one. But I'm not writing a biography; I'm just helping Sir John write what he wants to include. I don't think he'll want to put in anything that would hurt you or your mother's memory."

She tears up at that, smiling with relief. "Thank you. I'm not ashamed of her. But I'm still adjusting. I never really knew my mum, and now she feels even further…"

She trails off, and I find myself welling up, too. Damn this Sanctuary of Emotion.

"Don't worry," I reassure her, fighting back tears, "I didn't do it for a good story. I did it because Sir John was missing you, and I've become very fond of him."

She smiles gratefully, "Well, I can tell you that's mutual, even if he has the emotional dexterity of a teaspoon at times and can't express it. But whatever comes of this book – I'm glad he met you. You're a very good person."

At that, the damn breaks, and I suddenly go from polite and professional ghostwriter to sobbing snot monster.

"Oh, I'm sorry," Ophelia leaps up in alarm, "Are you OK? Did I say something…"

"No, no," I try to regain composure, dabbing my eyes frantically with something off the back of my chair, which I realise mid-dab is a sock from last week. "I'm just not such a great person after all."

It turns out that Ophelia, for all her intimidating elegance, is a good listener who makes a solid cup of tea. She hands me a Kleenex to sub in for the sock that I'm still clutching like a rag from a comfort blanket. I tell her all about the Ryan fiasco and what a terrible person I am.

She listens intently, her emerald-green Karen Millen dress and L.K. Bennett shoes contrasting with the chaos strewn all around us. Each item she's wearing is probably individually more expensive than anything I own.

When I finish, she takes a deep breath, "Well, I'm not going to lie to you. It looks like you have a very singular talent for getting into a mess. And some creative skills to make that mess ten times worse. BUT none of this takes away from what I said earlier. I think you are a kind person. You just happen to be a chaos magnet. And yes, you could have told him earlier (she sounded like a slightly less stern Sir John here), but ultimately, we all go along with the scenarios that seem easiest. It's human nature. Dad and I know that well. I don't think you should give up just yet. Give him time, continue to be honest. If he doesn't come round, then maybe he wasn't right for you anyway."

I sniffle, "You should take over my column."

Ophelia frowns, "I'm not sure how much good that's doing for you anymore, either. Anyway, I'm an excellent judge of character. Criminal lawyers have to be, you know, and I can tell that you're a keeper, faked Russian ancestry and dodgy advice columns notwithstanding. I do not doubt that."

She stands up, "I better go and see what mischief Dad's getting into. He's dusted off the old family album. Thank you, once again."

"Sorry for keeping you from him; I know you have lots of time to make up."

"Not at all," she dismisses me with a wave of her hand.

She smiles and hugs me.

It's like a shot in the arm, the sudden injection of self-belief that I'm not the most wretched and unlovable creature on the planet. It spurs me on to spend the rest of the day tidying the flat (or making a valiant stab at it) under the logic of a tidy home, a tidy mind. With my renewed energy, I determine to make some solid decisions to get life back on track.

I quickly draft an email to Stephen at *Ladditude* as Step One of The Plan.

Dear Stephen,

A huge thank you once again for giving me the opportunity to write for Ladditude. *I'm really sorry to do this; I've been mulling over my column and all those wise words I'm dishing out to our lovely readers. I've realised I can't do justice to the responsibility of handing out advice every week, and people deserve a lot more wisdom than the teaspoonful I've accrued over the last twenty-nine years. Besides, I've already tripped on the crazy paving my good intentions have laid down. So, respectfully, while I'm still on my probation period, I'd like to resign.*

While I'm heading out the door, I should also mention that I am a woman, so I don't even qualify. I'm afraid I bullied my housemate into doing the interview and going along with the charade because I really needed the money. Of course, I'll stick to our confidentiality agreement, and I hope you will accept this resignation and my apologies for misleading you, as the end of the matter.

Best wishes,
Alex

THIRTY-SEVEN

Finally, the flat is looking more presentable and less like a Tracey Emin exhibition, and I'm feeling much lighter now that I've said goodbye to *Dear Alex*. Amazing what a bit of a spring clean, both literally and metaphorically, can do.

The buzz of escaping my funk lasts all the way to Monday morning, and I float about for the rest of the weekend, confident in the knowledge that I am well on my way to being a better person. But when my alarm goes off in the morning, I'm pushed into a Monday malaise by an email back from *Ladditude*, where I'm not sure my vagina reveal (so to speak) has gone down too well. There's a very terse reply from Stephen:

Alex,
Got your email this morning. Before doing anything else, let's have a conversation. I'll call you at 11:00am.
Stephen

No 'Best wishes' or even a 'Kind regards'. God, I wish I hadn't woken up early enough to see this little missive.

Doesn't he know that 11am is when I watch my property shows and picture Alex of the future living in some of the more palatial ones? It's an important source of motivation for me. The idea of giving all that up to be yelled at by a magazine editor does not appeal. But running away is old Alex's behaviour, and I'm not allowed to do that anymore. I send back a reply agreeing and wait for the anxiety to start merrily knotting up my gut for the rest of the morning as we get closer and closer to the time.

Eleven comes and goes, and for an optimistic moment, I conclude he's decided not to bother wasting his time haranguing me for my little bit of identity fraud. Then, ten minutes later, the phone starts singing shrilly. Damn. It is Stephen. He hasn't forgotten. But he doesn't sound mad. More amused:

"So, am I speaking to the right Alex?"

"You are," I confirm sheepishly.

"Well, this is a first for me."

I grab the bull by the horns, "Look, I'm really sorry, Mr... Lippman. I know it was a bit of identity fraud. Although the person you met on Zoom was in on it, I'm not sure it was technically, but that doesn't matter. We did lie to you, and I'm really sorry. I'm a freelancer, and it was too good a..."

"Alex, look. I'm not too worried about the 'identity fraud', as you call it. We can handle it. What annoys me is that you're leaving because of it. Our reader research suggests your letters are going down a storm with readers. They're funny. They're kind of wise but a bit mean. I'm not sure anyone will care who they were written by."

"But... it's all a lie. We'd just be lying to all those readers."

"Oh, I'm sure there's a waiver our guys in Legal can add to keep us in the clear. Or maybe we can open it up a bit. Turn Agony Alex into an Aunt instead of an uncle – Test that with a few focus groups."

I think for a moment, picturing that lovely little income stream continuing to trickle into the bank account. But then I shake myself. "It wasn't just that I was lying about that. In fact, to be honest, I'm not sure I'd have come clean at all, except that I gave out some bad advice. And then, when I tried to correct it, I made the whole situation even worse. You don't know how lucky you are to be rid of me. Trust me."

(Full-on funk has returned by this point.)

"Well, I don't know about that, but it is just a bit of fun. You're not there pretending to be a fully certified psychiatrist."

"Thank God," I interject, "But you know – we never really know how good or bad a bit of meddling can make a situation. I don't want to take the risk after… that time."

"OK – well, I guess we can look at a few alternatives to make that work," Stephen says, disappointed. "But we'd be sorry to lose you. You're a great writer."

"Well, I'm off advice but not writing in general…"

"Hmm. What about cooking? We were thinking of doing some sort of easy recipe collection. *Baking for Bachelors*… that kind of thing."

I think about my collection of pot noodles and takeaway menus in the cupboard, "Possibly… You don't have anything on film, do you? Film's my biggest thing to write about." Suddenly, my heart is pounding. I've somehow slipped into pitching for my dream job.

The excitement ends pretty quickly: "We have a film critic, unfortunately."

"And he's not about to retire anytime soon?" I love this new assertive me. I'm not sure where it comes from. I only had Coco Pops this morning.

"I'm afraid not. He's twenty-three. But leave it with me," Stephen continues, "I'll have a think and come back to you if we have any other gigs. If you change your mind on Agony Alex, then let me know ASAP. I'll need to sort something for next Friday's issue."

"I will," I promise, "but I don't think it's likely."

I put down the phone, and despite the income worries, I feel free.

THIRTY-EIGHT

Two weeks later, it's still like living with a whole new Sir John. He still has the odd pre-morning coffee bout of crankiness, but generally, he's still approaching life with his new sunny attitude. I'm in the kitchen having a chat with Mrs Jenkins when he practically skips in, asking if anything needs to be carried into the breakfast room. Mrs Jenkins immediately pales and asks him if she should fetch the thermometer.

"No, my dear girl!" he bellows, "I don't have a fever! I'm just trying to be helpful. Ophelia tells me I could stand to work on my manners when it comes to people like wait staff and underlings."

"Oh. Thank you, Sir John," Mrs Jenkins says cautiously and slightly through gritted teeth before handing him a tray of bacon and his favourite silver coffee pot. He skips off joyfully, and we exchange glances.

"Dropping the word 'underlings'" would be a start," I observe as Mrs Jenkins chuckles and hands me the scrambled eggs and a rack of toast, and I follow him through to the breakfast room.

The only downside to Sir John's new cheerful demeanour is the fact that instead of engrossing himself in his morning paper, he now interrogates me about my life, currently mainly focusing on my relationship (or lack thereof) with Ryan.

"Any word from your bedfellow?" he asks for the seventh time this week before I've even sat down.

"None."

"Shame. He seemed a nice young chap."

"He is nice," I say, almost whispering. I take a large swig of coffee so that I can hide behind my mug.

"I was telling my friend Henry all about it, but I couldn't really remember how the Anastasia bit had happened, so the story sort of lost its punch. He's coming over for supper tonight, though, so you can tell him yourself then."

Oh, wonderful. I'm so glad my heartbreak is providing fodder to go alongside Sir John's drunken MP anecdotes. I've long since learned that he has no idea how insensitive he's being, so I bite my lip hard and try to ignore him, but as he continues, I know I'm fighting a losing battle.

"It's really quite mad that he believed you were a Russian émigré. Quite, quite, mad. I've never met anyone who knows *less* about Russia than you!" He starts chuckling, and I can't help but feel it's slightly unfair to remind me that through my blubbering in the immediate aftermath, I mentioned to him that I wasn't even 100% sure where Moscow was beyond "by those other cold cities like Stockholm."

Alongside his increased motivation to bond with waiting staff, he does seem to have developed ever so slightly more emotional intelligence, so when he realises that I'm not chuckling along with him, he stops and says in a somewhat more gentle tone, "Dear girl. You do realise if it is meant to be it will be, don't you? Relationships have survived worse. If he doesn't get past this, it just means he wouldn't have got past a whole host of things that naturally happen during a relationship."

"Thanks, Sir John, but I'm not sure that things like pretending to be someone you are not is a usual relationship problem…"

"Maybe not," chuckles Sir John, "But if you bring it back to its basic component, it's about deception. And deception *does* happen. And people do get past it. Laura deceived me, and I would have forgiven her and carried on if that was what she had wanted. Arguably, betraying someone in the way she did is worse because we were a family for such a long time. But I have never stopped loving her."

I'm touched that Sir John has been so open with me, and I manage a watery smile.

"I just don't know what to do. If he won't talk to me, I don't know how to fix it."

"Just give him time, old bean," he says gently. "Have you thought about a gesture?"

"A gesture?"

"You know! Like in the films. The hero makes a grand gesture."

"I think that only works in Hollywood, Sir John."

"I'm sure we could come up with something if we put our thinking caps on. What does he like?"

"Architecture? His family? Honesty in a girlfriend?"

"Architecture, you say... why don't you go... *on the line*...on your gizmo (laptop – a word he knows perfectly well), and we'll see if we can come up with some ideas."

I make a hotspot and fire up my laptop. I'm not at all certain about this, but I'm finding Sir John's interest quite sweet and wanting to indulge it.

He hovers behind me excitedly as I connect and open Google.

"Go to the internet homepage," he demands.

"This is my homepage," I explain.

"Oh. It's different from the ones I've seen before."

Before I know it, plans for romantic gestures have been replaced by a very frustrating half an hour teaching session on search engines and links.

This could go on for a while. I patiently explain to him that hyperlinks are a list of websites or documents connected to his original Googled word and that you click on the one that seems most relevant. He looks entirely lost, so I decide that it's probably easiest to show him rather than try and explain.

I type in 'presents for architecture lovers', 'architecture ideas', and 'presents when you've really messed up'. Sir John is staring, open-mouthed, in utter amazement as suggestions magically start popping up. I'm less than impressed by the results, which seem to consist mainly of 3D puzzles, books, and artistically shaped lamps. I'm not sure they particularly scream, "I'm so sorry," or "I am a nightmare and messed up utterly."

We Google for another hour, but by the end, even Sir John is jaded and cynical, occasionally muttering, "I wouldn't wish that footstool on my biggest foe." My patience is running dangerously low, so we give up and retreat for lunch. I suggest we work on the book after lunch, but Sir John insists on grilling Mrs Jenkins about what she'll be serving Henry for supper (sea bream and new potatoes with green beans, and then a summer berry trifle) and then taking a nap. I head back to my lair with a pile of Sir John's papers and continue combing painstakingly through the minutes of parliamentary sessions and highlighting anything remotely interesting so that it's earmarked for the book. I'm determined to make a success of at least one part of my life, and now, the only likely candidate is this.

THIRTY-NINE

Sir John wakes from his nap and, after some cajoling, joins me for writing. We hit a roll, and only when Mrs Jenkins pops her head around the door do I realise it's 6:45pm. I have exactly fifteen minutes to get ready before whoever this Henry character is arrives. Sir John told me in no uncertain terms that I was expected downstairs at 7pm sharp. I hastily pull a hairbrush through my hair before scooping it into a clip and refreshing my slightly smeared make-up. I pull on a dress and summery sandals, spritzing on some perfume and glancing in the mirror before dashing down to the hallway just as the doorbell chimes. It feels wrong to ignore it, but I know that if I answer the door rather than Mrs Jenkins, Sir John will be absolutely horrified by my "breach in protocol." A harried-looking Mrs Jenkins, face flushed from steaming the beans, rushes past me as I continue towards the reception room, and I feel even worse.

"Henry!" Sir John booms as a tall, distinguished-looking man, who looks to be in his late sixties, walks in. His dark hair is streaked heavily with grey, and he's got deep furrows across his forehead. He smiles as he greets me, and his blue eyes crinkle. "Alex, lovely to meet you. I've heard a lot about you."

I blush, knowing that Sir John has mentioned some of my "merry debacles" to him, but he's chivalrous enough not to mention specifics.

"Mrs Jenkins!" Sir John barks, a touch of the old Sir John emerging. "Don't forget Henry's coat!"

"I'll look after that!" I offer quickly. "I think Mrs Jenkins might be quite occupied with cooking."

Sir John glares at me, but before he can say anything I've whisked Henry's coat out of his hands and retreated to the hall closet.

Henry is great company, it turns out, charming, intentionally amusing, a good listener – nothing like the old incarnation of Sir John, and I wonder how they know each other. I'm a little worried about asking, in case it's somehow linked to Laura, but thankfully, Henry mentions that he's an antiquarian bookseller – having escaped the drudgery of being a parliamentary clerk, which was how they first met.

"That's so fascinating!" I tell him. "Do you have a speciality?" I ask, thinking if we get onto political books, I can fade into the background and let Sir John dominate as usual.

"Oh no," he answers. "I'm a generalist. Everything from Natural History to the Normans, from Physics to Photography. This morning, I sold a book on the biota of Finland, which was written in 1670, and another on the naval history of Europe from 1712. I'm an expert in nothing, unfortunately, but I know a little about everything."

"Wow! That's amazing!"

I'm about to probe further when Sir John, who has been looking thoughtful, pipes up, "What about architecture? Alex's chap is an architect."

"Ex-chap," I add hastily.

"For now," Sir John adds loyally.

"Ah yes, the unfortunate Anastasia incident. John mentioned." I turn fuschia, but he carries on, "Tell me more about his interest in architecture."

"Well, he works in quite a niche area – he's much more interested in conservation than in new buildings. He absolutely hates the Walkie Talkie, for example. But is obsessed with St Paul's. He actually lives in a converted chapel."

"Really? Does he own it?"

"Yeah. He bought it with a couple of architecture friends, and they converted it themselves. Definitely a labour of love. It's beautiful, though, and still has the original windows and everything. And you can see where the Baptismal font used to be."

"Interesting. Where is it?"

"South Wimbledon."

At that point, Sir John interjects. "Henry!" he says excitedly. "Do you think you might be able to source something suitable related to Alex's ex-chap's chapel?"

"That's practically a tongue twister, John… but I can certainly try. Why don't you drop by the shop tomorrow, and we'll see what we can do?"

"Excellent!" Sir John exclaims. "That's sorted then, Alex. Tomorrow, you can go visit Henry's shop, and we'll lasso Ryan back."

He looks so delighted that I can't bear to puncture his spirits. I'm not confident this will work, but I am determined to put my worries to the back of my mind and enjoy over-indulging in the port with Sir John and Henry, delighting in their many anecdotes.

FORTY

The next day, I'm up early despite last night's port indulgence with Sir John and Henry. I have an appointment with Henry at noon. Before that, I'm determined to show Adam I've taken his advice on truth-telling. I've sent him a couple of update texts in the past week, and he's responded, but a little noncommittally, clearly feeling a little tired of me and my constant dramas. I refuse breakfast and head to the Tube.

When I arrive, I knock on the door hesitantly, clutching a pack of Adam's favourite beers. Javier opens the door and smiles broadly. "Alex!" he pulls me into a hug. "I haven't seen you for ages! How are your parents?" he adds, with a wink.

Clearly, Adam hasn't told him much about my latest escapades.

"Haha!" I say. "They're good. Adam around?"

"I think he's sleeping – alone for once – come on in!" Javier's enthusiasm for life is infectious, and I find myself smiling back.

We head through to the kitchen, and Javier raps on Adam's door as we pass, shouting, "Alex is here!" before sitting me down at the kitchen table and putting the kettle on. There are occasional sounds suggesting life is stirring in Adam's room, only broken by the increasingly urgent bubbling of the kettle.

As if on cue, Adam emerges as the kettle clicks off.

"Alex. You know it's beauty sleep time until 10am when I'm not training."

"Well, I certainly miss your morning sunshine," I say.

"Oh, tell me about it," says Javier, disappearing off to his room.

"I brought you beer by way of saying... thank you. You called me out in a pretty helpful way. And I am totally trying Truth Week. Maybe even Truth Century."

He inspects the beer, and his eyes light up like a baby meeting Tickle-Me-Elmo, "My fave!"

"It's my way of saying you were totally right. I was a complete mess, and I'm still a bit of a mess. But I'm working on it. I haven't told a lie since I revealed your West End debut," I say.

Adam laughs. "If I'd known I'd get beer every time I told you your life's a mess."

I wince. "That's not quite how this little transaction works, but..."

"So, no lies since my theatre debut? And what about news from the boy? Did you follow my advice there, too and give him a bit of space?"

"I haven't seen him, and I think your advice was right..."

Adam looks sceptical.

"I'm telling the truth! I swear."

"Wow. You *are* speaking the truth! And no messages?"

"OK – some messages. But not bunny-boiler level."

Over the next hour Adam even manages to get me to laugh myself out of my funk, powering up the fancy coffee machine helps (and the sound also summons Javier from his room). I tell Adam all about my appointment with Henry, and he insists on coming along to make sure the present is "blokey" enough.

At 11:55am, we arrive at Henry's shop, a beautifully mahogany book-shelved gem hidden away on Charing Cross Road. It's exactly what a rare bookshop should be: all brown leather armchairs for perusing your finds, matching mahogany ladders to reach the higher bookshelves, and dim lighting so as not to wash out the books' colours.

We find Henry at the back of the shop, poring over the hand-coloured drawings in an ancient manuscript with a magnifying glass, looking thoughtful.

"Hello!" he says, seeing us approach. "I've been thinking about the chapel architecture project all morning!"

I introduce him to Adam, and he smiles broadly. "So, tell me more about Ryan and his particular architectural work. The more detail, the better."

I fill Henry in with as much detail as I can remember from my conversations with Ryan.

"Let me make a few calls," he says, looking excited. "I have a friend who specialises in these kinds of books."

He dispatches his shop assistant to make us tea and immediately phones his friend.

Henry describes to his friend what I've said about Ryan's interests and chapel, and then for about ten minutes, all we hear is, "Uh-huh… yes … that's right… Oh, really?"

"Well?" As soon as Henry hangs up, Adam, who seems even more invested in this than I am, demands.

"Well… it's good news! That chapel of your beau – it looks like it's the only surviving part of a 19th-century barracks. And it won't be hard to track down the original architectural plans!"

"What!" This is amazing news. Ryan would love this."

Surely, as gestures go – this might make it at least halfway.

"Yes!" continues Henry, oblivious to my internal plotting. "He says he'll know for sure later today, and if he can source them, he can get them to you by the end of the week."

"How much will they be, though?" Adam asks, putting an immediate damper on my joy.

"It depends on their condition and age, obviously, but I've seen similar pieces go for anything between £500-£2,500."

"Oh…" I say, crestfallen. "I don't think I can cover that."

"Well, I'll investigate anyway. We don't have to purchase it."

By the time I get back to Sir John's, I'm exhausted. My emotions feel like poorly skilled acrobats, flipping about in every direction with joy, excitement, and hopelessness, with no real sense of purpose and a greater-than-average chance of broken limbs.

"Well?" Sir John greets me excitedly. He's clearly been waiting. "How was the appointment with Henry?"

I fill him in, and he looks delighted. "That's perfect!" he exclaims. "If Henry can source that, that will do the trick, alright."

"It mightn't matter, though," I explain, telling him the price range.

Sir John's smile stays. "Well. I'm sure we'll figure out something else," he says, unusually comforting.

The next day, Sir John and I head to Henry's shop, even though I know I'm being ridiculous, and I can't afford whatever Henry finds. We arrive around 2pm. We discover Henry in the back again, poring over what looks to be architectural plans.

He breaks into a broad smile when he sees us. "I found them. And they're in mint condition!"

Henry has clearly bought into my romantic debacle, so it breaks my heart when I have to tell him we can't afford them. I can see the romantic in him battling the business owner, who won't let him discount something worth so much money… especially not to a price I can afford.

Sir John has been entirely silent and is just quietly examining the manuscript. After about ten minutes, he looks up. "I'll take it," he says quietly. I start to protest, but he just turns to Henry and ignores me.

"Henry, this girl has reunited me with my daughter. She's given an old bean a source of happiness in his dotage. Please package it up and send it to Ryan. Alex will write the address down for you."

Henry hands me a pen, and I wordlessly write down Ryan's address, a tear of gratitude running down my cheeks.

FORTY-ONE

Days go by after the present is dispatched, and I hear nothing. I double-check it went to the right address. Yes. I triple-check it was delivered. Yep.

Friday morning, in what feels like an inappropriately early hour, I'm roused from sleep by my phone ringing. I glance at the bedside clock. It's bloody 7am. I panic immediately. Are my parents OK? Has something happened? Nobody who knows me would ever try to raise the dead at this ungodly hour without it being an emergency. Could it be Ryan finally reacting to my gift? My heart does feel like it stops for a moment as I pick up the phone.

It's only Adam.

I greet him with, "What the hell, Adam? Are you OK?"

"Where are you?" he demands.

"It's seven in the morning. Where do you think I am? I'm in bed."

"It's actually closer to 8am. Did you just decide not to bother with changing the clocks this year? Become your own timezone again?"

"I just didn't get around to it when the clocks went forward," I mutter.

"Three months ago," Adam helpfully adds.

"OK, well. I'll start again then. It's 8am. Where do you think I am?"

"Well, a lot of people might be grabbing breakfast or doing a morning jog. Some people are already at work. Some are on their way," Adam continues with his not-unreasonable list.

"Gah! Why are you being so annoying? What about that time I interrupted your 10am beauty sleep, you hypocrite? Where are you? What do you want?! Tell me now so that I can go back to sleep."

"I'm in Regent's Park. I've just been here since six this morning doing military fitness with a few clients. No big deal. Just a normal day for us plebs who aren't snoozing on their chaise lounges."

"This hasn't answered my question," I reply through gritted teeth.

"Look, it's better if I show you. Can you come to the park? I've got another session about to start, so say 9am? You'll actually have to vacate your mattress. I don't reckon they can get it into your Sudan chair."

"I think you mean 'sedan' chair, and there is nothing I have any desire to see in Regent's Park enough to lure me out of bed right now." I snuggle down further into my duvet.

"You'll want to see this," Adam replies confidently. "Trust me. I'm not going to tell you, though. Better for you to see. I want to see your face when you see it."

I groan in annoyance. "Are you trying to trick me into exercising again? Like that time you told me there was 50% off at Oddbins so that we had that run across Clapham Common? Because if you are…"

"I'm not," Adam insists. Look, you're wasting time. Get up and get over here. I'm by the boathouse."

I mutter dire threats against Adam all the way through the shower, my hasty breakfast and Tube journey. By 9:05am, I emerge from Regent's Park Tube to a barrage of impatient texts, eventually getting there a quarter of an hour later.

Adam is tapping his foot. "Good job you're not in the emergency services."

I roll my eyes, "Yes. I think we agree on that. I'm not in the emergency services; I don't have a pole to slide down into my clothes…"

"I think that's Wallace and Gromit," Adam points out.

"Or a blue light…"

"No, I figured that. I'm into my next session now."

I look around for a client, "Oh, where?"

"It's OK. I sent him to run around the lake a couple of times. He's just starting out and was a bit of a fish and chips fan, so I reckon we've got ages."

"For what?" I plead. "Why am I here at the crack of dawn?"

Adam pulls out his phone. "For this!" he says triumphantly, bringing up the latest edition of *Ladditude* on his browser like it's a winning lottery ticket.

I take his phone very coldly. For this, I missed Coco Pops and my usual nine hours of slumber?

I mutter dangerously as he instructs me to flick to the *Dear Alex* pages. There may be a whole new Alex, but they've kept everything the same, down to Alex's muscly silhouette. The only new thing is the disclaimer at the bottom of the page and the small print: "Alex is a pseudonym for one of our writers."

I look up in irritation. "You dragged me here for this? I already knew they were keeping Dear Alex and just adding a bit of a disclaimer. I spoke to the editor the other day. I can't believe I've been dragged…"

"Not that bit," Adam says, more gently than usual. "This." He points to the letter on the page:

Dear Alex,

This letter has taken me a long time to write. I've got a problem, and you're probably the only person who can fix it. I fell for a girl. This funny, beautiful writer. She's made me laugh more in the last few months than I have for years, and I really fell for her. But then, three months in, I found out quite a few things had been made up, and some stuff happened that left me feeling betrayed like I had been once before. Except it felt even worse than before because this girl seemed so far above that.

So I was left feeling really shitty, and we broke up. Since then, I've been thinking about her every day, and instead of missing her less as time has gone on, I've been missing her more. The other day, I got a birthday present from her via post. And it brought back everything we'd talked about and how thoughtful she was. And the more I thought about it, the more I pretty much decided life really is too short not to be with someone you've fallen for. Dumb lies or not. And if she forgives me, too – for how I reacted – then I guess what I'm hoping for is a second chance for both of us.

Always,
Ryan

I never understood what 'heart soaring' really felt like before. But suddenly, in Regent's Park, mine not only soars but also does a few loop-the-loops around passing aircraft. I hug Adam. "He wants to get back together! He's forgiven me!"

"I told you it was worth it!" Adam replies smugly. "Oh shit, but wait. You need to read the response."

"Oh yeah, I forgot… the new Alex." My eyes leap back to the page:

'Ryan, man,

You got it bad. You're sounding pretty loved up, but all that says to me is that you're not thinking straight. You don't go into details, but what you're basically saying is that you had a relationship for three months, and it hit the rocks. I have worn underwear for longer. Give it up, man. If it takes twelve weeks for things to go so badly wrong, it sounds better for both of you to call it a day. It's lonely splitting up, and it's pretty normal to miss your ex, but you made your decision for a good reason. Stick with it.

Yours
Alex'

Arrrrrrrrrrrrgggggggghhhhhhh. "Damn it, damn it, damn it! I hate that Agony Uncle! I hate *Ladditude*! Ryan doesn't know I resigned! What if he thinks this is the final brush-off from me? I have to get to him. Now."

Throwing his phone back to Adam, I start a sprint out of the park, barreling past the sweaty form of Adam's latest client/victim as they stagger through their second lap.

"Good luck!" Adam calls after me. "I knew I'd get you running eventually!"

FORTY-TWO

I'm running as I've never run before, not even when I was about to miss the bus and be late for my Geography A level (which I subsequently arrived for thirty minutes after it had started, sweaty and tearful. I got a C, in case you're wondering). I make it around fifteen minutes before I've slowed down to a slow jog, and then a fast walk… and then a slow walk. It's fine, I rationalise, as I catch my breath. Better to arrive and see Ryan for the first time when I'm composed and stunning, rather than the Helena Bonham-Carter as Bellatrix Lestrange creature I currently mirror. I catch sight of myself in a car wing mirror and think I might need a bit of a detour before going to Ryan's work. My cleavage is glistening with sweat, my eyeliner has smudged under my eyes, making me look like I haven't slept in days, and my top has a coffee stain. I know Ryan is used to my haphazard appearance, but I feel like our reunion is going to be one of those moments I tell the grandkids about. I'll probably be expected to show them a selfie or something, so I should take a moment to regroup and at least let my hair get reacquainted with a brush.

Shouldn't I?

Then I think how ridiculous that is. The grandkids. The selfie. The make-up. That's the kind of tram tracks my brain always runs away on. To what end? I don't need the make-up. Ryan either won't care because he doesn't care, or he won't care because he does care.

I ditch the make-up pitstop idea and carry on running.

A text beeps in from Adam: "Are you with him? Are you back together?"

I make an executive decision to ignore him. He knows I'm not a runner, and there's no way I'd have made it to the Tube station by now, let alone actual Ryan. At last, I head down to Regent's Park Underground. The stupid Tube is, as ever, like a cross between one of the warmer circles of hell and a neglected gym locker, complete with unloved socks, and I can almost *feel* its scent oozing onto me. Eau de Tube. Maybe I should have done a quick perfume spritz in Boots.

I take the escalator back to the surface two at a time, tutting impatiently at the gates and clicking my tongue behind a poor elderly woman who is clearly a tourist and is trying to feed her shiny new Oyster Card into the ticket slot. Disregarding all the rules of London, I interact with a stranger on public transport and impatiently explain that she just needs to tap it, so desperate am I to get to Ryan. She smiles gratefully, and I smile indulgently, hoping this can go into my good karma bank. As I get closer to the building Ryan is currently working on, my palms start to get a little sweaty. I haven't felt this nervous since the time I had to participate in a debate about whether schools should have uniforms or not in primary school. I was assigned to the "For" side, and I was so nervous that everyone would think I agreed with the motion that I threw up on Rachael Jenkins in the first row. So, everyone made fun of me for that instead.

The site looks pretty empty when I get there, and I poke my head around the door, calling Ryan's name a couple of times. There's no sign of life, so I wander inside, picking my way through mounds of plans and empty coffee cups. As I make my way up the stairs towards the terrace, I can't stop thinking about the magical date we had here. My heart is pounding as I round the top of the stairs, and there he is… standing with his back to me, pouring over some plans that have been set up on an easel.

"Ryan…" I murmur.

He turns and looks pretty shocked. "Alex… what are you doing here?"

It was not quite the greeting I had been hoping for. "I… I saw the letter in *Ladditude*. There's a new "Alex," but Adam showed me. I ran here as quickly as I could."

"Yeah. I figured that when I got the response. Didn't sound like you."

"Well?" I look at him, hopefully. "Did you mean what you said?"

He looks down, and my heart plummets. "I did… I did at the time. But the response from the new Alex sort of made sense to me. I don't know. I just think maybe he has a point."

"But… but the chapel plans!" I almost wail.

"Yes, I love them. I really, really do. They are so thoughtful. But Alex, I just don't know. Like the letter said, it's been three months, and the entire thing was a lie. I don't even know you, really…"

"You do! You do know me. I was still me, just by another name. Everything meaningful and important about me is true. OK, so I'm not a Russian émigré, but my clumsiness, my love of films and writing, my love for you… that's all totally true. Even my stupid ex, who, by the way, I met for a drink the other day. I have to tell you that. I was brokenhearted over you and sad and needed something from it. I don't know what. And all the way through, I couldn't stop thinking about you. How awful he was, but mostly how amazing you are."

I pause briefly for breath but don't want him to cut in and say anything. I want to hold onto this moment where things can still work out. I press on. "I didn't lie about anything important. I totally get it… I understand why you feel this way… but please, don't let a stupid letter change your mind."

I resist tears for once. It isn't right to make Ryan feel sadder about what's probably a wise decision on his part. "Anyway, that's all I had to say. Thanks for listening. I didn't have a right to expect it."

I take a deep breath and turn to leave. Dignity. No sobbing. Dignity. No sobbing. I turn the words around in my head like a mantra. But suddenly I feel a hand take mine and turn me around.

He takes my other hand.

"What if I stopped listening to Agony Uncles? And you stopped with crazy stories? And we just spoke to each other instead?"

My eyes glisten. "That would be… good," I swallow.

"Come here, Alex," he says gently. He enfolds me in his arms, and as his familiar Ryan scent washes over me, he kisses me softly. I know that even though we have a lot of talking to do, everything is going to be OK.

EPILOGUE

A year later...

"I'll get it!" I shout to Ryan as the doorbell rings. I'm heading down the corridor to inelegantly drag open the heavy chapel door and welcome the first of our living-as-a-couple housewarming guests.

Sir John, whom I have accompanied on several more shopping trips, thanks to the lure of Emma's discount, is on the front step in his brand new 'casual barbecue apparel' (pastel rather than striped tie). He hands me what looks like a very expensive bottle of wine, which I resolve to squirrel away at the back of the fridge.

He greets me with his usual bluster, "Is this a church? Why the devil does he live in a church? Is your young bedfellow a squatter?"

I steer Sir John towards the garden, "No, no, it's a chapel, remember. He converted it. He did the... architecting. Remember the present from Henry?"

"Hmm. It's very small," Sir John mutters, glancing around the place. "Is there enough room for the two of you here?"

I smile as I pour him a glass of wine in the kitchen. "Is this your way of saying you miss me, Sir John?"

He harrumphs as he takes the glass. "Don't be ridiculous." After a beat, he says, "It is a little quieter, I suppose."

"I'm around for a writing session every weekday! And you're never in on the weekends anyway!"

Today is one of the rare Saturdays when Sir John isn't staying with Ophelia's family in Sussex, having taken to grandfathering with aplomb.

"Well, perhaps you are missed a little," Sir John says without his usual bombast, "but as long as you're happy."

I think back over the last two months of squabbling, cuddles (and yes, more squabbles). "I am," I say truthfully. Sir John smiles and pats me on the shoulder before wandering out into the garden. I follow him. Ryan is keeping a watchful eye on the burgers while Cecille stands beside him, giving him a long list of helpful tips. Sir John wanders over to add his own views despite the fact he never mastered toast, and I grin as Ryan's frown furrows further. Adam is flirting outrageously with Ryan's mum, and Ryan's dad is fruitlessly trying to engage Javier in football talk. Emma looks on, thoroughly bored. I wonder if the kind thing to do would be to redirect Gareth towards Adam, who would enjoy the football talk, but I remember Javier's haiku and decide to let him suffer.

Emma makes a break for it and wanders over to me. I feel my heart rate quicken. Emma and I have an unspoken truce, but we're still guarded with each other. In all of our meetings since Ryan and I got back together, I've felt her studying me. I totally get it; she's looking out for her brother like any good sibling, and it'll take a while before she trusts me. Today she offers a quick smile and cheers her wine glass against mine, and I almost relax. We trade stories about Ryan's annoying tidiness (which has thankfully been the only real source of our quarrels since moving in together two months ago), and we laugh. Things are easier than they've been since the Anastasia reveal. Her smile seems genuine as she wanders back and rescues Javier from her dad's "seventy-eight interesting facts about Tottenham Hotspur." I'm not quite there yet with her, but it's better.

An arm drapes over my shoulder; I turn my head to Ryan's grin. "Third degree again?" he asks. "No, we were mostly complaining about you," I grin back.

"Me?" he laughs indignantly. "What is there to possibly complain about?!"

"Well, the fact that you've abandoned your post for a start. Why aren't you tending to the burgers?!"

"Too many cooks. I've left Sir John and Cecille to duke it out."

"Sir John doesn't know anything about cooking!" I protest. "He only ever enters a kitchen to hurry Mrs Jenkins' breakfast along and possibly for some sociological research. And I'm not sure he's even had a burger! But he does like opinions."

Just then, the doorbell goes again, and it's my parents and Bea – looking remarkably cheerful for a city-phobe who's also had a long journey with my parents.

"Bea – you survived," I cry, hugging her.

"Why shouldn't she have survived?" my mother mutters indignantly.

Bea whispers urgently in my ear, "Point me directly to the beers, now!" I do, with the greatest sympathy.

Mum and Dad are next in the line-up. They hug me and Ryan, my mother managing to simultaneously make me feel guilty for not visiting recently while also telling me it's a good thing I've finally moved in with a man, as it's about time I became an adult who didn't rely quite so much on her parents. They head straight through to the garden, Dad immediately going to add his unneeded support to the barbecue crew and Mum making a beeline for Joy to compliment her dress / interrogate her about whether Ryan visits his parents more than I do mine.

We watch them all for a minute – a motley crew of friends and family. It's not what central casting would assemble for a Jacob's Creek summer party advert, maybe, but it gives me the warmest glow to see them all there together.

Adam places Ryan's chef's hat on Sir John, who, somewhat miraculously, has taken up the task of dishing out the burgers. Narrowing his eyes and without turning around, he stiffly removes the hat with wounded dignity. While everyone else is distracted, Ryan nuzzles my neck. I lean into him, relishing the hardness of his chest, taking in the smell of soap and charcoal.

"So, Agony Alex, I need some advice," he whispers. "I'm the happiest I've been in a long while. How do I keep that going?"

"No more advice for starters," I whisper back.

"No?"

"No," I say adamantly, "We muddle through like everyone else and just take it one day at a time."

Ryan kisses the back of my neck. "Agreed," he says happily.

ACKNOWLEDGEMENTS

From Miranda

I am deeply grateful to so many people for their love and support while we wrote this novel.

At the risk of leaving someone out, special thanks to Ellie, Carmel, Kathleen, Jeni, Emer, Julia, Caz, Hannah, Becky, Frances, and Adrian for reading early drafts, and for your feedback and encouragement. *Dear Alex* would not be what it is without your comments. I appreciate you all, and the time that you took to give positive, constructive feedback.

Thank you to Chris for so gracefully sharing your name with the "bad guy", and to Catherine B and Catherine McC for your endless patience while listening to me go on *ad nauseum* about the trials of the publishing process. Thanks to Crystal, Emily and Jemma for your relentless cheerleading, and for being amongst my biggest supporters, and to Molly and Tom for always being there when I've needed you most. Much love, also, to the Mount Anville class of 2003 – that so many of you jumped to pre-order more than twenty years after we left school is humbling, and I can't adequately express how grateful I am to have such a supportive group of women in my corner. Thanks to Ursula, the best coach I could wish for, for encouraging me when I wanted to give up, and for believing in me when I didn't believe in myself. Kelly, Heidi, Nailia, Morag, thank you for letting me brainstorm with you, and always seeing the glass as half full.

Thanks also to Holly Porter, Carolina Santos, Sophie Morgan and Rosie Lowe, for your invaluable guidance throughout the publishing process.

Finally, and most importantly, to J-P. Co-writing a novel is not a small undertaking, and I'm sure it would test the strongest of friendships. It's a huge testament to us that we were still laughing during the copy editing stages. Thank you for your love, friendship, and support, and for being someone I can always count on. I'm so grateful for our friendship and you mean the world to me.

From J-P

I'm hugely blessed by a collection of people who unfailingly cheer me on and cheer me up through all my endeavours, not least this book!

It's been in gestation for some time – so the full list of lovely people who've provided encouragement would run into several chapters.

With advance apologies for any omissions, top of the short version is a second appearance for the people in my dedication for their unconditional love and support.

Thank you to Caz and Mariah for holding me to New Year's Resolutions through all our travels and misadventures, as well as to Paolo, Catherine and Jon for the listening ear and/or wine at various crucial moments, and to Chris for lending us a name!

I'm very grateful too for the friendship of a brilliant set of funny, kind people, from the Welsh cohort through to the contingents from university, from work, the "Sofa Club", and from many years of bumbling around London.

Thanks to the Book Guild, including Holly Porter, Rosie Lowe, Sophie Morgan, Carolina Santos and the wider team.

And finally, Miranda, I'm so grateful for your encouragement and your can-do, never-say-die attitude that kept us typing away past any marker I'd ever reached in writing before. Thank you for being such a fabulous, kind and loving friend, I couldn't wish for a better partner-in-crime on this adventure! XXX.

ABOUT THE AUTHORS

Miranda Seymour grew up in Dublin, before moving to Canada to study English Literature and Theatre & Film at McMaster University. A hopeless romantic at heart, her debut novel, *Dear Alex*, is fittingly a romantic comedy.

J-P Jones grew up in a small Welsh village, reading anything and everything. Now living in London, writing became a passion in lockdown. *Dear Alex* is one of J-P's first completed works, along with four short plays.